The Cottage on Strawberry Sands

HOLLY MARTIN

To Skipper, my beloved best friend. I love you and miss you every single day

CHAPTER ONE

Roo laid out all the ingredients to make fairy cakes on the tiny kitchen counter. She was so nervous about starting her new job the next day. Not about the job itself, she was really excited about that part, and she knew she was more than qualified to do it, but she just wanted everyone to like her. She didn't know why that was so important to her – it had never been something she had worried about before. Probably because she always knew she wasn't staying, that in a few months she would probably move on, do something new, something different. Nothing stuck. But this job was different. She wanted to make a home for herself here in Apple Hill Bay. She was tired of moving on.

She'd decided to take her beloved dad's advice. He'd always said no one can hate you if you have cake. So, she was going to make a big batch of cakes and try to persuade people she was lovable.

She smiled as she remembered her dad standing next to her in the kitchen as a child as she made some cakes, dipping his finger in the cake mix and licking it 'just to test if the mixture was OK'. She rubbed an ache in her chest. It had been nearly fourteen years since he'd died but there wasn't a day that went by that she didn't think of him.

Being back in Apple Hill Bay was bringing back loads of memories of him, of growing up here and playing on the beach with him. Her mum was never around back then, she was always off on holiday or having affairs. She'd left her dad more times than Roo could count and then returned to him a few months later once the affair had ended. Every time her dad would take her back, hopeful they could make things work, and every time she would leave him again a few months later. And Roo. Her mum never made any apologies about leaving her only child. A family life was not something her mum had ever wanted.

Roo pushed that thought away and looked at the ingredients and the recipe she'd brought up on her phone. It really shouldn't be that hard. Except she hadn't made cakes since she was a little girl, and the tiny beach hut that would be her home for the next few weeks, until she found somewhere more permanent, was slightly lacking in the kitchen department.

It was a pretty little wooden house, tiny lounge with a small dining table in front of the large French doors opening out onto a wooden deck with stunning views over Strawberry Sands. Upstairs there was a large double bed on a mezzanine level and a little bathroom and shower. This beach hut was called Narwhal and there were whimsical smiling narwhals playing together painted on one wall. It was very cute and was perfect for a week's holiday but clearly wasn't made to live in long term. The kitchen had the world's smallest oven, a tiny fridge, one cupboard of bowls, saucepans, cups and glasses and one drawer of various cutlery and cooking utensils.

But she could make it work.

She washed her hands before realising she'd already done that a few minutes ago but as she turned back to the counter she slipped on some water on the floor, her legs flew up in the air and she made a grab for the side to stop herself falling, hit the chopping board with her flailing hand and sent the thankfully unopened bag of flour soaring through the air. She landed on her bum hard, which knocked the wind from her but before she had chance to recover from that, the bag of flour landed next to her with a thud and exploded, sending white dust all over her, the kitchen and probably the lounge too.

She coughed and spluttered, flour in her eyes, her mouth, her nose. She couldn't even see. She sat up as the dust settled and she quickly scrambled to her feet and rinsed water in her eyes and mouth. She patted her face dry with a towel and turned around to survey the damage.

Flour was everywhere, the floor, the worktops, the cupboard doors, the carpet in the lounge, the sofa, chairs. She couldn't believe how far it had spread. How could the act of doing something nice for her new co-workers go so badly wrong? She didn't even have any flour left to make the bloody cakes now.

She sighed and set about cleaning the place up: hoovering, sweeping, mopping, wiping down the work-tops and cupboard doors. Finally, it was done, but she thought she'd be finding flour for weeks after – it was one of those things, like sand, that never really went away.

She decided to leave the cake making until later and go and grab a tea from the cute café near the reception area of The Little Beach Hut Hotel.

She stepped outside, gave her hair a quick shake to rid it of any flour and was surprised when a thick cloud escaped into the air. She brushed down her clothes, gave her face a quick wipe and closed the door behind her.

She started walking along the cliff path. The view over the turquoise sea was stunning and one she had missed over the years, and she hadn't realised quite how much. It had been fourteen years since she had walked the cliff tops of Apple Hill Bay but surprisingly, looking at the view now, it felt like she'd come home and that was a weird feeling to come to terms with.

She sat down on a bench and looked out on the three stunning beaches that made up the large bay. White sands, crystal waters that sparkled with almost every shade of blue and green, the hot sun shining overhead, it was as if she was somewhere far more tropical than the south coast of Cornwall. On the far side of the bay was Cranberry Cove, in the middle was Blackberry Beach and at the bottom of this headland was Strawberry Sands. She had such fond memories of all three beaches but especially

Strawberry Sands and the little shack at the bottom of the headland right above the beach. It was there she and her childhood best friend, Theo Lucas, would spend hours watching the local wildlife together.

Just thinking about him made a lump form in her throat. If she had one regret in life it was losing contact with him. She wondered where he was now. Probably New York or Tokyo or some other important city in the world, living his dream.

They'd first met when they were fifteen and he'd just moved to Apple Hill Bay with his family. They'd shared a love of skateboarding, watching wildlife, drawing and coming up with crazy business ideas to take over the world and make them billionaires. She smiled. They thought they were invincible back then; the world was their oyster.

She had been desperate to get out of Apple Hill Bay and they'd planned to travel around Europe together and leave that life behind. But looking back now, it wasn't so much Apple Hill Bay she wanted to get away from, it was her parents' volatile relationship; the rows, the multiple affairs, her mum constantly leaving and breaking her dad's heart then coming back and doing the same thing all over again.

Just then an old retriever came trotting over to her. She could tell he was old from the white fur around his face but there was still plenty of life left in him – she could see the spark in his eyes that said he was still loving life. He wagged his tail and plonked a soggy ball on her lap.

'Hello, do you want me to throw the ball for you?' Roo said, stroking his velvety soft head. She went to pick up the ball, but he grabbed it before she could touch it, chewing it with his big head on her lap. She laughed.

An elderly lady walked towards them, and Roo instantly recognised her as her old science teacher.

'Mrs Kimbleford!'

The woman looked at her and broke into a huge smile. 'Aurora Butler. I never forget a face.'

'It's Clarke now, I changed it to my dad's name after he died.'

She nodded. 'I was sorry to hear he'd died, he was a good man.'

'Yeah, he was,' Roo said.

The dog nudged her and she turned her attention back to him again. 'Wait, is this Max?'

'Yes it is,' Mrs Kimbleford said, her face beaming like a proud mother.

'Hello Max. God, he was a tiny puppy the last time I saw him. I used to put him in my bike basket when I was looking after him for you.'

'It's been a long time since he was that small. Is this the first time you've been home since then?'

Roo smiled at the word home. 'Yeah, it is.'

'Well welcome back. I'm sure there will be lots of people happy to see you again.'

Max walked off as if he was done with this exchange and Mrs Kimbleford smiled after him. 'He knows his own mind, that one. It's good to see you again. I'll see you around.'

She waved goodbye to her old teacher and watched them both walk away. It was funny to think of Max still ambling around and chasing his ball after all this time. When she'd come through the town in a taxi earlier that day, she'd been surprised how much had stayed the same, even the people.

The Little Beach Hut Hotel was new, though. Each of the guests had their own little beach hut just like hers to stay in, which was a wonderful idea. When she'd left Apple Hill Bay this was just hills and trees and an old stone cottage where Theo's mum Carrie lived with Theo, his brother Shay and his sister Fern. She wondered if Carrie had sold the land to developers who had built the beach hut resort.

Roo got up and walked down the path to Seahorses, the clifftop café. She pushed open the door. It was late Sunday afternoon and the café was quiet, just a few stragglers sitting in the corner laughing about something. She moved towards the counter and smiled when she realised who was serving – her old friend, Orla. Orla had been in the year below her at school so they hadn't really been friends until they were older. They'd bonded when Roo's mum had an affair with Orla's dad and the subsequent divorces that ripped the two families apart.

Orla looked up to serve her and she smiled when she saw her. 'Roo!'

Orla hurried round the counter and gave her a big hug.

'Oh, it's so good to see you again,' Roo said, embracing her. She'd lost contact with her friend when Orla had gone off to university in London shortly before Roo moved to Chicago with her dad. She'd never been one for Facebook and with an ocean and a time difference in the way she'd slowly lost touch with all her friends. Apart from Theo – she'd talked to him every day until her dad died, then she'd cut him out of her life, and she hated that she'd done that. She should have tried harder with all her friends.

She pulled back to look at her friend, her long red hair, her freckles all over her cheeks and nose, her sparkling green eyes. 'You look stunning.'

Orla grinned. 'I wish I could say the same. Did you have a fight with a bag of flour?'

Roo laughed. 'I did. I thought I'd got it all.'

'Not quite. There's a lot in your hair and your face.'

Roo gave her hair another brush and then shrugged. 'I'll head back and grab a shower in a minute. I was trying to make cakes and there was a minor explosion.'

Orla laughed.

'You working here?' Roo said, stating the obvious.

'I own here. This is my place.'

'Oh, that's amazing. You were always so good at cooking and baking. I figured you'd have your own restaurant one day.'

'I love it. I get to see all the regular walkers and hikers, the tourists, the locals and I work with food – it really is my dream job. What about you, what are you doing now?'

'I've just got a job as a lead designer at a small publishing company on the other side of town.'

Orla moved back behind the counter. 'How wonderful, you're back for good then?'

'Yes, I hope so.'

'We must catch up then, we'll have a glass of wine one night.'

'Yes, you can fill me in on all the village gossip and everyone who is still here. I figured there'd be hardly anyone left that was here fourteen years ago, but I've just bumped into Mrs Kimbleford and now you.'

'Mrs Kimbleford will always be here. Rumour has it she's a vampire and never ages.'

Roo laughed. That was the rumour when they were at school because some of the kids' parents had been taught by her too. Even now, all these years later, she seemingly hadn't aged at all. Maybe there was some truth to it.

'And I love it here too much to ever leave,' Orla said. 'But are you saying no one knows you're back?'

Roo shook her head. 'I lost contact with everyone here over the years. But I wasn't expecting a big welcome-home party.'

Orla's eyes flicked to the door behind Roo. 'So Theo doesn't know?'

'Theo's here?' Roo said, in surprise. She'd thought he would have moved on years ago.

'Did someone say my name?' said a male voice behind her.

Roo froze. 'Theo is *here*?'

Orla nodded, her eyes wide.

Roo turned around and her heart stopped because the man who'd just walked in was Theo Lucas. He was older and so much bigger than the scrawny kid she remembered. He had filled out in all the right places, his hair was shorter than the mop of blond curls he used to have but it was undoubtedly him. Christ, he was hot. She'd like to say she never saw Theo like that when they were kids or teenagers but that would be a lie. She'd always had the biggest crush on him. Nothing had ever happened between them, and she'd valued his friendship too much to ever tell him. She had no idea if he ever felt the same but he certainly hadn't said anything to her. Of course, she was standing there with flour in her hair and on her face while he was looking more gorgeous than ever.

She wanted to run forwards and hug him but it had been fourteen years, they couldn't exactly pick up where they'd left off. He probably wouldn't even recognise her.

Although that fear was soon put to bed when his eyes widened in shock.

They stood frozen, staring at each other.

Eventually he spoke. 'Roo?'

CHAPTER TWO

She nodded, her voice croaky. 'Hi.'

They stared at each other some more. What if he just said 'hi' now and went about his business? That would be too painful, but exactly what she deserved.

He seemed to shake his head to clear it of the shock and then in two large strides, she was suddenly wrapped in his arms. 'I can't believe you're here, after all this time.'

She smiled in relief and slid her arms around him too.

He pulled back, holding her at arm's length. 'You look amazing.'

'I have flour in my hair.'

He smiled. 'You still look incredible.'

'So do you. You're all grown up.'

He laughed. 'What are you doing here?'

'I have a job here, I start tomorrow.'

'A permanent job or just a few days or—'

'Permanent, I'm back for good.'

The smile spread across his face and that warmed her from the inside. 'This is the best news I've had in a long time.'

Her heart filled with joy at that comment. It was her fault they had lost contact and he had every right to be angry or standoffish with her or not want anything to do with her, but the way he was looking at her, he clearly wasn't holding any grudges. Theo was too laid back to be bitter and twisted.

He let her go. 'Can I get you a drink?'

'Oh, let me get them.'

'No no, let me.'

Roo nodded and glanced at Orla who was grinning at them both. 'I'll have a chai latte please.'

'Just a tea for me please, Orla.' Theo said. 'To take away.'

Orla started making them.

'Thank you,' Roo said.

'My pleasure, I can't believe you're here.' He was looking at her like he'd found a pot of gold.

'I can't believe you're *still* here. We always had such big plans. I thought you'd be a big swanky city boy now.'

'And leave that view?' he gestured to the sea behind them.

She looked out over the bay. 'Yeah I know what you mean.'

She turned back as Theo paid for the drinks. She couldn't take her eyes off him, drinking in every little detail. He looked at her, his eyes filled with so much affection for her and that made her smile so damn much. Her heart was beating so fast at seeing him again, she felt sure he would hear it. She cast around for a suitable topic of conversation that didn't involve her squealing in excitement.

'How is Fern?' Roo asked, which was a rather sensible question considering how he made her feel.

'Happily married and heavily pregnant.'

'That's wonderful. I'm happy for her. Is her husband a good man?'

'Yes, Fletcher is one of my friends actually.'

'Oh,' she laughed. 'Your friend and your little sister. Did you go all protective big brother?'

Theo smiled. 'Maybe a little. They're great together, though, and he's really good for her.'

'That's great. Are they local?'

'Yes, I'm sure you'll see her around town. She has her own mural-painting business now, she's very much in demand.'

'She was always good at drawing and painting. You both were. Are you working in that field too? You were always brilliant at graphic design.'

He frowned slightly. 'There are... design elements to my job but I'm more on the boring admin side of things.'

She looked at him in confusion. How did someone so brilliant and creative with graphic design and digital illustration end up doing an admin job?

'Here are your drinks,' Orla said. 'Why don't you take them outside and enjoy them in the sun together.'

Roo smirked at the blatant matchmaking. She'd never told anyone about her feelings for Theo when she was in her teens but she wondered if it had been obvious to anyone looking in. She hoped it hadn't been obvious to Theo, that would be mortifying.

Theo didn't seem to mind. 'Shall we?' He gestured to outside.

She nodded. He took both drinks and she followed him outside.

She glanced back at Orla as she walked out, who gave her a smile and wink. Roo smiled and shook her head.

Theo sat down on a picnic bench and she sat down opposite him. He looked out over the sea and she followed his gaze.

'I do love it here,' Theo said.

'It's a good place to call home.' She glanced over at the multi-coloured beach huts that dotted the clifftops and went all the way down the hillside to the beach. 'And a perfect place for The Little Beach Hut Hotel. Did your mum sell the land?'

'Oh no, she owns it. This was all her idea. My brother Shay oversaw the building of it and he's the manager here now.'

'What a wonderful idea. I'm staying in one of the huts, at least until I can find a place of my own. It's lovely.'

'Yeah, she and Shay worked hard on it. Which hut are you in?'

'Narwhal.'

'I know Fern enjoyed painting that one especially.'

'She did the narwhals inside? They are beautiful.'

'She has an incredible talent.'

And how is Carrie?'

'Mum is great, she has a boyfriend, Antonio and they're very happy together.'

'And Shay, is he with anyone?'

'No although I think he secretly has a thing for our lovely Orla.'

'I've always thought it was reciprocal. It's strange they've never got together.' She cleared her throat. 'And you, any girlfriend, wife, kids?'

He grinned. 'Free as a bird.'

She felt her cheeks flush, focusing her attention on picking the nail varnish off her thumbnail. She shouldn't have asked him that.

'And you?'

She looked up at him. 'No significant other.'

A smile touched his lips. He glanced at his watch and his face fell.

'I have to go, I promised I'd help someone... with something,'

That was vague enough for her to see it as the excuse it was. He was clearly done with this little reunion.

'Oh OK. I guess I'll see you around.'

'I really do have to go but we have so much more we need to catch up on, I want to know what you've been doing all these years. Will you have dinner with me tonight in the Smuggler's Inn? Say seven o'clock?'

'I'd love that.'

He stood up and she stood up too. He came around the bench and gave her another hug, but this time he placed a kiss on her cheek and the warmth of his lips made her heart leap in her chest.

'It's so good seeing you again,' Theo said. 'I'll see you tonight.'

'I can't wait.'

He smiled and gave her a wave and then hurried off, but as he disappeared she could still feel his lips on her cheek.

Roo finished her drink and took her mug back inside. Orla was waiting for her, eyes filled with excitement.

'Well?'

Roo laughed. 'Well what?'

'How did the reunion go?'

'It was short, he had somewhere he needed to be.'

'Oh.' The smile fell from her face. 'I wouldn't take it personally. He is always so busy.'

'I'm not taking it personally. I can't expect that we're going to suddenly be best friends again, not after all this time. But he is taking me to dinner tonight.'

Orla's face brightened. 'Well that's more like it. I always thought you two should have got together.'

'Oh no, he never saw me like that. We were best friends. It was never anything more than that.'

'Not from what I saw. He adored you.'

Roo smiled sadly. Theo had had many girlfriends before she'd left for Chicago but he'd never looked at her in that way. She decided to change the subject because if they did become friends again, she couldn't pine after him again. She'd been there and done that.

'What about you and Shay, if ever there was a couple that should be together, it's you two.'

Orla blushed and shook her head. 'Shay and I… we have a complicated past.'

'You have a past? Did something happen while I was away?'

'No. It's really not something I want to talk about. I've shoved it away in a box in my mind marked "do not open" and I don't think it's something I'll ever get past. We're friends. I like it that way. No complications.'

'Well that's intriguing.'

'It really isn't. It's ancient history. It's not going to happen. Whereas you and Theo—'

Roo held up a hand. 'Let's just agree we're not going to interfere in each other's love lives.'

Orla's mouth snapped closed. 'OK, fair point. I'm just happy you're back and I'm pleased you and Theo will be friends again. I'll say no more.'

Roo nodded. 'I'm happy to be back too. I better go and have a shower before I meet him for dinner tonight.'

'Good idea,' Orla smirked.

Roo laughed and rolled her eyes. She gave Orla a wave goodbye and walked out.

As Theo drove to the woods on the opposite side of White Cliff Bay, he phoned his brother, Shay, and put him on speakerphone.

'Hey,' Shay said.

'Hey, I have a problem.'

'Is everything OK with Molly?'

'She's fine, she's sitting next to me and making a lot of noise,' Theo said, trying to tune out the incessant squeaks and squeals from his passenger. 'No, it's not that. Erm… Roo's back.'

There was silence from Shay for a moment. 'Wow, I wasn't expecting that.'

'Me neither, we just bumped into each other in Seahorses. She looked amazing.' He shook his head. He didn't want to go down that road again. 'We chatted a bit but I obviously had Molly to take care of. So I'm meeting her for dinner tonight.'

'So what's the problem? It's good that she's back, she was your best friend.'

Theo sighed. He wasn't sure he could even begin to describe the turmoil he'd felt over seeing her again. At work he was confident, made decisions, got stuff done. Even outside work he had to make quick judgement calls and that never fazed him, but with Roo he suddenly felt lost.

'If I were you, I'd tell her.'

Theo stared at the phone in disbelief. 'I'd rather eat a live cockroach.'

'Nice, be sure to fill her head with such lovely images, right before you tell her.'

'Why would I tell her?'

'Because it means you can put the past to bed and start over with a clean slate. It's something you should have told her years ago. Trust me on that.'

Theo sighed. 'Shouldn't you be taking your own advice?'

'That's entirely different. It's... complicated.'

'How many times have I heard that?' Theo said.

'I cocked up the past spectacularly, I'm surprised Orla even talks to me. You two can still be friends as long as you're honest with each other.'

Theo looked out the window at the sea. 'I'd better go. Thanks for the pearls of wisdom.'

'Anytime,' Shay said, completely missing the sarcasm.

Theo hung up and shook his head. That wasn't going to happen.

CHAPTER THREE

Roo closed the door to her little beach hut and walked over the headland into the town of Apple Hill Bay. Her stomach was twisting and fluttering like she was on a rollercoaster, and her heart was racing, which was silly. She knew Theo, this was simply two friends catching up, there was nothing more to it than that. But her stupid heart didn't believe her.

She focused on the incredible view that was now her home instead. The sun was on its way into the sea, leaving behind clouds of flamingo pink so it looked like little tufts of candy floss in the sky.

And there was the little town. Houses of every colour huddled together in the valley as if sheltering from a storm. Strings of lights were already lit up around the harbour and many a window already had a golden glow spilling out onto the street.

In many ways, Apple Hill Bay hadn't changed at all

since she'd left. It was still the sleepy little seaside town with a fleet of small fishing boats and trawlers that went out every day. This image from up here on the headland was on every postcard they sold in the shops and it was probably the same postcard image fifty or a hundred years ago.

There was something achingly familiar and comforting about seeing this view again. It was good to be back home after all these years. It had felt like fate when she'd been offered a job on the far side of town. All she needed now was a new home; a flat or cottage to rent. Staying in The Little Beach Hut Hotel was only a temporary thing, no matter how much she loved the view over Strawberry Sands.

As Roo walked closer to the town, she could see some of the shops had changed names or uses and some stalwarts were exactly the same, even down to the displays in the windows. It made her smile.

Her favourite Indian restaurant was still here, although it was quite obviously closed tonight. The Smuggler's Inn appeared round the bend. She had many fond memories in there, although a lot of those memories were connected to Theo.

She pushed open the door and looked over to the pool table where they'd spent many an hour thrashing each other at pool. The pub was exactly as she remembered it, old wood-panelled walls, steps up and down to little nooks and secluded seating areas. It was there, underneath a painting of the Golden Hind, that she and Theo had sat and planned out a round-the-world trip, where they wanted to visit and what they wanted to do. Over there, near the bookshelf of forgotten books, they'd talked about starting their own business, although the nature of the business changed every week. They'd always had big ideas and dreams that had never come to fruition.

She looked around and saw Theo at the same time he spotted her. He stood up with a big smile on his face and as she hurried over to him, he held out his arms and enveloped her in a big hug. She held him tight, probably longer than was necessary but he didn't seem to mind. He smelled amazing, the scent of vanilla, grapefruit and cedar wood that reminded her of summer nights on a tropical beach.

She pulled back and looked up at him. 'Hey.'

He smiled. 'Hi.'

She couldn't help but just stare at him. 'I missed you so much.'

He frowned slightly and she instantly regretted saying that. 'Roo, losing you was like losing a limb.'

She felt a soft gasp escape her lips.

He cleared his throat and let her go. 'I didn't know what drink to get you, whether you're drinking wine or beer or something soft as I know you're starting your new job tomorrow, so I got you that rose lemonade you always loved.'

She loved that he remembered that. 'What a lovely dose of nostalgia.'

As was sitting here with him again after all this time.

They sat down and she took a sip, which brought back so many memories.

Theo handed her the menu and she took a few moments to look at it.

'The burgers are always good here,' Theo said.

'I was leaning towards the burger.'

'Two burgers it is.' Theo stood back up. 'I'll get these.'

'Oh no, let me, you got our drinks—'

'Please, let me get them.'

It was so sincere she couldn't help but nod. 'But I'm getting the next meal.'

'I'm just happy you already want another meal with me, so I'm fine with that.'

He went off to the bar and she couldn't take her eyes off him. As he waited to be served he kept looking round at her too, with a big grin on his face. She felt like she needed to clear the air with him. He didn't seem like he needed that, but she knew she must have hurt him all those years ago.

After a few minutes he returned to the table, still sporting a huge smile.

'Theo, I need to apologise for—'

'You have nothing to apologise for.' Theo frowned. 'It's me that needs to apologise, I should have been there for you when your dad died.'

'You tried, so many times.'

'I should have tried harder.'

'I cut you out. It wasn't your fault. I was so angry at the world, so lost and confused. I was alone in Chicago and there was a lot to deal with. There was so much paper-work over his death. His accounts were frozen because he'd died and there were bills to pay. It was just the worst time and I didn't know how to handle it. And you were so excited about going travelling around Europe and when you said you were going to fly out to see me instead of your trip I knew I couldn't let you do it. You'd talked about that trip for months. So I stopped replying to your messages and eventually you stopped texting me. I lost my best friend and it was entirely my fault but you have to know that broke me just as much as losing my dad. It's my biggest regret and I'm sorry.'

Theo reached out and took her hand. 'I hated losing you too. I thought about you so often over the years. I wish I could have been there for you when your dad died but I never blamed you for us drifting apart. You were grieving. When you stopped messaging me, I figured you needed space and that when you were ready you'd get in touch. I should have tried harder to make sure you were OK. I did text you about six months after your dad had died but the text came back undeliverable. I didn't know what to do after that. You've never been one for Facebook or other social media. I thought you were angry at me for going to Europe without you.'

'Oh no, of course I wasn't.'

'But we'd planned that trip together, right over there.' Theo gestured to the table in the corner.

'That was never going to happen, not for me. It was lovely talking about it, but I think I knew even then that it wasn't going to happen. When Dad moved us out to Chicago after he finally divorced Mum, that was my exciting future. I had a place at a college in Illinois. But I was excited for you. I was never angry at you for that. I suppose if I'm honest, a part of me was angry that your life was so exciting and wonderful when Dad's life had just stopped and it felt like mine had stopped too. But I wanted you to go to Europe. That was important to me. If you can forgive me for how I acted, then maybe we can move forward. I'd love to get to know you again.'

'There is nothing to forgive,' Theo said, without hesitation.

She smiled and looked down at her hand wrapped in his. It felt so right.

'Tell me about Europe then, what were the highlights?'

'Oh, that feels like a lifetime ago, but undoubtedly the Plitvice Lakes in Croatia were the most beautiful place I've ever been.'

She gave a little mock gasp. 'That wasn't in the plan, did you deviate?'

Theo laughed. 'A little… well maybe a lot. It was very easy to go with the flow out there. You would have loved it. Me, you, Custard and a canopy of a million stars.'

Roo laughed.

'Custard only had one bed,' she said, referring to his bright yellow camper van.

Something sparked in his eyes she'd never seen before. 'We would have made it work.'

The way he was looking at her she was left with no doubt how he wanted to make it work. Her mouth was suddenly dry. Had he really felt that way? She'd last seen him when they were nineteen. He always had lots of girl-friends, however fleeting, but he'd never looked at her like that, well not to her knowledge. She always had no confidence back then, and while he had a different girlfriend every week, she never went out with anyone – she was too shy, too awkward, apart from with him. Fourteen years ago she would have blushed, and changed the subject, but that was a long time ago and she was a different person now.

'How exactly would that have worked?'

He grinned. 'Well, some parts of Europe were very hot. I ended up sleeping naked many nights.'

She laughed. 'You were always such a flirt.' She had watched him turn on that charm with everyone he met and most of the time it didn't mean anything, it was just harmless flirting. Maybe she could try it too. 'If you'd said that to me when I was nineteen, I would have floated out of here on air, I had such a crush on you back then.'

She expected him to be taken back by this but he squeezed her hand. 'Roo, I was head over heels in love with you.'

'Two burgers.' the waitress appeared between them, placing two oversized plates of burgers, chips and all the trimmings on the table. Theo let go of her hand to make room.

'Thanks Becca,' Theo said, flashing the woman a big smile. She scurried away, blushing and Theo took a big bite of his burger.

Roo stared at him in shock. 'What did you say?'

He chewed, a smile on his lips. He was playing with her. He swallowed his food. 'I was in love with you.'

She had no words at all.

'Your burger is getting cold,' Theo said, taking another bite.

She looked down at her burger and back at him. 'You loved me? Do you mean you loved me as a friend?'

'I loved you in the sense that I wanted to get married to you and have lots of babies.'

She sat back in surprise. 'You... You wanted to marry me?'

'It was something I thought about a lot.'

'Why did you never say anything?'

'Why didn't you tell me how you felt?'

Roo sighed. 'God, Theo, I was so in love with you but you always had lots of girlfriends, I didn't think you were interested in me.'

'I was always interested in you, but I didn't think you felt that way for me either. And I never thought I was good enough. Your mum made it very clear you'd be scraping the barrel by dating me.'

'She said that?' Roo was horrified.

'Oh yes, many times. In many different ways, but mostly it was how I would ruin your life if I got involved with you.'

She reached out to take his hand again. 'That isn't true, not at all and I'm so sorry she said that and for how that must have made you feel. She's a vile woman, you know that.'

'I know. I did consider telling you how I felt but then your dad started the move to Chicago and you were so excited. I didn't want you to miss out on that.'

Roo put her head in her hands and let out a moan. She

wanted to cry over the missed opportunity. Neither of them had been brave enough to tell the truth.

'Hey, come on. It was a very long time ago. We've both changed and grown.'

'But we could have grown together,' Roo said.

He smiled wistfully. 'We have no idea how long we would have lasted, if at all. We were kids.'

'We loved each other. We deserved a chance. I'd rather have had six months together than nothing at all.'

'I would too, but it is what it is. Maybe it just wasn't our time.'

'I think we would have made it work,' she echoed his words back to him.

They stared at each other, both thinking about what could have been. She turned her attention to her burger, though she really wasn't in the mood for eating now. She didn't know what to say. All these years she had thought about Theo, missed him, ached for him and he had probably been feeling the same. He'd wanted to marry her. What would have happened if she had stayed here instead of going to Chicago with her dad? Would they really have ended up married with kids?

'I've made you sad and that wasn't my intention,' Theo said. 'I never told you back then but I thought you should know you meant the world to me.'

'You meant the world to me too. I'd really like to be friends again.'

He nodded. 'I'd like that too.'

They were silent for a while as they ate. She had to let

go of this disappointment. It was a long time ago and would they really have lasted all this time?

She cleared her throat. 'So how did Custard perform around Europe?' she asked.

'Admirably. We went up mountains and travelled miles. For her age, she was a star.'

'Well I hope you gave her a fitting retirement when you got home.'

'Fern has her now, she uses Custard for her mural painting business.'

'Oh I love that Custard is still going after all this time.'

'And what about you? What have you been doing for the last fourteen years?'

She frowned. 'My life has been a bit of a mess. I didn't go to college in Illinois, I was grieving and I just didn't want to stay in Chicago when Dad had gone. With my dual citizenship, I could work anywhere, so I worked in Florida at Disney, Universal Studios and Busch Gardens, there's a lot of seasonal work out there. I worked in Colorado, San Francisco, Rhode Island. A different place, a different job. I went to Australia, learned how to be a dive instructor and did that for a while. I worked my way through Europe for a while, working in bars and restaurants, picking fruit, worked on farms, I travelled all over Europe doing jobs here and there, I worked in the ski resorts in the winter. Moved back to America about eighteen months ago and ending up working in the big hotels in Vegas for a few months. I got married, got divorced very quickly. I guess I'm still trying to find my place in life. Nothing fits, not long term.'

'Not even a husband,' Theo said.

'That was a huge mistake. Cole and I just had one of those crazy passionate whirlwind affairs and one morning, after we'd been seeing each other for a week, we decided to get married. It was silly and Vegas does crazy things to a person. We got a licence half an hour later and were married by lunchtime. A few days later he came home drunk, wanted sex, I said no and he slapped me round the face.'

Theo went very still. 'What?'

'It's OK. Well it wasn't, but it was one slap. I packed my bags and got out of there, filed for divorce and thankfully never had to see him again. It was then I realised I'd lost my way in life and I'd become someone I didn't even recognise or like. What kind of person would marry someone they barely know, just for fun? I didn't love him, I knew that. It was a huge wake up call for me.'

She chewed her lip. 'Since Dad died, and since I lost you, who was the best thing that's ever happened to me, I've been moving on, never staying still long enough to form attachments. I don't know, maybe I was trying to protect myself from getting hurt again, or maybe I'm just like my mum, restless, always trying to find something better? I looked back at my life and wondered when was the last time I was truly happy and it was here, with you. And while I didn't think you'd still be here, I knew I wanted to come home to Apple Hill Bay. I haven't had somewhere to call home for the last fourteen years and I've missed that. Once the divorce was final a few months ago, I came back to England and now I have a job here I'm really excited about and I'm just so happy. I'm ready to settle down in one place and now I feel like I can finally start the rest of my life.'

'I'm happy for you. Being in foster care for most of my childhood, with hundreds of different foster homes, I was always so desperate for somewhere to call home. When Carrie adopted me and brought me here, I knew this place was it. I feel at peace here and there's nowhere in the world I'd rather be.'

She nodded. He understood the need for home more than anyone and it explained why he never moved off somewhere else.

'What's the job?' Theo asked.

'It's in design. Graphic design was always something I loved, even when I was here. It was something you got me interested in and I stuck with it for the last fourteen years, did more courses, taught myself on loads of different software. No matter what job I was doing, wherever I was in the world, I always had design side hustles. I've worked on book covers, marketing, brand design, logos, packaging, I've even worked on character design for some computer games and illustrations for children's books. The company I'm working for are starting a new project and I will have free rein to design it how I see fit. I'm really excited.'

'That's wonderful. When you find that thing that you're really passionate about, there's no feeling like it.'

'What about you, what is it you do?'

He let out a heavy sigh. 'It's not something I'm passionate about, not anymore. When I started, I loved it, but there's a lot more paperwork and meetings than I ever thought was possible in a job and I find that stuff mind-numbingly boring.'

She studied him, she knew what it felt like to work doing something she didn't enjoy, or to find herself stuck in a rut. 'What are you passionate about?'

He was quiet for a while. 'I think I'm like you in that respect, I haven't found my niche in life. Although it sounds like you've finally found yours.'

She finished her burger as she thought, maybe she could help Theo find the thing he was passionate about now she was back. She wanted him to be happy, he deserved that much.

'So other than your ex-husband, any great love stories?' Theo asked, wiping his mouth and moving his plate to the side of the table.

'No, and not even with him. I never stand still long enough to fall in love. And I certainly didn't grieve for losing that *love story*. In fact I'm grieving more for my lost love story with you than I ever did for Cole.'

He grinned. 'If we'd have got married, we'd have done it properly and it would have lasted a hell of a lot longer than a week.'

'Don't. I don't want to start imagining what our wedding would have looked like. I never even imagined it fourteen years ago as I had no idea that future was a possibility. I did imagine kissing you a lot. And other things. But I always felt woefully inadequate in that department. When I left here at nineteen, I'd slept with one man, you'd slept with tons of women. I'm half grateful that we never got that far. You'd have been very disappointed.'

'There was no way I could ever have been disappointed with that. It would have been different for us. Making love to the woman I loved, it would have been perfect.'

She smiled and rolled her eyes. 'We need to stop talking about making love. This is not helping me to stop lamenting over what might have been.'

'Sorry. I'm sure it would have been rubbish really.'

She laughed. 'What about you?'

'You were the only woman I've ever loved. I've never met anyone I wanted anything serious with. And a few years ago I started my own business and it took off. My life is filled with early breakfast meetings, late-night meetings, weekend meetings, I'm not sure any woman would put up with that. And for the most part, the only women I see now are the ones in my company. And I certainly never want to mix business with pleasure.'

'I get that. Work and relationships should never mix.' She looked at her watch. 'Talking of work, I should probably go. I want to be fresh for my first day in my new job.'

He nodded. 'I have an early breakfast meeting so I probably need to go too. I'll walk you back.'

'You don't need to do that, it's not far and Apple Hill Bay is very safe.'

'It's no problem and I don't like the idea of you walking around on your own at night.'

She smiled. She wasn't ready to say goodbye to him

just yet so she was happy to spend a few more minutes in his company.

They left the pub and he took her hand as if it was the most natural thing in the world. It made her feel warm inside. They started walking out of the town. She had so many memories of this place or rather so many memories of Theo in this place, it was wonderful to be back here again with him. Over there, at the back of the doctors, they had started their own car-washing business, well, Theo had and she had helped. They were both good at art and they would sell hand-drawn caricatures of people's pets outside the supermarket. He had even designed websites for some of the businesses around the town when he was sixteen. He had always been entrepreneurial, so it was no surprise he owned his own business now.

As they left the town behind them and started walking over the headland, the moon seemed to shine brighter as they walked through the darkness. Thousands of tiny diamonds peppered the heavens above them. The sea sparkled under a moonlit blanket.

'What are you thinking?' Theo said.

'How happy I was here with you. I have so many good memories of my life here, doing our car-wash business, doing our pet caricatures and all those happy, fun times. Swimming in the sea, paddleboarding, surfing, racing our bikes over the hills. I've had some friends in my life, albeit temporary ones, but I never had what I had with you and I know we were kids and my friends were obviously adults but we shared an incredibly close bond.'

'What we had was special, even outside of the seemingly unrequited love, it was something rare and wonderful.'

She liked that. It really had been.

They arrived at her beach hut too soon. She unlocked the door and considered inviting him in. She wanted more time with him but he was already looking at his watch.

'Can I see you tomorrow night?' Theo said. 'I'll take you out for dinner again.'

'I'd like that but this time, I'm paying.'

He smiled. 'We'll see about that. I'll pick you up at seven then?'

'Sounds good.'

He smiled and bent his head to kiss her on the cheek but as she leaned up to hug him, he ended up kissing her on the corner of her mouth. His eyes flashed. Her heart leapt.

He stroked her face, staring at her with a look of adoration. 'Roo, can I kiss you?' he asked softly.

'I'd be disappointed if you didn't.'

He smiled and bent his head, her heart thundered against her chest. She closed her eyes and then his lips gently met hers. It was sweet and wonderful and utterly divine. She'd wondered if it would feel weird to be kissing her best friend after all this time but it didn't. It felt completely perfect, as if they should have been doing this all along. She slid her hands round his neck, stroking the short hair just above his collar. He made a noise that sounded like a moan and suddenly the kiss changed to something needful, something more. This was everything.

It was too much but not enough. He powered her back against the door, kissing her like he couldn't get enough of her. His hands wandered down her body and she pressed herself up against him.

Suddenly he pulled away making her feel bereft.

His breath was heavy as he stared at her. 'I should go, otherwise this kiss is going to turn into a hell of a lot more.'

'Yes, we should be sensible about this,' Roo said, grabbing his shirt and pulling him back to her, kissing him hard. This was the best kiss she'd ever had in her life, how could it be so good? Was it because it was Theo, was it their connection, their past or was he just some kind of god of kissing? Whatever it was, she didn't want it to stop.

'Do you want to come in for coffee or something?' she said, breathlessly.

He nodded as he kissed her again. She fumbled around with the door handle and they fell through the door. He caught her before she hit the floor and lifted her back on her feet. He kicked the door shut as he pinned her to the wall, not taking his mouth from hers for even a second.

He rocked his hips against her and she made a strangled noise of need against his lips.

'Roo, I need to be honest.' Theo moved his mouth to her throat.

'About?'

'I don't drink coffee?'

She laughed. 'Neither do I.'

He kissed her again. His hands slid her dress up her thighs and with one swift movement he dragged it over her head and threw it across the room. He made quick work of her bra and then his mouth was on her breast.

She clutched the back of his neck. 'Oh God, Theo.'

He paused, lifting his head. 'Is this OK?'

'Yes, don't stop.'

He smiled and kissed her hard, his hands roaming over her body.

For a brief moment, she wondered if this was a good idea. She wanted to be friends with Theo again, would this ruin everything between them? But the part of her that was celebrating that she was kissing Theo Lucas after all this time, the part that had often fantasised about what it would be like to kiss him and make love to him was screaming with joy that this was happening. This was Theo Lucas with his hands on her breasts. She owed it to her nineteen-year-old self to let this play out. She had spent years thinking about this moment and now it was finally happening.

She wrestled him out of his shirt and then unzipped his jeans and pushed them off his bum. He grabbed his wallet, yanked out a condom and then wriggled out of his jeans. She ran her hands over his chest and arms. He was deliciously strong, his body rock hard with muscles. He kissed right over her heart then trailed his mouth lower to her stomach as he knelt down to remove her knickers. He kissed up her leg until his mouth pressed gently inside her thigh before he stood back up again.

He kissed her again, skimming his hand over her waist and then between her legs. She gasped against his lips as he touched her in the exact place that made her go weak.

Her stomach tightened with need and she felt that delicious feeling building through her body like a wildfire spiralling out of control. She cried out against his lips as that feeling exploded through her. Her legs were weak and she would have sunk to the floor if he hadn't been holding her up.

As she struggled with her breath while she came down from her high, he kicked off his shorts, ripped open the condom and put it on before he lifted her. She wrapped her arms and legs around him and in one exquisite move he was inside her. Her breath shuddered at the feel of him and she cupped his face and kissed him as he moved against her. That feeling that had started to subside immediately started to build again. He was utterly perfect, every movement sending her mindless with pleasure, taking her higher and higher until she was falling apart in his arms, moaning against his lips, making noises she'd never made before. The noise he made as he fell over the edge was nothing short of a roar. She pulled back to stare at him, her breath heavy on his lips. She stroked his face, barely able to believe that had just happened.

He carried her over to the sofa and lay her down. He quickly dealt with the condom and half lay on top of her, stroking her and kissing her until she fell asleep.

Roo woke in the early hours of the morning as Theo climbed off her and started moving quietly around the room. He was obviously going to try and sneak out, which she wasn't totally surprised about. When she knew him in his late teens, he said he never spent the night with a woman. He'd said that cuddling with a woman in bed, spending the night together made it feel more intimate than it was. It was always just sex and he'd never wanted that intimacy with anyone. Although that had been fourteen years ago, she wasn't surprised that attitude hadn't changed. He'd had a damaged childhood before she'd met him, living in foster care until Carrie adopted him at thirteen. No one, apart from Carrie, had ever shown him any love so running away from intimacy was understandable. But it didn't stop it hurting. She wondered if he regretted it and what would happen between them now he'd slept with her. She couldn't regret what happened, it had been incredible but if he didn't want a relationship with her, could they really go back to being just friends after this?

She watched him quietly picking up his clothes and then putting them down again as if he was looking for something. Maybe his underwear. She smirked, that had probably been kicked across the room in a moment of passion.

He came back to her, obviously having found what he was looking for.

'Hey,' she said, softly. 'You OK?'

'I can't sleep here.'

She felt the kick of disappointment.

He pressed something into her hand, although in the darkness she couldn't make out what it was. He bent down, slid his arms underneath her and lifted her.

She let out a little shriek and quickly wrapped her arms round his neck.

'Don't lose that. It's my last one and I'm going to need it shortly.'

She glanced at the thing in her hand again and as he walked across the room and the light caught it, she realised it was a condom. Her stomach clenched with need.

'What are you doing?'

'Why sleep on a hard, uncomfortable sofa when there is a huge, soft, comfortable bed upstairs.' He started carrying her up the stairs. 'And if you're willing and awake enough, I'd like to make love to you in that great big, comfortable bed.'

'I'm definitely awake enough.'

He hit the light switch with his elbow as he got to the top and laid her down on top of the bed. She scooted over and he lay down next to her immediately wrapping her in his arms and kissing her softly. She stroked his face.

'Do you think we've ruined our friendship now?' Roo asked.

'I think we've made it stronger.'

'We don't even know each other. Fourteen years is a long time.'

'We can get to know each other again, doesn't mean we can't have some fun along the way.'

'But what if the person I am now is not someone you want to be with, long term, or we break up for another reason? Can we go back to being friends after we've seen each other naked and done rude things to each other?'

'And what if we fall head over heels in love with each other, get married, pop out a few kids and live happily ever after?' Theo said.

She smiled at the lovely rose-tinted image. 'I never thought I would see the day that Theo Lucas would be talking about marriage.'

'I'm just saying, let's not worry about the future just yet, it might not be this big scary thing you're making it out to be. It could be utterly wonderful.'

'Live for now?'

'Exactly.' He kissed her. 'Are you happy now?'

She smiled. 'Blissfully so.'

'Then worry about tomorrow, tomorrow.'

She pressed herself up against him and kissed him. 'I like that attitude.'

He kissed her and rolled on top of her then he pulled back to look at her, stroking her face.

'Never in a million years did I ever think we'd be here like this,' Theo said.

'Me neither. Even when I saw you tonight, I didn't think I'd be taking you back to mine for incredible sex.'

'It wasn't even on my radar. I figured as it hadn't happened fourteen years ago, it wasn't about to start now. And then we kissed and suddenly it made sense.'

'As if we should have been doing it all along.'

He nodded. 'I don't know what the future holds for us, but I do know making love to you tonight was something more than it's ever been for me.'

She swallowed. 'Me too.'

He kissed her again and she smiled against his lips.

He pulled back again. 'Can I make love to you again. I promise it will be much better than last time.'

'That is a hard act to follow, Theo Lucas. The last time was pretty spectacular.'

'But I want to take my time with you. I want to explore every single inch of your body. I want to spend the rest of the night making love to you.'

'Well, that doesn't sound like a total hardship.' She wrapped her legs around him, sliding her hands down his back.

He laughed. 'I think you might enjoy it.'

CHAPTER FOUR

Theo woke the next day with Roo wrapped in his arms. It felt so perfectly right, as if she belonged there. He had never been with a woman he wanted more with. Every single woman in his past had been one night, nothing more but for the first time in his life he was excited about what would happen with her.

He looked at his watch and groaned. He had an early breakfast meeting this morning, he had to go.

He quickly slipped from the bed, Roo didn't even stir. He wasn't surprised. It had been several hours before they'd finally fallen asleep the night before.

He went downstairs and threw on his clothes, he'd grab a quick shower at the office and he knew he had spare clothes there too.

He found his wallet and keys and shoved them in his pockets and then went back upstairs. He shook her gently awake. She stretched and opened one eye and her smile lit up her entire face when she saw him.

'I have to go to work. Can I still take you for dinner tonight?'

Her smile grew. 'Yes, I'd really like that.'

He leaned over and kissed her and she stroked his face. Christ, he wanted to climb back into bed with her and make love to her again. He had an insatiable need for her that he didn't think would ever be sated.

He pulled back. 'I really have to go.'

She let him go. 'I know.'

'Good luck at your new job, I want to hear all about it tonight.'

He realised that he had no idea where she was even working or what the big project entailed. There was so much he needed to know about her, but they had all the time in the world to get to know each other again.

'Thank you and you can tell me all about your job and why you're not passionate about it. Maybe I can help you find your joy in life.'

He wondered if she already had.

'I'll tell you all about it,' Theo said.

He kissed her again, this time on the head because he knew if he kissed her properly, he would be late. He gave her a wave and quickly ran out of the hut and straight into his brother Shay.

Shay had been responsible for building all the beach huts at The Little Beach Hut Hotel and now the place was up and running he was the manager of the place. It was just Theo's luck to bump into him now.

44

'Hey, what are you doing here?' Shay looked at the hut suspiciously. Theo wondered if he knew who was staying there.

'I'm running late for work, that's what.'

'Did you stay there last night?'

'Yes, I...'

He didn't have an explanation, or at least not one he wanted to share with his brother. What he'd shared with Roo was private, just between them.

'Is everything OK at your house?' Shay asked.

'Yes, everything is fine.'

Shay looked back at the hut and back at him, his face clearing with understanding. 'Am I going to get complaints from my guests for bad behaviour?'

'Why would you assume I've treated anyone badly?'

'You're not known for your commitment. You're sneaking out of here at six-thirty in the morning, presumably to avoid the awkward morning-after conversation. It doesn't bode well for when she wakes up.'

'I can assure you there won't be any complaints.'

Suddenly the penny dropped, he could see it on Shay's face. 'Is this where Roo is staying?'

Theo sighed, it would take Shay five seconds to look up which guest was staying there, so there was no point denying it. 'Yes.'

'Bloody hell. When I said put the past to bed, I didn't mean literally.'

Theo rolled his eyes and patted Shay on the shoulder. 'Best advice you've ever given me. But I really have to go.'

He left Shay before he could say anything else and ran down the hill towards the town.

Roo practically floated into Orla's café a while later. She must have had a maximum of two hours sleep the night before, she was exhausted but she couldn't have been happier. When Theo had made love to her the second time he'd spent an inordinate amount of time kissing every single inch of her body, adoring her, worshipping her. No one had ever done that before. And when he'd eventually made love to her, the way he'd looked at her was with so much adoration. No one had ever looked at her like that either. She knew she had so much to learn about Theo but she was looking forward to finding out.

Orla looked over at her as she finished serving a walking group and her face lit up in a big grin.

The walking group moved over to the tables and chairs and Orla leaned over the counter to talk to Roo.

'I was going to ask how your dinner with Theo went last night, but I'm guessing that it went really well.'

Roo laughed. 'Is it that obvious?'

'You look like you've had the most amazing sex of your life.'

Roo blushed, knowing there was no point in denying it. 'Wow, I really need to work on my poker face. Can I get a tea to go please?'

'That was fast work,' Orla said, as she started preparing Roo's drink.

Roo nodded. It was fast. She had never jumped into bed with a man so quickly before in her life. But with Theo it was different.

'It really was and so completely unexpected. Even when he walked me home, I don't think either of us expected the night to end the way it did. Then he kissed me goodnight on the cheek and suddenly it was a hell of a lot more than a kiss.'

'I'm happy for you,' Orla said, wistfully. 'I wish all relationships were that simple. So are you two together, dating, or was it just a one-time only thing?'

'I think we're going to give it a try. We have to get to know each other all over again but from the way he was talking it didn't seem like a one-night stand to him. He's taking me out to dinner tonight, so yeah I guess we're dating.'

Orla grinned. 'That's fantastic news. I'm excited for you.'

'I'm excited too. But can we just keep this between us for now? It's all so new and I would prefer no one else knew until we can figure it out for ourselves, especially not Theo's family.'

'I know what Carrie's like, my lips are sealed.' She handed Roo her drink. 'Have a good day in your new job.'

'I'm sure I will.'

The door opened behind her and she glanced round to see Shay walking in. She looked back at Orla and saw her face light up. It was so obvious she was in love with the man, she might as well be holding a neon flashing sign above her head. Roo looked back at Shay who only had eyes for Orla. He didn't even seem to notice Roo at first.

'You have a good day too,' Roo said, backing away to give them some space.

Suddenly Shay realised she was there. 'Roo, hey, I heard you were back.'

He gave her a hug.

'Shay, it's good to see you again.'

He pulled back and studied her, a smirk playing on his lips. 'You look… happy.'

God, was she that obvious? 'I'm happy to be back.'

'Sure, yes, that's the kind of happiness I can see,' Shay said, clearly trying to suppress that smirk.

Roo flushed. 'Well, I must go, I'm starting my new job today. I'll catch you both later.'

Shay nodded and watched her go but by the time she was at the door he was already giving his undivided attention to Orla again, and Roo was completely forgotten.

Roo smiled and hurried out.

Right now she had to focus on her job and make sure she shone. Charlie, her new managing director, had approached her after she started posting images from her design portfolio on local Facebook groups and pages asking if anyone knew of any design jobs in Apple Hill Bay. She wanted to ensure that Charlie felt he'd made the right decision in taking her on.

She saw Mrs Kimbleford ahead, walking Max, and she waved. Max bounded over and she gave him a scratch behind the ears.

'You're looking very smart in your suit, dear,' Mrs Kimbleford said as Roo drew closer to her.

'I start my new job today, I'm not sure if it's a suit-wearing kind of place but I thought I should try and make a good first impression.'

Especially as she hadn't had time to make the cakes as she'd planned.

'Oh yes, first impressions are important, you want to show people you are fun, serious, hard-working, flexible, reliable and likeable all in one hit. I think you can't go wrong in a suit, unless they're all wearing jeans and shorts and t-shirts, then you'll stand out like a sore thumb. But I'm sure management will be impressed with a suit even if no one else is.'

This wasn't filling her with confidence.

'Where are you working?' Mrs Kimbleford asked.

'Pet Protagonist on the other side of town. It's a small, illustrated book publisher and printing press where people's pets are cast as the main character in a personalised story.'

'Oh I love the idea of that.'

'It's a great concept isn't it? And very popular. I've been hired as a lead designer and I'll be in charge of creating the illustrations for a brand new story they're publishing soon. I'm really excited about it.'

'Sounds wonderful. What a great job. In my day you were either a secretary or a teacher, but nowadays there are so many more exciting opportunities. I must check out this Pet Protagonist, it would be nice to immortalise Max in such a way.'

'Oh you should! I've seen the stories, they're very cute.'

'Well, you go and knock 'em dead.'

Roo grinned. 'I will.'

She gave her a wave and hurried off. Charlie had suggested she started at ten so she wasn't lost in the crush of everyone arriving. She absolutely didn't want to be late.

Charlie was waiting for her as she walked into reception and he came over to shake her hand.

'Aurora, lovely to see you again.'

'Hello, Mr Roberts.'

'Charlie, please. Mr Roberts makes me sound so old and I'm in denial that my thirty-fifth birthday is at the end of the month.'

She smiled. 'OK, Charlie it is.'

'I thought I'd give you the tour first, so you get a rough idea of where everything is. Although if you forget or get lost, just ask someone. We're a very friendly bunch here.'

'Good to know.'

There was a very good chance she wouldn't remember any of this. Her mind was half asleep and half thinking about Theo. She needed to focus, she had been so excited about starting this job for weeks and she definitely wanted to make a good impression.

Charlie gestured to a pair of doors and she followed him through.

'In here is the elf workshop.'

She laughed as she looked around at a load of people working massive machines in high-vis vests.

'This is our printing room – once the book is finished up there in the graphics department, it's sent down here and our elves print them off. It's a big production because we have machines printing out the pages, a different machine that prints out the cover, another machine that laminates the cover, one that binds it and another that trims it.' He gestured round to all the different machines that were churning out pages and books as they walked through the room. 'When we first started, we would make the book on the computer and then send it to a small local printers in the town, but as the demand has grown we've had to expand our company to incorporate our own printers too. We have a rigorous checking system as well – the last thing we want is bad reviews because we've cocked up. Once a book is printed and bound, Tasmin and Bex here will check every single page to make sure it's in the right order, the colours are all fine, and the right pet is portrayed for each customer.'

Bex and Tasmin both smiled and waved and Roo waved back.

'OK, let's head on up,' Charlie said, opening the door to a set of stairs.

She followed him up the stairs and into a huge open plan office.

'Over here is the Marketing department. These guys are doing TikToks, Instagram posts and reels, Facebook posts and ads, Amazon ads, sponsored listings on Etsy, eBay, Not on The High Street, Buy a Gift, Virgin Experiences, Into the Blue, and loads of others. We also have ads in newspapers and magazines, and sometimes on the London Underground too. Everyone, this is Aurora, she'll be working in Design.'

Everyone waved and then carried on with their work.

'This is the story department.' Charlie gestured to a small area with three people busily working away on their computers. 'There are currently five different adventures that the pets go on in our books. But the more choice we have, the more likely we will get repeat customers. So we are constantly working on new ideas and new stories. By Christmas we hope to have twenty stories for people to choose from.'

The three people here had headphones on so Charlie didn't disturb them. He walked onto the next area, which was around fifteen desks all pushed together to make one big area.

'This is Design, where you'll be working. There are multiple roles here and eventually you'll learn them all. Meryl over there, for example, creates the blank templates for each pet, no details or colours, just a Labrador or cat or guinea pig shape and makes the templates for each page in the story where the animal will be in different poses. Nate is our lead designer and will create the images for each story page. Brooke does all the fonts and text layout – some of our text will be in a curve or diagonally across the page depending on the images of the story, so Brooke sorts all of that. You'll be working on one area of design for a month and then we will rotate you to do a different aspect of design. Everyone gets rotated. This way you'll bring your skills and experience to each area of design and we feel that helps to improve all the areas. You will find the best way to do something and others can learn from you as you'll learn from them. It keeps it fresh for you too, so you don't get bored.'

Roo frowned. She had been hired as lead designer and was told by Charlie she'd be working on one of the new books, creating the images to go with the story. Although she knew there would be an element of training and getting used to the software, she wasn't expecting she would be learning all the areas of design like she was a trainee with no design knowledge at all. She was happy to be part of the team but this didn't sound like the job she was promised.

'You'll be training with Danielle first.' Charlie gestured to a young blonde woman with her hair in plaited pigtails. She was wearing a bright yellow retro t-shirt with Bagpuss on. Roo felt decidedly overdressed in her suit. 'She adds the details to the templates that make the pets look like the customer's pets. She'll add markings on the fur or body, add collars in the right colour, make sure the eye colour is correct based on the photos the owners provide us with.'

Already Roo could see there would be an easier way to do that which would save hours of time. Maybe she'd suggest it once she'd been there a few days.

'Hello, I'm looking forward to working with you,' Danielle said with a big smile.

Roo thought that probably wasn't true. No one wanted to be lumbered with the trainee. Fortunately Roo knew her way around most design programs so she hopefully wasn't going to be too much of a burden to Danielle.

'I'm really excited to be working here. I actually bought

one of your books last year for a friend and I just loved the concept of it. It's a brilliant idea. And now I'm here and I get to be a part of it. I'm really happy to be here.'

'Oh it's wonderful here,' Danielle said. 'We're one big family. I can't imagine working anywhere else.'

'Right, I'll just quickly introduce her to upstairs and then I'll bring her back to you,' Charlie said.

Danielle nodded.

Charlie gestured for her to follow him up another flight of stairs to the top floor.

'The editorial team works up here. They will check every book before it goes to print. Are the pets and children's names correct, the locations, have the right pictures of the pets being applied to every page?' Charlie peered through a window to a large office. 'Ah they're in a meeting right now, but I'm sure you'll meet them soon enough. Monday morning is always the time for meetings. I have a managerial meeting in ten minutes which will be in the conference room here, where we'll meet with all the department heads but let me just quickly introduce you to our CEO.'

He peered through a crack in the door and then opened the door, talking to whoever was inside.

'Hey, can I just introduce you to our new girl?'

'Sure,' said a male voice.

Charlie stepped back to let her in the room. 'This is Aurora Clarke.'

She stepped into the room and froze because standing up behind the CEO's desk, smiling, was Theo Lucas.

CHAPTER FIVE

Theo was the CEO of Pet Protagonist. The man who had made her scream in pleasure multiple times just a few hours before, was her boss. The man who had kissed her *everywhere* was standing a few feet away from her, the smile slowly sliding off his face.

Her heart thundered in her chest, the blood roaring in her ears. How was this happening?

Charlie looked confused that they were both simply staring at each other, and she had no idea how to play this. She didn't want anyone knowing she'd slept with the boss.

She moved forward and stuck out her hand for Theo to shake. 'Aurora Clarke, pleased to meet you.'

Theo stared at her hand in shock. Probably because that hand had touched him very intimately a few hours before. She went to remove her hand but suddenly he took it, giving it a shake.

'Theo Lucas. I hope you'll be very happy here.'

He had made her very happy. She had been looking forward to being made happy again tonight. But she couldn't do that now and that made her want to cry.

She quickly removed her hand as he was holding onto it for too long.

'Well, I should go and start my new job,' Roo said. 'I'm sure Danielle is waiting for me.'

Theo nodded. 'I have a meeting shortly.'

They stared at each other for a moment longer before she turned away. 'Thanks for the tour, Charlie.'

'Can you find your own way back?'

'Yes, thank you.'

Charlie flashed her a smile and then closed the door behind her as she walked out.

'What the hell is going on between you two?' she heard Charlie say to Theo.

She paused to listen.

'Nothing,' Theo said.

'Jesus, Theo, I have eyes. The tension was sparking between you.'

'We… knew each other at school,' Theo said.

That was skating over the biggest cause of tension, the fact they'd spent the night wrapped in each other's arms.

'And?' Charlie asked.

'And nothing.'

'Really because she was shooting daggers at you.'

Theo sighed. 'I… was an ass to her.'

She cringed that Theo was now being forced to tell Charlie a lie, but they could hardly tell the truth. But now this was making Theo look bad and he was getting it in the neck.

'Excuse me young lady, I don't think you should be eavesdropping outside the CEO's office,' said a woman's angry voice directly behind Roo. She whirled round to see an older woman, looking furious with her.

Unfortunately, it was deliberately loud enough for Charlie to hear as he opened the office door and he and Theo were standing there. She couldn't even deny what she had been doing. This was a terrible impression on her first day. The older woman was staring at her with her hands on her hips, her lips pursed like she was sucking a lemon.

'Sorry, I umm... heard you talking about me.'

Theo pushed his hand through his hair. 'I think Aurora and I should have a few minutes to clear the air if we are going to work together professionally. You two go ahead to the meeting, I'll catch you up shortly.'

Charlie hovered. 'Are you sure? I can stay to mediate.'

'No, it's fine,' Theo said.

Charlie looked at her and she nodded too.

Charlie sighed and left the office, ushering the other woman into the conference room further down the hall.

Theo gestured for her to come in and he shut the door behind her. Immediately he wrapped her in his arms. 'Roo, I'm so sorry, I had no idea you were starting work here today. I saw your name on some paperwork but... I've always known you as Roo and Clarke was not the surname you grew up with.'

'I changed it to my dad's name after he died. I didn't

want anything to do with my mum, after the way she treated my dad, so I eradicated her name from my life too,' she said, wrapping her arms around him as well. She closed her eyes, relishing in the feel of him holding her. She looked up at him and he stroked her face. 'What are we going to do?'

She saw the hesitation in his eyes and she already knew the answer. She'd known it as soon as she'd seen him. She really wanted this job, she couldn't be the person that was sleeping with the boss. Everyone would assume she only got the job because of her relationship with Theo, not her skills and experience in design. And it would reflect badly on Theo too if people found out he was screwing the new girl. He'd said it himself when they were in the pub, that he never wanted to get involved with the women at work and for good reason.

'We can be discreet. Nobody needs to know,' Theo said. Although he didn't sound sure. 'Hell, Charlie met his wife here so he can hardly have a go at me.'

She rested her hands on his chest and swallowed the lump of emotion in her throat. 'We can't do this, you know that. I don't want to lie to people. If I do, eventually they will find out and they won't trust me after that. It will look bad on you as the boss, sleeping with one of his employees and I don't want that for you. You're a wonderful man. And it will look bad on me too. Sleeping with the boss within five seconds of me arriving here or getting the job because I'm sleeping with the boss. People will talk, you know that.'

He shook his head and looked away.

'Look, if we had something serious, then I would fight for it, I'd say, to hell with what anyone thinks. But we don't know each other. Not really. We had a wonderful friendship fourteen years ago and one night of incredible sex last night,'

His mouth tightened. 'Just one night of sex, yeah, why would we fight for something so meaningless?'

'It was not meaningless, not at all, I didn't mean it like that,' she frowned and concentrated on the buttons on his shirt. 'I'm not long-term relationship material. I've dated so many men and they all end it after a few weeks. I've been hurt so many times and I just... I've stopped looking for serious a long time ago because I don't think it exists for me. Or maybe I didn't want serious because it meant I could get hurt again like I was after I lost you and Dad. And you obviously feel the same as you've never had a serious relationship either. Why would you want to go through weeks of gossip and people judging you, judging us for something you'll probably run away from in a few weeks' time. And then what, we have the awkwardness of having to work together after you've broken up with me too.'

He tipped her chin up to face him. He studied her for a moment before he kissed her. She felt her body immediately ignite and she instinctively pressed herself closer to him, melting into the kiss, maybe their last kiss.

He pulled back slightly to look at her. 'I'm not like other men.'

'No you're not, I think you have the potential to hurt me so much more than the others. Losing you again would hurt too much. I'm not sure I could see you at work every day with my heart smashed into pieces after you got bored of me.'

He nodded and took a step away from her and she saw the hurt in his eyes as he rubbed his chin. 'So we'll just be friends then?'

'Don't you think it'll be for the best?'

'What I think doesn't seem to matter but you're probably right. I really need to go to this meeting.'

He opened the door for her and gestured for her to go ahead. She walked out the office and he followed her out. They walked down the corridor towards the conference room in silence. So much for it not being awkward.

'Hope you have a good first day,' Theo said, before disappearing into the conference room and closing the door.

She went back downstairs feeling numb. Why did it feel like she'd just lost the best thing that had ever happened to her?

from: officemanager@petprotagonist.com
to: everyone@petprotagonist.com

Please can I remind all staff that office doors are closed for a reason, do not stand outside and listen.

Following on from last's week's debacle, please do not heat fish or eggs in the microwave

If you have taken Kevin's coffee mug please return it

No sandals in the office. Some people are offended by feet.

Regards

Betty Dimble - Office Manager

'So what we're doing here is making sure that the animal characters in each book actually represent the pet the book is based on,' Danielle said. She had already spent an hour showing Roo around the computer system they used at Pet Protagonist. It was a whole computer program designed specifically for making these story books with people's pets as the star. It was really clever and intuitive and Roo wondered if this was something Theo had designed himself. 'We have hundreds of templates we can choose from for the different animals, but it's not enough to choose an English Setter for example, we want the markings to look like the pet. So we add an English Setter to the book and we add the correct colour spots to the paws, nose or wherever else and try to make sure they are in the right place and pattern based on the photos the owners have sent us. We have to do this on every page of the book. When we make books for a black cat or some dog breeds that are one colour like a lab or a westie it's a bit harder to individualise it, but we always make sure the collar and eye colour is correct and if they have spiky fur on top of their head or their muzzle we can add that in. Do you want to have a go at editing the spots on this one? You have to go into edit template.'

Roo clicked on the button and a whole multitude of tools appeared on the left-hand column, from different brushes, pens, spray pens to get different effects and every possible colour on the spectrum. She could have a lot of fun playing with all these tools as she got to know the program. Many of it was very similar to other design programs she had used in the past, so she guessed she'd learn her way around this very quickly.

She looked at the spots on the photo of an English Setter called Skipper, the brown speckles on his white paws and the brown and black spots on his face. He also had really tatty black ears, they could definitely add that in. He had a big mane of fur around his neck and a big bushy tail they could add to the book as well. She started adding spots to the English Setter template in the book, playing with the tones and shades of brown to get it exactly right.

'Aurora, can I have a word?'

She looked up to see Charlie standing next to her desk. Oh God, was she going to get into trouble for listening to his and Theo's conversation? Even Danielle looked worried.

'Umm sure.' Roo stood up and followed him into a small empty meeting room.

He closed the door behind her.

'Look I'm sorry about before and listening to your conversation with Theo. I—'

Charlie held his hand up to stem the tide. 'It's fine, I mean it's not really appropriate to listen to other people's private conversations but we were talking about you so it was only fair, I suppose. I just wanted to make sure you were OK. It's clear you and Theo have history and it's none of my business what happened between you in the past, I just want to make sure that you two have cleared the air and it's not going to be awkward for you working here under him.'

She had to suppress a smirk at that choice of phrase.

'It's fine, we're fine. We were friends and...' How could she even begin to explain their past and present situation? 'It was just a shock to see him here but we're good now, we had a chat and everything is fine.'

Everything was definitely not fine. She'd slept with her boss and then pushed him away and hurt him in the process. He'd said he still wanted to be friends with her and she wasn't sure she could do that without hurting him or herself. But Charlie didn't need to know all that.

'OK good, just wanted to make sure it wasn't going to be weird.'

It was definitely going to be weird because every time she thought of Theo, she thought about how he'd made love to her the night before, how he had stroked and kissed every single inch of her body, how he had looked at her with complete adoration and how she had thrown all that away so easily.

'Nope, definitely not weird,' Roo said, forcing her voice to be happy and bright.

Charlie narrowed his eyes as if he didn't quite believe her. She didn't blame him. 'OK then.' He opened the door for her and she stepped outside.

She spotted Theo straight away as he was talking to someone and she found herself stopping dead as she watched him.

He finished his conversation and as if he knew she was there, his eyes immediately found hers. The look he gave her was pure heat before he quickly turned and walked away.

'So definitely not weird?' Charlie said, with a sigh.

She bit her lip. 'OK, it might be a bit weird but it's not going to affect my work. It will just take us a few days to get over it and then I'm sure we'll be fine.'

It was going to take a hell of a lot more than a few days to get over Theo Lucas, but she knew she could be professional about it. And how often would she really see him when he was upstairs in his office and she was down here? It was going to be fine.

It was definitely not going to be fine. Theo had been down on her floor a grand total of seven times so far, talking to various members of staff. She wasn't sure if this was the norm for him or whether he was just trying to make it awkward for her. Surely the man could email these people rather than running up and down the stairs every few minutes.

'I see you looking at Theo Lucas,' Sally, the woman at the next desk said, in between eating handfuls of popcorn.

Roo looked at her in alarm. 'There was no look.'

She looked around to see if anyone else was listening to their conversation. Danielle had gone to help someone on the other side of the design team, leaving Roo to finish turning the English Setter on every page into Skipper. Everyone else was busily working away on their own projects and not interested in what Sally was saying.

'There was definitely a look. People-watching is my favourite way to spend my time. People never take the time to really see everyone else, but I do. I see it all. Ordinarily, I'd say you don't stand a chance with him. He never dates anyone from work. But I see the way he keeps looking at you too. Something is afoot.'

'There is no foot.' Roo sighed because there was no point denying it. 'We were friends, back in our teens and lost contact fourteen years ago. It was just a shock seeing him today, for both of us, that's all it is. Does he always come down here?'

'Yes, Theo always likes to talk to the staff face to face. He says he can discuss things better when they are both looking at the same thing. Charlie is much more the efficient, fire-off-an-email type. We're on the verge of launching a new adventure story for the pets so it has been a bit full-on the last few weeks as everyone has been trying to get it ready.'

She'd seen the new story. *Captain Pet's Name and the*

Search for the Lost Treasure. Obviously when people bought the book their pet's name would become the captain's name in the title. Now seeing all the departments that were working on it, she could see how much work had gone into it. But some members of the design team were already getting ready for the launch of the next book. There was certainly no resting on your laurels here.

'So you're really not interested in Theo?' Sally asked.

Roo thought she'd managed to escape that topic.

'I don't know him to be interested in him,' Roo lied. 'We haven't seen each other for fourteen years.'

'I don't know Chris Hemsworth, doesn't mean I can't fancy the arse off him.'

'But Theo is the boss, don't you think it'd be weird to fancy the boss?'

'Every single woman in here fancies him. He's hot. Now, sleeping with the boss – yeah, that would be weird. When Beth first started working here, everyone liked her. She had been here for six months when she and Charlie got together at the Christmas party. Although no one realised at that point apart from me. I'd seen them leave in a taxi together. But pretty soon everyone here knew they were together, despite them desperately trying to keep it a secret.'

Roo wondered how much of that had come from Sally spreading the gossip of seeing them leave together at the party. People would have been looking for clues every time Charlie even talked to Beth if they knew they'd got together before.

'He would come down here on the pretext of work and

he'd leave her little notes on her desk that would make her blush. Charlie had a lot of very important meetings with her in his office and people would see them together around town outside of work. It became a bit of a running joke, especially when he'd call her up to his office for another meeting. I walked past Charlie's office once and could blatantly hear them going at it. It was hilarious. They had no idea we all knew.'

Sally ate another handful of popcorn and Roo couldn't help thinking how unpleasant this conversation was. She didn't even know Beth and had only spoken to Charlie a few times but she didn't like hearing this gossip about them. It was unkind and unnecessary. But this was her first day, she could hardly tell Sally that this behaviour was inappropriate. Although it was clear she wasn't the only one. Ginny, on the other side of Sally, was looking horrified, although maybe that might be from hearing that Charlie had been having sex in the upstairs office.

Sally carried on. 'I personally found it a bit… distasteful. I'd always respected Charlie for being a professional businessman and I lost all respect for him knowing he was calling her up to his office for sex. And there is always so much work to do here, we couldn't afford for her to swan off for an hour every day. When they announced their engagement, we were all relieved the big secret was finally out. Anyway, they got married very quickly and she had a baby. She's a stay-at-home mum now so we don't have to watch them sneaking off for sex every day.'

Roo turned her attention back to the computer. This was exactly the kind of thing she was worried about, people gossiping about her and Theo behind their backs, laughing at them, losing respect for Theo for sleeping with one of the members of staff. She had done the right thing, despite how much it hurt. Although she couldn't imagine sneaking off during the work-day for sex with the boss. She could understand people being pissed off with that, especially if it was a daily thing.

'So if you're not interested in Theo, do you mind if I ask him to the summer ball?'

'You just said it'd be weird to date the boss,' Roo said.

'But I'm leaving soon. I have a job in Newquay. It's better money. Theo has always had a bit of a thing for me but he's respected that employer employee boundary. Once I'm out of here, we could have as much sex as we want.'

Roo's stomach twisted at the thought. There was no doubt that Sally was pretty and she was the kind of woman that Theo had always gone for back when they were teens.

She cleared her throat. 'Go for it.'

God, the thought of him going out on dates or sleeping with someone else made her feel sick and she had no right to feel that way. She'd told him she didn't want him.

She had to stop thinking like this. It was for the best.

So why did her heart not agree?

from: charlie@petprotagonist.com
to: everyone@petprotagonist.com

One week until launch of *Captain Pet's Name and the Search for the Lost Treasure*. Thank you to everyone for your hard work on this project – we're really excited about publishing this one on Monday. If you do want to share about the new book on your social media, Marketing have created some visuals you could use on Facebook, Instagram and a short video you could share on TikTok. Thanks so much if you are able to share.

I'm sure you are all aware the summer ball is in two weeks. Tickets are £10 which includes a buffet. All the money raised at the ball will go towards Little Paws, our charity partner. Final numbers must be given to Merryport Castle next Tuesday so the last chance to buy tickets will be a week today.

Betty has asked me to say that Kevin's mug still hasn't been returned.

Thanks

Charlie

CHAPTER SIX

Theo parked his car in the car park of The Little Beach Hut Hotel and walked up the hill a little way to get to his mum's house.

He waved at Antonio, his mum's boyfriend, who was tending to the garden, and let himself into the kitchen.

His mum was taking a batch of what smelt like apple cakes out of the muffin tray and placing them in a tin. Carrie turned to look over her shoulder and her face broke into a huge smile when she saw him.

'Theo, what a lovely surprise.'

'You make it sound like I haven't been here for ages! I was here just last week for dinner.'

'But you don't normally pop by after work, you're always so busy.' She poured him a tea from a steaming hot teapot, adding sugar and milk just as he liked it.

'I wanted to talk to you about something.'

She passed him the mug and offered him a cake. He took both, and sat down at the breakfast table, picking a big chunk of cake off to eat as he thought about what to say.

Carrie took a sip from her own mug as she sat opposite him.

'Roo's back.'

She paused mid-sip and lowered her mug as she stared at him in surprise. 'For a visit or—'

'For good. She's staying here actually, at The Little Beach Hut Hotel, at least until she can find a place of her own.'

Carrie frowned. 'How did I not know that?'

'She goes under Aurora Clarke now, her dad's name.'

'Oh my God, I didn't make the connection when I saw the booking.'

'Neither did I, I've always just known her as Roo.'

'Have you spoken to her?'

'Of course, she was my best friend for four years or more.'

'She was a bit more than that,' Carrie said.

Theo sighed. He hadn't realised his feelings for her had been so clear to his mum back then or to anyone, although it was obvious Shay had known.

'I bumped into her in Seahorses and we had dinner together last night. It was just like it was fourteen years ago.'

'Did she explain why she cut you out of her life?'

'Mum, don't be like that.'

She sighed. 'You know I adored her. She was round here so often it was like having a second daughter. But she hurt you when she cut you out.'

'She was grieving for her dad and angry with the world. She was alone out there in Chicago and I just don't think she dealt with her grief in the best way. And partly she did it for me. I kept on messaging her about coming out there to be with her after her dad died and I was due to go on my trip around Europe. She didn't want me to miss it. She knew how excited I was about it. She apologised and said she'd always regretted it. Regardless, it's in the past, I certainly don't hold any grudges and I don't expect you to either.'

Carrie nodded. 'I'd like to see her again.'

'I'm sure you will. I'll see if I can get her to come to our family dinner night tomorrow, I'm sure she'd love to see Fern and Shay again too.'

'That will be lovely.'

Theo concentrated on his cake.

'There's something you're not saying,' Carrie said.

'I told her how I felt for her, back when we were friends.'

Carrie smiled. 'That was brave.'

'It didn't feel like that, it's been fourteen years. Shay said I should tell her and put the past to bed. At the time I didn't think it was a good idea but when we were having dinner, it felt right. And it turns out she felt the same.'

Carrie's eyes widened in surprise.

'I walked her home with every intention of leaving her

at her door and meeting up again tonight, but then we kissed and—'

Carrie gasped. 'And?'

'It was incredible. Our connection was so wonderful and I never expected it. I ended up spending the night with her and it was just perfect. We made plans to see each other again tonight.'

Carrie gave a little squeal of excitement.

'And then Charlie introduced me to the new girl at work this morning and...'

Carrie's face fell. 'No.'

Theo nodded. 'Roo doesn't think we should see each other anymore. She thinks people at work will get the wrong idea, that they'll judge me for sleeping with one of the staff and judge her for sleeping with the boss within seconds of her starting there. And she's right. The gossip wasn't kind when Charlie started dating Beth. I don't want that for her.'

Carrie took a sip of her tea as she watched him.

'She says we don't know each other and that it will inevitably end, so why go through all that gossip and people judging us for just a few weeks of fun. But it felt so much more than that last night and I think she felt that too. Part of me feels like I shouldn't let her go that easily. I let her go before and I should have done more to keep our friendship, to be there for her. I don't want to walk away from her this time. But maybe she's right. Maybe last night was about rekindling a memory. We were so excited to see each other again, and maybe that's all it was.'

Carrie finished her drink. 'I think she's right. You don't

know each other, not after fourteen years apart, how could you?'

Theo sighed. With all Carrie's perpetual enthusiasm, this was not what he'd hoped to hear.

'I think you need to be her friend, take the time to get to know each other properly. You've never had a long-term relationship and she needs time to trust in you. If that connection you felt last night is real and something more than just two old friends meeting up again, it will still be there in a few weeks, maybe even stronger. And if it was just sex and she doesn't want anything more then at least you will have your best friend back and that's something wonderful.'

He smiled. 'You're right. I realised last night in the pub how much I've missed her, how much I want her in my life again, even if that is just as friends.' He finished off his tea and stood up.

'Where are you going?'

'I'm going to get my friend back.'

Roo sat on a chair out on the decking of her beach hut, watching the sun make its descent into the sea. It wouldn't set for a while yet but the clouds were already turning a beautiful shade of bubble-gum pink.

As first days go, hers had been rubbish. Sally had insisted on telling her who was dating who at the company. Apparently, it was fine for employees to date each other as long as it didn't involve the management team which was definitely inappropriate. She'd started telling Roo who had kissed who, who had slept with who and Roo didn't want to know any of it but wasn't brave enough to tell her to stop. In the end, Roo had insisted she must get on with some work and put her headphones in so she wouldn't have to listen to any of it. Sally obviously thought this was rude and refused to speak to her for the rest of the day, which was a relief in some ways, but frustrating in others when Roo needed help on one part of the computer program and Sally had completely ignored her. She'd figured it out for herself in the end – she'd always been good at teaching herself how to use programs like that.

But the worst part of the day had been seeing Theo walking around the office talking to people, not talking to her, sometimes not even looking at her. She didn't blame him. She couldn't stop reliving his expression when she said she just wanted to be friends. That had hurt him and she hated that. She had dismissed the night before as not being serious when it had been everything. She had pushed him away so easily and she regretted that so much.

She knew that part of it had been because she'd been scared. It had been so wonderful, not just the sex which had been incredible, but their connection which had felt so real and rare, she'd known she could fall in love with him so easily. And that scared her because what would happen when it ended? And of course it would end. He had the potential to break her heart when he got bored of her. And then she'd have to see him every day at work where everyone would know they'd slept together and he'd dumped her.

But she couldn't escape the feeling she'd made a big mistake, that maybe she'd walked away from something life changing. But what was the alternative? She'd spoken to a few people at work, and everyone loved Theo, they respected him for building up the company from scratch and for his friendly, hands-on approach. She'd hate for people to lose that respect because he'd got too hands-on with one of the staff.

She was so wrapped up in her thoughts that she didn't notice someone approaching the beach hut. She looked up as they stopped next to her. Her heart leapt when she saw it was Theo and she scrambled to her feet.

'Hey, you looked so sad when I walked up, are you OK?'

She smiled sadly. 'Thinking about you, about us. I hate that I hurt you.'

He shook his head. 'Come here, I'm fine.'

He opened his arms and she immediately stepped up and he enveloped her in a big hug. She wrapped her arms around him too. She felt so comfortable with him, like nothing else mattered when she was with him.

She looked up at him. 'What are you doing here?'

'I think you're right; we should just be friends.'

She couldn't help feeling disappointed by that even though that's what she'd said that morning.

'And last night, before I pinned you to the nearest hard surface and mauled you like some crazed wild animal, I offered to take you to dinner again tonight as friends. So I'm here to do just that,' Theo said.

She smiled in relief; she didn't want to lose him. 'I'd really like that.'

He let her go. 'Come on then, it's not far.'

She quickly locked the door and stepped off the decking. He started walking down towards the end of the headland, which confused her as there was nothing down that way.

'How was your first day in your new job?' Theo asked as she fell in at his side.

'Well I found out the boss is some bloke I had the hottest sex of my life with and instead of grabbing him and making love to him on his giant desk, I told him I just wanted to be friends.'

Theo burst out laughing. 'That sounds like a rough day. I've never thought about my desk as a place to have sex before.'

'Really? It's huge. Both of us could easily fit on that desk. In a multitude of positions.'

He laughed again. 'Christ, this isn't helping my resolve to just be friends.'

'Sorry,' Roo giggled. 'I've just never seen a desk so big before.'

'That's so I can spread out the story in its entirety and view the whole thing, I certainly didn't pick it with sex in mind. Anyway, let's stop talking about sex or we're never getting through dinner. Your smoking-hot boss aside—'

'I never said *he* was smoking hot.'

'Is he?'

'Well, apparently all the women in the office fancy him.'

He smiled. 'I'm sure that's not true.'

'I'm sure it is.'

'So how was your day apart from drooling over your hot boss.'

She laughed. 'There was no drooling, I was too busy adding spots to an English Setter.'

He frowned. 'What?'

'I had to make the English Setter template look like this English Setter called Skipper, who has brown freckles on his nose and on his paws and now all I can see is spots behind my eyes. And I got familiar with the computer program, which I love, did you design that?'

'Yes, sorry, you spent the day adding spots to an English Setter?' It was clear he was angry about this.

'Yes, but I'm new, I'm supposed to start at the bottom.'

'No, you were hired as lead designer to work on the illustrations for our new stories. The plan was to start on the designs for *A Knight's Tail* this week. That was something me and you were going to do together. Has Charlie mentioned when you're going to start that?'

'No, he said I had to learn all the areas of design.'

'What? Oh hell no, I'm not having this. Let me give Charlie a call and talk to him about this.' He fished his phone from his pocket.

'No way. I'm OK with this. I expected there would be time learning it all. You've built a whole program here to create your books and stories. I need time to get used to the software.'

'Yes, a day or two, but you should be shadowing Nate, our other lead designer, not working on bloody freckles. I can fix this. I'm the CEO, that should come with some benefits.' He swiped his phone.

'No please don't. I hate the thought that Charlie thinks I've gone behind his back and complained to you that I'm not happy. I'm fine with learning the ropes.'

'For how long?'

'What?'

'How long will you be happy with doing something like freckles or other basic design tasks? You told me last night how excited you were about having free rein on a new project. That's what you were told you'd be doing when Charlie approached you. That's what he told *me* you'd be doing when he hired you. And by the sounds of it, he wants to rotate you round every design department instead. Will you be happy with that?'

Roo sighed. She had been a bit disappointed not to be getting her teeth into designing the illustrations for the new story that day. But it did make sense that she would have a few days of becoming familiar with the software before she did that. But Theo was right, the thought of being on freckle duty for the next month, then moving on to learn one of the other basic design tasks did not fill her with joy.

'No I wouldn't be, but this is my problem to solve not yours. You going to Charlie to tell him I'm not happy would put me in a really awkward position and I don't want anyone to think I'm getting preferential treatment because I know you or had the best sex of my life with you.'

Theo burst out laughing. 'I'm sure that isn't true but I'll take the ego boost. And it's not preferential treatment if you're doing the job you were hired to do. That's just common sense. I've seen your online portfolio. Charlie was really excited about all the things you've done. You have an incredible talent and we should be using that for something more than just freckles.'

She smiled at that. 'That's kind of you to say.'

'It's the truth. I'm not just saying that because I had the best sex of my life with *you*.'

She laughed. 'You're such a flirt.'

'That's the truth too.'

She stared at him, an overwhelming desire to step forward and kiss him, but she couldn't do that.

'The point is, I need to handle this, not you,' Roo said.

'But will you? Or will you just suffer it for the next few weeks before handing in your notice through complete boredom. The Roo I knew hated confrontation.'

The Roo she was now hated confrontation, she always tried to avoid it as much as possible. Handing in her notice in a few weeks would be much more likely. Although she really didn't want to do that.

'I will fix it,' she said, feeling sick at the thought of going to Charlie to complain. Theo looked doubtful. 'I will. Promise me you won't say anything to him.'

'Look, as far as I know, you were going to start *A Knight's Tail* this week. I'm pretty sure my diary is blocked out from Wednesday onwards to work on it with you and I will be pissed if Nate turns up instead. Not because he isn't a brilliant designer, he is, but because *A Knight's Tail* was supposed to be yours. Charlie hasn't told me any different so if you or the new book come up in conversation, I'm going to act like that is the case because I haven't heard from you or anyone else to say differently. But right now, Charlie is undermining you in front of the rest of the design department. I agree that you need a few days to get to know the software but any longer than that shows the rest of the design team that you haven't got the skills or experience to be a lead designer. So if you're going to fix it, it needs to be this week.'

She nodded. 'I will, I'll talk to him.'

Just then Theo's phone rang.

'Sorry, I'll turn it off after this call. I only turned it on to call Charlie.' Theo frowned as he looked at it. 'It's Ginny.'

'From work? Does everyone from work have your personal number?'

'No, thankfully, or they'd all be ringing me to tell me that someone had brought tuna sandwiches or egg into work again. Ginny is Charlie's little sister, although no one knows that as she didn't want anyone to think she'd got the job because of him. She's his step-sister so she has a different surname and they've successfully flown under the radar without anyone finding out. We swapped numbers when we were trying to organise a surprise birthday thing for him a year or so ago, but she never phones me. God, I hope Charlie's OK.'

He quickly answered the phone. 'Ginny, hi, is everything OK?'

'Yes, well no,' Ginny said and Roo realised the phone was on loud speaker. 'I'm sorry to call you outside of work and I know I should have come to see you or Charlie about this but I didn't want anyone to know I was making a complaint and it's awkward telling Charlie this stuff so I didn't know what to do.'

'Ginny it's OK, what's the problem?' Theo said, kindly. Roo smiled, he was a good man.

'I was sitting next to Sally today and she was talking to Roo. Remember all those horrible lies she was spreading last year about Charlie and Beth having sex in his office.'

'Of course, she had several warnings about that, although if it was down to me I would have sacked her on the spot for that. It was defamation of character. And it was all because Charlie promoted Beth to lead designer instead of Sally, not that Sally would ever be promoted to lead designer, but it was just petty jealousy. She should never have been allowed to get away with that.'

Roo stared at him in shock. All of that had been lies and Sally was still spreading that rubbish to all that would listen.

'I know,' Ginny said. 'They were creating a new book, they weren't having sex, it was complete bullshit. And I know I'm biased but Charlie is a good man, he doesn't deserve that. Well I was horrified to hear Sally telling Roo those lies again today, how they were sneaking off to have sex every day.'

'What?' Theo glanced at Roo to see if it was true and Roo nodded. His face turned to thunder.

'Sally was trying to make out there was something

going on between you and Roo because apparently you kept looking at each other, although I didn't see it. Sally said it was inappropriate for management and staff to be fraternising and then told Roo all about Beth and Charlie and how everyone lost respect for Charlie because of it. But everyone lost respect for him because of the horrible lies she's telling and I just couldn't let it lie. I know I should have been brave enough to tell her to shut her stupid mouth but... I'm not.'

'No, that's hard to do when you have to work together every day, I understand that,' Theo said.

'She's leaving,' Ginny went on. 'She has a job in Newquay, starting in a few weeks I think. So I know I probably should have just put up with it until she's gone but... he's my brother and I just can't bear for these lies to be spread all over again. And then what? She'd walk out of here with a leaving gift and a pat on the back and a big thanks for all her hard work when she's a lying little bitch.'

Roo smirked at the forcefulness of her little rant. Ginny looked so sweet and innocent.

'No I get it. I'm going to deal with this tomorrow. This needs to stop, for good this time. But I am going to have to tell Charlie that this came from you.'

Ginny sighed. 'I know.'

'But neither Sally nor anyone else will know. Sally will be told that complaints have come from multiple sources, which will be true if Roo corroborates your story, which I'm sure she will.' He glanced at Roo and she nodded again. 'And we'll ask around to see if anyone else heard something too. So don't worry.'

'Thanks Theo.'

They said their goodbyes and Theo hung up.

'I can't believe she would tell those lies again. Why would she do that?' Theo said.

'I don't know. It's attention seeking, I suppose. People will listen to her if she has something juicy to say, even if it's not true. It was really unpleasant to listen to today and completely inappropriate. But Beth and Charlie weren't the only ones that got the Sally treatment. I had to put my headphones in to stop her talking about everyone in the office and who had slept with who.'

He groaned. 'I hate dealing with stuff like this. As you can see, I'm really not cut out to be CEO material.'

He turned his phone off and shoved it in his pocket. He started walking again and she followed him, taking a path that would lead them down towards the beach.

'I don't know about that, everyone respects you there, that much was clear today. They like your hands-on approach, dealing with people face to face.'

'I think it takes a bit more than people skills to run a company. Charlie makes that place run like clockwork.'

'You were always entrepreneurial. How did Pet Protagonist start?'

'Well I love graphic design, it's something I've always enjoyed doing and I love animals so I wanted to do something that combined the two. It was just an idea I had one day. There were lot of things like it on the market for children, books where children starred in their own stories, and I thought, why don't we offer the same thing for people's pets? People love their pets. So I created my own story with people's pets as the main character? I just used some basic art and design software to start and only offered a choice of maybe ten different dogs – Labrador, Border Collie, a few spaniel breeds, the typical dogs. The story wasn't even mine; I did a version of Jack and the Beanstalk but with the dog stealing bones, a roast chicken and a squeaky toy from the giant.'

'I like that.'

'I set up an Etsy account but people really need to search for something specific there for them to see it. So I did a few craft fairs locally and people were really into it. Of course I started getting requests for weird dogs I hadn't even heard of – 'Do you do the Russian Borzoi?' 'Do you do the Komondor?' Of course, I always answered yes and went away and quickly designed one. Then people wanted one for their cat, their budgie, even their goldfish. And it started to grow, people told their friends, they told their friends. I was doing really well, selling ten or fifteen copies a week.'

She smiled at that humility of being really happy with ten or fifteen sales a week.

'I quickly realised that I could produce them a lot faster if I was to build my own software where I had the basic storyline and background images, but I could swap out the different pet templates accordingly and that worked perfectly. It was quite rudimentary to start with, the program you were using today is mark four.'

He took her hand as they started walking down a more rocky part of the path and it felt like the most natural thing in the world.

'Charlie was my best friend back then. He'd done a business marketing degree, so he was helping me by doing some Facebook and Instagram ads and some TikTok reels. Sales started increasing massively. I was getting fifty to a hundred sales a week. I told him if he got me five hundred sales a week, I'd take him on as my business partner and give him forty-five per cent of the profits. It was just a bit of a joke. He worked in a bank at the time. I didn't honestly see this thing bringing enough money to build a career out of it, I was just happy playing with my design program and producing the books. But Charlie took the challenge, the sales built and built. Soon we had to take on a few staff members to help with it all.'

Theo took another path that led them away from the main path to the beach. They were now heading to the very end of Strawberry Sands.

'One day, we had a TikTok go viral and it was ridiculous. We had nearly six thousand sales in one day. Then we had some big celeb talking about our book on their social media and it went nuts. Charlie quit his job and he's worked his arse off building the company up to what it is now. We were still working out of my house at that point. Charlie found the office which was empty and we used the money we'd got from going viral to build our own printing press and we've never looked back. It's got so much bigger than I ever imagined it would be. We sell all over the world now working with translators to produce books in German, French, Spanish, Portuguese, Chinese and Japanese. We have printing companies we work with in the States, Canada, Peru, Belgium, Australia, China and

Japan so we can ship to different countries quicker. I can't keep up. I never hoped for this. I was just enjoying drawing dogs on the computer and making a few quid from it.'

'It's very impressive.'

'It's all Charlie, and the brilliant staff he's hired. If it wasn't for him I'd still be working out of the craft fairs. He is incredible. He took another degree in business management and he really knows his stuff. It's his company really. I do all the technical stuff, he makes us shine.'

'Your part is equally important.'

'I don't know about that.'

They walked on in silence for a moment, Theo leading the way, still holding her hand.

'When I asked you last night about your job, you said it wasn't something you were passionate about.'

'It's not. And how ungrateful does that make me sound? So many small businesses would give their left arm to be where I am two years after starting their company. Pet Protagonist is hugely successful and I have more money than I know what to do with. But I started this because I loved working in graphic design. It was something I was good at.'

'I remember us starting our own pet caricature and portrait business when we were younger. You loved it. You've always been really arty.'

He turned back to her, a huge smile across his face. 'Yes, that was fun. When I started Pet Protagonist I would do everything from creating the animal templates, the background, play with the typesetting and font, the layout.

I loved it. Now we have staff to do all that for me. I sit in meetings all day and I'm bored. I work closely with the designers when we create a new story, but that's the only time I get my hands dirty so to speak. And I miss it. I never envisaged I would be a CEO of a big company, I never wanted that. Do I sound like a complete shit?'

'No, you have to have joy in your work. So many people go to work in a job they hate just so they have money to pay the bills. You could have done that any time, worked for a big company doing web design or building computer programs, you were always so good at that. But you chose to do something you love with creating these books and now you can't even do that.'

'I'm not sure what to do about that. If anything, I feel like I should just put up with it. It's gone too far now. I have nearly eighty people that depend on us for their income, and that's just in the UK. I can't start changing things now.'

'Maybe you can demote yourself. Be a lead designer instead, let Charlie take control?'

Theo was silent as they carried on walking, and she wondered if he was thinking about that proposal.

'Where are we going, anyway?' Roo said. 'I thought you were taking me out for dinner.'

'You'll see.'

She laughed. 'You're so infuriating.'

They rounded a corner and the rest of the headland opened out in front of them. She stopped, letting out a little soft gasp as she took in the cottage at the very furthest edge of the beach.

'Is this yours?'

'Yes.'

'You bought Little Haven?'

'Yes I did. Well it belonged to my mum, it's on her land, but I gave her a fair price for it.'

She stared at it in shock. When Theo had moved to Apple Hill Bay with Carrie, Shay and Fern, Carrie had inherited a strip of land from her grandfather, which was where The Little Beach Hut Hotel now stood. Little Haven, an old, dilapidated building on the beach, had been part of that land and when she and Theo became friends, this was where they always hung out. It had been structurally sound, well the walls were, a small part of the roof had fallen in but there were several rooms that were still protected by it. They used it to watch wildlife: the birds that nested on the cliffs, the foxes and badgers that had made their homes in the trees and bushes, the dolphins that would often swim round the headland, the seals that would rest on the rocks at the end of the beach. Even the bats that nested in the eaves of the roof provided hours of entertainment. When Carrie found out they were down there every day after school, she'd replaced the roof and windows and made sure the place was structurally sound. She'd given Roo and Theo some paint and they had helped to clean and redecorate the place, but it was still a bit of a hovel. There was no electricity, no plumbing, no facilities, just a few solid walls and a roof.

But now the place had been completely transformed. There was a large balcony that stretched the whole length of one side of the cottage. Fairy lights were strewn round the top of the balcony and they were glowing in the receding light of the evening sun. The roof had been redone with beautiful sleek slate tiles. The walls were painted a lovely, warm, sunshine yellow and there were flowers and plants flourishing in the garden.

'Theo, it's beautiful. I can't believe you bought it.'

'I spent so many happy hours here, it felt like the perfect place to call home. Mum had electricity and plumbing put in to all the beach huts down here on the beach for guests to stay in. So it wasn't that hard for me to get the cables and pipes extended to incorporate Little Haven too. The way we came down is the quickest but there is a much safer concrete path to it that I use when I have to transport furniture and anything else I need down to the cottage on a quad bike. I've loved doing this place up and every day, I wake up to this incredible view.'

'I love it.' She couldn't take her eyes off it.

'Come on then, wait until you see inside.'

He led her down the last part of the path, pushed open the red wooden gate and led her through a garden that was a riot of colour with flowers tumbling over from the borders and pots.

'I'm not great with the garden, so I choose plants that are hardy and can take care of themselves.'

They approached the front door and Roo felt a lump in her throat when she saw the house name sign was the one she had made for Little Haven many years before. It was a wooden plaque with twigs nailed to it spelling out the words Little Haven. Little Haven had been on a rusty old name plate above the door when they had first started coming here and she had felt like it needed a new sign. They hadn't changed the name though, because it had always been a haven for them too. Her sign had obviously been painted and varnished over the years to preserve it.

'I can't believe you still have this.'

'It was inside when I came to look around with the view to buying it. The house protected it, so I had to keep it. It's a part of our heritage.'

She smiled at that.

He opened the door and moved back to let her in.

She stepped inside the lounge and smiled. It still held that rustic, traditional charm but with a modern twist. The velvet sofa was a deep, forest green with cream and gold cushions. The rug in front of the fireplace was a deep, fluffy cream flecked with gold. The chimney breast was painted gold but the rest of the room was in a warm cream. There were fairy lights twisted around the log beams in the pitched roof. Double doors opened out onto the balcony and the incredible view of the sea and Strawberry Sands.

'This is lovely, it's quite romantic.'

'Well that wasn't really the intention.'

'This isn't your little love shack then?' Roo teased.

'Hardly, the only action this place has seen is the rabbits who are breeding quite happily in the garden. Beyond my mum and Fern, you're the only woman I've brought here. This is my sanctuary. I like that's it's just me here. I can spend hours out on that balcony watching the sea or the wildlife that live in the cliffs. It's peaceful here.'

'I get that,' Roo said, feeling touched that he had brought her into his haven.

Her stomach gurgled loudly and Theo laughed.

'Let me get you some dinner.'

CHAPTER SEVEN

Roo was sitting next to Theo on the balcony looking out over the sea. The light of the day was almost gone now, although it wasn't completely dark yet. The only sound she could hear was the waves gently lapping on the beach below them and the birds calling to each other as they settled down for the night.

She felt so content here, more so than she'd felt in a long time. Part of that was the tranquil setting and being back in Apple Hill Bay and Little Haven after all this time but another part of it was the man sitting next to her. It just felt so easy with him. It was as if those fourteen years apart had never happened. They had talked and laughed constantly over dinner, reminiscing over old times, catching up over the years they'd missed. But since they'd come out onto the balcony there had been more talk but also long comfortable silences where they just enjoyed looking out over the sea and being with each other without the need to fill the silence. She'd never had that, with anyone. Silences were always awkward and she always felt like she had to find something fun and interesting to say. But not with Theo. She felt relaxed in the silence.

She leaned her head on his shoulder and let out a happy sigh. He put his arm around her and kissed her on the forehead and she knew he wouldn't take it any further than that. She'd said she just wanted to be friends and he respected that. Although there was still a huge part of her that regretted it.

She looked up at him and he looked back at her. She really wanted to kiss him right now.

His phone suddenly rang, saving her from any inappropriate actions.

He swore under his breath and grabbed his phone from the table. She noticed for the first time that he had two phones; the one he'd picked up was red, different to the one he was using earlier.

'I'm so sorry, our lovely evening has come to an end,' Theo said, standing up.

She frowned in confusion and he snagged her hand, pulling her to her feet and leading her back inside. He quickly locked the French doors as he swiped the phone with one hand and answered it, wedging it under his chin.

'Hello?' Theo said. He led her across the room, wrapped a coat around her and pulled one on himself as he listened to the person on the other end. 'Yes I know it. OK, I'll be right there.' He hung up. 'Sorry, I have to go. I'll walk you back.'

'Where are you going? Is everything OK? Can I help?'

'It's late and you didn't get much sleep last night.' He smirked and she laughed. 'I'm probably going to be dealing with this for the next few hours, let me take you home.'

'If something's wrong, I want to help.'

He paused. 'Well, you asked me last night what I was passionate about. Let me show you.'

'This isn't work-related?'

'Thankfully I don't get emergency work calls at nine o'clock at night. This is something else.'

'A non-work emergency?'

He ushered her out the door. 'It could be an emergency. It could not be. I won't know until I get there.'

'Is it Fern, is it the baby?'

'No I'm sure they are fine. Fletcher takes very good care of them both. I'll explain on the way.' He grabbed a torch in one hand and Roo's hand in the other. 'We'll take the main path this time of night. We're no use to anyone if we fall off a cliff.'

She followed him as he lit the way ahead. The concrete path wasn't rocky like the other path they'd come down but it meant that Theo could go at a fair speed, and with his long-legged stride, she was having trouble keeping up, having to jog along in his wake.

They reached the top of the headland and Theo followed the path back to the car park where his Land Rover was parked. This was not the executive car she was expecting from a CEO. He opened the passenger door for her and she hopped in. He quickly ran round the other side, reversed the car out of its space and drove off. He took a little country lane that would take them out of Apple Hill Bay and towards the next town of White Cliff Bay. This was the lesser-used road of the two that led between the two towns but it was definitely more picturesque so was quite popular with the tourists who wanted the scenic route.

'Do I get some kind of clue where we're going?' Roo said.

'Yes, sorry, I was just thinking ahead. So Pet Protagonist has a charity partner called Little Paws and a percentage of our profits goes to them. They are a wildlife hospital and rescue centre that deal with any injured, sick or orphaned wild animals. When we first partnered with them, we spent a week with them volunteering. Not everyone, every day, we had staggered shifts so that everyone in the company had at least an hour there to understand the work that they do. Those who wanted more time there might have spent a whole day or a couple of afternoons.'

He slowed down as he drove through some road works.

'I was there for the whole week and I loved it. It felt like I'd finally found what I wanted to do with my life. It's hard work and sometimes it's heartbreaking work, but it felt like I was really making a difference. I've worked with some animals I've never or rarely seen in the wild like badgers and otters. After the week was over, I wanted to do more with them. My work as CEO doesn't give me much personal time, but I work with Little Paws at least one day most weekends and a couple of evenings a week. Sometimes I'm just on call for any wildlife emergencies. Like tonight. Sometimes I won't get a single call, sometimes I'll get two or three in an evening. This time of year, most of our calls are about orphaned baby or juvenile animals, or at least perceived orphans.'

She watched him, her heart filling for this kind, wonderful man. He had always had a love for wildlife and now he was actively involved in it.

'What made you decide to partner with Little Paws?'

'I knew Joseph, the former owner. We used to surf together. Well, he owned the land and Violet leased it off him to create Little Paws. He started coming down to help her make the different enclosures. The outdoor enclosures are as close as possible to the real thing in the wild so we have setts and dens for badgers and foxes, a few small ponds and lakes for the otters and rivers for the voles. Hedges were put in for the hedgehogs. Joseph helped a lot even after Little Paws was up and running and I never knew whether he was going there for the animals or for Violet but pretty soon they were head over heels in love.' He smiled. 'He was her toy boy, only seventy-two to her seventy-nine. They never married though. I wish they had as it would have made things a lot simpler. He died last year and I just wanted to get involved to honour him, not realising how much I would love it.'

'He sounds like a great man. And he was surfing in his seventies?'

'Yes, put most of us young ones to shame.'

She smiled at that, but frowned as she thought back over what he'd just said. 'What do you mean, you wish he'd married Violet because it would be simpler?'

'His grandson, Adam, owns the land now and the lease is up at the end of this year and at the moment he's dragging his feet about renewing it. Though I can't see that he would sell, the land is waterlogged in many places, which is great for some of our water dwelling creatures but not so great for building houses on. There's a river that runs straight through the middle of it so I can't see that the land would be of interest to any developers, but I know Violet is worried.'

'I'm guessing Little Paws doesn't have enough money to buy it off him?'

'No. Nowhere near enough. I have a fair bit in my savings and if Adam sold the land for arable or grazing use, I could probably buy it off him, but if he somehow gets planning permission approved on the land, the price of the land would be significantly higher, probably four or five times as much, which would make it over a million. Land with planning permission is worth a fortune and Little Paws has a lot of land. There's no way I could afford it then.'

'Do you think the local council would step in and help?'

'I doubt it. Rescuing wildlife just isn't seen as a priority. It's not something that serves the community and a lot of people aren't sympathetic to saving animals like foxes or rats. But our concerns might be completely baseless. Adam might renew. He was very close to his grandad and he would have known how much Little Paws meant to him.'

'Let's hope so. What are we rescuing tonight?'

'Fox cubs. Three of them. Vixens are normally really good mums and don't abandon their cubs lightly. If one is sick they might remove it from the den to give the others the best chance of survival, but they don't generally abandon their whole litter. They do go off hunting though, and sometimes the cubs might venture out to look for Mum if she has been a long time and that's when kind members of the public find them and think they've been abandoned. They pick them up and bring them to the hospital and that's it, their connection with Mum has been severed. We've tried to take the cubs back to the spot they were found and Mum almost never comes back for them once they've been handled by humans. We try to encourage people to leave the cubs alone for a few hours when they find them. Normally, if left alone, Mum will come back for them. But there is a risk that Mum won't come back, she might have been hurt or killed by a car, she might just have been scared off, and if the cubs are really young they will die without heat and food, so it's a tricky balance. Sometimes we have to act quickly because the cubs have been out of their dens for too long.'

Roo loved that he'd obviously taken the time to learn this stuff.

'The woman who phoned me tonight said she was driving along and had to stop when the cubs were crossing the road in front of her. No sign of Mum. She's picked them up and put them in an open cardboard box away from the side of the road to try to keep them from getting run over and she's done the right thing and watched from a distance for half an hour before she called us, but Mum still hasn't come back for them. There's an old tin mine up here which they are working on to make it into a museum. They're widening the road in parts and creating a car park. My guess would be that they've disturbed the den either when Mum was absent and the cubs have panicked and ran, or Mum was moving them from one den to another and got disturbed mid-move. There's been so much noise up here the last few days, I'm not surprised if it's scared Mum away. We've had numerous calls to this area in the last week, baby rabbits, birds, hedgehogs. This area has been relatively undisturbed for years apart from the cars going through and the walkers, so the heavy machinery has obviously upset the wildlife.'

'What will you do?'

'I need to see how young they are. If they still have their eyes closed then I'll take them straight to the centre because at that age they can't regulate their own body temperature and rely totally on their mum for milk. If they're a little bit older and appear uninjured, I may leave them for another hour. We'll watch them from a distance. If Mum still doesn't come we'll take them to the centre tonight.'

'We'll do a stakeout?' Roo said.

'Yeah, I should have brought doughnuts. Look, that must be the woman.' Theo pointed to a car parked at the side of the road, right next to the remains of an old tin mine. There were traffic cones blocking the entrance to the makeshift car park and heavy machinery parked up in the darkness surrounding the building.

They got out their car and the woman did too.

'Hello, I'm Theo from Little Paws and this is my colleague Roo.'

'Hello, I'm Daisy. I'm sorry for calling you so late. I just didn't know what to do. I couldn't just leave them. My husband is going nuts that I'm sitting in a dark country lane by myself.'

'I'm not surprised. If you were my wife, I'd be worried too. I'd be getting in the car and driving up here to sit with you.'

'Oh well, he's busy tonight. Football's on the TV.'

Roo watched Theo's face fall, probably at the lack of support from her husband and then he quickly rearranged his features to something more professional. 'Oh yeah, of course, umm… Football is important too. Well we're here now so we won't keep you. Just point us in the direction of the foxes and you can be on your way.'

'They're in that box over there,' Daisy pointed.

'Did they look injured at all?'

'No, perfectly healthy, like three cheeky little puppies.'

Theo smiled. 'We'll check them out and help them if need be. Thank you for calling us.'

Daisy hovered. 'Will it be OK if I call you tomorrow or in a few days to see how they are?'

'Yes, please do.'

Daisy gave them a wave and got back in her car and drove off.

Theo turned to Roo. 'We have to be really quiet when we go over there. And no matter how tempting it is, we can't pick them up and give them a cuddle.'

Roo grinned. She couldn't deny that she was excited to see them. 'I will refrain from going doe-eyed.'

'That's good. If we have to take them in, we try to keep human contact to a minimum. Obviously, we have to feed them and treat them if they are sick or injured. But we don't want them to develop a bond with us or become dependent on humans if we want a successful release back into the wild.'

She nodded.

They walked over to the box. Daisy had placed a towel roughly over the top but as they drew closer, Roo could hear them snuffling and making little yapping noises. She wondered if they were calling for their mum.

Theo carefully drew back the towel and shone a torch inside. Three pairs of eyes blinked up at them, the cubs shrinking back into the corner. They were beautiful with their dark, fluffy coats. Despite her promise, she did desperately want to give them all a cuddle, they did look like puppies.

'These are around four or five weeks old,' Theo whispered. 'They appear to be in good health so Mum probably left them at some point today, maybe she got disturbed by the builders. I'm going to leave them for another half-hour or so and we'll watch from the car to see if Mum turns up. They were quite vocal when they heard us coming. If Mum is nearby, she would have heard them too, but foxes can travel a couple of kilometres whilst hunting so she might not be anywhere near us.' He draped the towel back over the box.

'Can we cuddle them before we go?' Roo teased.

Theo grinned and opened his arms. 'If you want to cuddle something cute, I'm always willing.'

She stepped up and wrapped her arms around him. He stalled for a moment, clearly not expecting her to take him up on it, before he wrapped his arms around her and held her tight.

'This is becoming a bit of a habit,' he said.

'It's a habit I could get used to.'

'Me too.'

She bit her lip, wondering if she should tell him she thought she'd made a mistake by saying she just wanted to be friends. But then she remembered what Sally had said, how everyone had lost all respect for Charlie when he was dating Beth, and she couldn't do that to Theo.

Theo stepped back. 'Come on, let's give these cubs a chance to get back to their mum.'

He walked back to the car and she followed. He opened the boot and handed her some weird contraption that looked like a pair of binoculars with a head strap. She looked at it in confusion.

'Night-vision goggles,' Theo explained, grabbing a pair for himself.

'Oh my God, I was joking when I said we'd do a stakeout.'

'We can have a good look around the hills and trees from the car. It'll be a lot easier to see if she's lurking around in the bushes somewhere.'

They got back in the car and she watched as Theo pulled his goggles on. He looked so ridiculous she couldn't help bursting out laughing.

'Sshhh!' Theo whispered. 'Foxes have really good hearing so we will have to be really quiet. We can whisper but no big noises.'

She found the fact that he was telling her off with the goggles on even more amusing and she had to stifle her laughter in her sleeve.

She pulled hers on and looked around. 'I can't see anything.'

She felt Theo's hand on the side of her face and heard him flick a switch on the side of her goggles and suddenly the world around her turned green. 'Wow, this is amazing, I can see really far.'

She turned to look at Theo who was now bright green in her vision and with the weird goggles covering his face, he looked like an alien from Doctor Who and she couldn't help laughing again. Theo smirked and shook his head in despair.

'So do you do this often?' Roo asked, quietly when she recovered herself.

'At this time of year, it happens a lot, not just with foxes but other animals too.'

'Do you do it alone?'

'Sometimes, sometimes I have Lizzie for company.'

'Who's Lizzie?'

Theo looked at her, a smile playing on his lips. 'Was that jealousy I heard in your voice?'

'No, not at all,' Roo said, knowing full well it was.

'Lizzie is an absolute badass. She loves her leather trousers and her motorbike, hair down to her waist, she takes no nonsense from anyone, heart of gold, oh and she's eighty-three years old.'

Roo grinned. 'I like how you left that part to last.'

'I was building suspense.'

'I wasn't jealous.'

'Uh-huh,' Theo said, clearly not believing her.

He glanced out the window in the direction of the box. Roo looked too but there was no sign of life anywhere.

'Sally said she was going to ask you to the summer ball, I was jealous about that.'

He turned to look at her. 'How could you possibly be jealous of her?'

'She's very pretty, and very similar to the women you used to date when we were teens.'

He shook his head and took off his goggles and she did the same. 'Those women were meaningless. I know that's a shallow and horrible thing to say but they were and they saw me in the same way. I haven't left a trail of broken hearts in my wake as none of the women I've been with ever wanted anything more than just sex. I deliberately wasn't looking for a proper relationship back then. I've never wanted that actually, apart from with you.'

He rubbed the back of his neck. 'I had spent most of my life, certainly almost all of my childhood not being wanted. My family didn't want me, I was passed from foster home to foster home, no one cared, no one loved me, until Carrie came along. But even then it took me a long time to trust her enough to love her. And, when

Carrie adopted Shay and Fern, it was a bit easier to love them. They had been through the same shitty upbringing I had. But apart from my family I've always found it hard to hand over my heart. Doing that means laying myself open to getting hurt and rejected. I'd already had a lifetime of that. It's better to have sex with meaningless women who can't possibly hurt me. It's a wall I've built around me and I've never met anyone who made me want to pull it down. Until you crashed into my life. Quite literally.'

She smiled at the memory. She'd been at the local skateboard park very early one morning. Most times she was the only one there at that time in the morning. She had been very proficient at doing various tricks and jumps, she'd been doing it for years but she liked going early as she never did her skateboarding tricks for show; they were just for her. She had been practising the 540 spin, something she had done successfully many times and as she'd done the first flip in the air, a pigeon had taken off nearby, clipped her face with its claws and she had caught the skateboard on the ramp badly and landed in a heap at Theo's feet. 'You're spectacular,' had been the first words he'd said to her and then they'd both realised that the poor pigeon had come off badly in the fall and they'd bundled it up and taken it to a nearby wildlife rescue.

'We became friends instantly, bonding over our love of skateboarding and wildlife,' Theo said. 'I fell in love with you almost as quickly too. But it didn't feel as scary as I thought, it felt safe, no one knew, I never told you so I could never be hurt by your rejection. It was just easier that way. It makes me die inside knowing that you felt the same way and you had to watch me go off with all these random women, when you were always the one that had my heart. That had to hurt, thinking that I wasn't interested in you.'

'It did. I was always insanely jealous that we'd spend the day together, watching wildlife or practising our skateboarding tricks, or running our little business schemes and then you'd run off in the evening to sleep with a random woman who you didn't even like.'

He rubbed his hand across his face. 'You have to understand that I felt so worthless growing up because no one wanted me. Then suddenly, I turned seventeen, I was voted the hottest guy in college in some random poll and suddenly every woman wanted to be with me. And even though it was fleeting, for that short time I was with them, they would look at me like I was worth something, like I meant something.'

'I always looked at you like that,' Roo said quietly. 'You just didn't see it. You meant the world to me.'

'I am sorry I wasn't brave enough to put my heart out there and tell you how I felt. I just couldn't do it. I had been hurt so many times as a child, suffering rejection after rejection, that I couldn't risk getting that from the most important person in my life.' he paused. 'Is that why you called a halt to us, because you think that last night was just another meaningless shag to me?'

'Originally, I worried what people would think about you sleeping with your employees and after talking to Sally today and she said that everyone lost respect for

Charlie when he started dating Beth, I know that's something I don't want for you as well. But I suppose I'm cautious with my heart too. I've always been the woman that men's eyes skate over when they walk into a room. I'm not like you, I'm not the kind of woman that every man wants to be with, they were never queuing up around the block like they were with you. But even the men that did date me, it never lasted long. I wasn't special enough for that. I've been hurt too, but you were the one to hurt me the most. I am sorry that your shitty childhood meant you were too scared to open your heart to love, no child should have to go through that, but you're in your thirties now and that still hasn't changed. You've never met anyone you've wanted more with, or is it that you're still too scared to want more? Either way, I'm not naive enough to believe I'm the one to change that.'

Theo sighed. 'Your self-esteem is as damaged as mine is, but it kills me knowing I was the first of many to damage it. You were my best friend, I would never have done anything to hurt you.'

Roo looked out the window to see if there was any sign of the cubs' mum, but without the goggles, she couldn't see particularly far. 'I loved you despite the heartache you caused me. It would have been so much easier to think, he's not interested in me, so I won't love him anymore, but the heart doesn't work like that.'

They were silent for a while.

'Last night meant something to me,' Theo said. 'It meant something as soon as we kissed, as we tumbled through the door and I knew we were going to make love,

I knew it was going to be so much more than sex. But when we did, we shared a connection that was beautiful. And I know you felt that too. I would take all the judgement and giggles and bitching at work all day, every day to have a chance to explore that connection, to build it, to nurture it into something more. But I do understand if you don't want to take that risk with me.'

The irony wasn't lost on her that the roles were now reversed, with her being the one too scared to take the risk, the very thing she was berating him for. It was so tempting to lean across and kiss him right now, and then make love to him out here under the stars because of course she'd felt that connection too. She hated that she was too scared to take that step with him. Work was a big part of it but protecting her heart was even bigger. Getting over Theo Lucas, once he'd had his fill of her, was going to be heartbreakingly hard. But she knew she would regret walking away from him too, not giving it a chance. Could she be brave?

'Last night meant something to me too but I think I need some time. This has come out of the blue for me. A relationship with you has never been on my radar and I never expected to come back to Apple Hill Bay and find you here, become friends with you again let alone have the best night of my life with you. We need to get to know each other. I need to get my head around what a relationship with you would look like.'

A slow smile spread across his face. 'So it's not a no?'

'It's definitely not a no.'

He reached out and stroked her face. 'I have waited

fourteen years for a second chance with you. I can wait a little longer.'

She smiled and kissed his palm. He took her hand and kissed it too, his mouth lingering long enough to make it intimate. He pulled back and looked out the window again, but he was still holding her hand and it made her feel so warm inside.

'Or we can always have a friends-with-benefits arrangement,' he said.

She laughed, knowing he was joking but that thought was suddenly very, very tempting. Amazing sex with her wonderful friend and no chance of getting hurt because they both knew it was just sex.

She shook her head. What was she thinking? It would never just be sex with him.

She decided to change the subject.

'What's the summer ball anyway?'

'It's a thing we do every year as a way of saying thank you to all the staff for all their hard work. We invite all the staff and volunteers from Little Paws too. We pay for everything but we charge a small ticket price which goes straight to Little Paws. We also do a raffle on the night to raise more funds. Most people bring a date or friends and everyone loves getting dressed up. We could go together. As friends.'

She loved the idea of wearing a beautiful dress and going to Merryport Castle, which was such a fabulously grand location. But most of all she loved the thought of being swept around the dancefloor in Theo's arms, but they couldn't do that.

'What would everyone at work say about that?'

'They'd say, oh look how happy Theo is. That woman must be someone incredible and really special to make him smile that much.'

She smiled. 'Do you not worry that people will judge you as CEO for shagging the new girl.'

'I wasn't planning on sleeping with you in the middle of the dancefloor. But no, their judgement doesn't bother me. It bothers me what they say and think about you, it bothers me that you have to be exposed to people's comments and gossip about us, while I'm closeted away upstairs, but I don't care what they think or say about me.'

'That's very bold.'

'Being CEO affords me some luxuries. And I would take all the giggles and comments for one dance with you.'

Her heart leapt at the way he was looking at her. 'Maybe we can dance in the garden, under the moon and the stars and where no one can see us.'

'I'd do that in a heartbeat. We can spend the whole night out there and forget everyone else.'

'As CEO aren't you supposed to be there, do the big speech, shake everyone's hand?'

'I may have to show my face from time to time, but I wasn't planning on doing any speeches. Despite the grand location, it is a fairly casual affair. That's why we opted for a buffet rather than a formal sit-down meal so people can just eat and mingle and dance whenever they want. Or wander out into the gardens and dance with beautiful women under the stars. There's a lake and little lights all the way around it. In the middle, there's a little wooden band stand type thing and there's lights around that too. I intend to sit out there and wait for one dance with the most incredible woman I've ever met.'

Her breath caught in her throat. 'Then I'll be there too.'

He nodded and swallowed. When he spoke, his voice was rough. 'Thank you.'

He pulled his goggles back on and she did the same, but as soon as he'd fitted them on his head, he took her hand again.

They took some time to look out of the window for the cubs' mum.

'Can you see anything?' Theo asked, looking out of his side of the car.

She looked all round them but nothing was moving. Her heart leapt. 'Oh, there's a badger over there.'

Theo turned to look. 'Oh amazing. I love them.'

They watched the badger waddle around for a little while, before it disappeared into some trees.

'Sadly, I don't think our badger friend is going to come and help our cubs. I think we're going to have to take them in, they'll be hungry. I hate doing this. They stand so much more chance of survival when they're with their mum, but she might not ever come back.'

They got out the car and straight away they could hear the cubs whining and crying and Theo shook his head. 'She would have heard that and come back for them by now. And there's a bad storm coming later tonight. Let's get them back to the rescue centre.'

He walked over to the box, picked it up and carefully put it in the back of the car.

'We will be a while feeding them and getting them settled. I can drop you off if you'd prefer. It's getting late now,' Theo said.

'No, I want to help.'

'OK, but I don't want you falling asleep at work tomorrow.'

She grinned. 'I promise, I won't.'

They got back in the car and drove off.

'OK, the first thing we need to do is feed them,' Theo said, taking one of the cubs out of the box and weighing it on the scales.

They'd arrived at the rescue centre and were now in the treatment room, which had a large stainless steel work bench in the middle of the room and cupboards all the way round the edge filled with medicines, first aid equipment and food for various animals. At this time of night there was no one else there, although if there was a medical emergency, Eloise or her husband, Jack who were both vets, would be more than willing to come out.

'Can you make up some puppy formula?' Theo said. 'There's some in that cupboard there, the instructions are on the side of the can. Make a big batch in that jug and then I can measure out the right amount for each cub, depending on what they weigh.'

Roo set to work making the formula. He made a note of the sex and weight, and sprayed the back of the fox's neck with a small patch of non-toxic blue paint, so they could identify which fox was which. He did the same for the other two cubs but used red and green paint and then moved over to help Roo measure out the right amount into some small bottles.

'Two boys and a girl. So you get the pleasure of naming them.'

'You give them names?'

'Yes, firstly to help with identifying which cub is which while they are in our care, but secondly to help promote us on social media. We'll do some photos of feeding them shortly and share our new arrivals on Facebook and Instagram. When people see some cute fox cubs they might be more likely to donate some money to help them.'

'OK then, how about Thunder, Storm and Rain.'

He grinned. 'Great names. We can add how we rescued them from a storm, that will pull on the heartstrings a little and it's technically true, it's supposed to be horrible out there tonight.'

He quickly added the names to the chart, Thunder was the cub with the blue spot, Storm was the red spot and Rain had the green spot.

'Right want to have a go at feeding them?' Theo said.

'Yes please.'

He sat down on a stool. 'Take a pew.'

She looked around for another stool and he smirked as she realised what he meant.

Roo smiled and sat down on his lap. He grabbed Rain from the box.

'This is how you hold her, lifting her head up slightly.'

Roo took the cub from him and he manoeuvred her hands to get the right position.

'The bottle needs to be held almost horizontally so it doesn't go in too quickly. That's perfect.'

He sat back and watched as Roo fed Rain. The cub was clearly really hungry and took the milk easily and happily. The smile that spread across Roo's face was immediate and completely infectious. He couldn't help smiling too though he was watching Roo enjoying herself rather than the cub.

'This is incredible,' Roo said, softly.

'Yeah it is.'

He took his phone out of his pocket and took a few pictures of Rain guzzling away at the milk, ready for posting on social media later. Then he took a few of Roo, a huge smile on her face, that were just for him. Whatever happened between them, he wanted to remember that smile always.

Roo got out of Theo's car in the car park of The Little Beach Hut Hotel and as they started walking up the hill towards her beach hut, he took her hand again, which made her smile.

The predicted storm was on its way in. Over the bay she could see dark clouds gathering, blocking out the moon. In the distance she could hear thunder rumbling above the sea, with the odd flash of lightning, subdued by the clouds. She could feel the static in the air – it wouldn't be long before it reached Apple Hill Bay.

Tonight had been fun, working alongside Theo again, just as they always had. He made her feel happy. It had taken them a while to feed the three cubs and get them settled in their cage with blankets to hide under and keep them warm. The vet would be in early to check on them and once they were transitioned onto solid food in a few weeks, they'd be moved to an enclosure that was more in keeping with their natural environment. She had loved feeding them, she couldn't stop smiling throughout the whole experience. Although she could totally appreciate that working in wildlife rescue was not always going to be sunshine and roses. But it was clear that it was something Theo was passionate about.

He'd shown her around the rescue centre – well, the cages and the vet surgery. There were acres of enclosures beyond the building, like a little mini zoo. Theo had been keen to reiterate that the intention for all the animals they rescued was to rehabilitate them back into the wild, although with the babies and juvenile animals that some-times took many months. A lot of the residents inside were hedgehogs, which was the animal they rescued the most. There were also baby rabbits, a juvenile badger, and a few baby birds, although there would be plenty more of those as the year progressed. There was also a vole and shrew, animals she had never seen before.

As they reached the top of the hill, the heavens opened above them and what felt like a monsoon of rain was unleashed on top of them. Within seconds they were soaked and they made a run for her little hut. Thunder rolled above them and a little way up the hill, lightning suddenly struck the ground.

'Oh my God, quick,' Roo said, sprinting as fast as she could to her hut. She opened the door and bundled them both inside, shutting the door as another fork of lightning lit up the sky, seemingly right above them.

'I'm soaked!' Roo laughed.

'Me too. I know heavy rain was predicted but I wasn't expecting a month's worth of rain in the first few minutes.'

Lightning lit up the sky with a deafening crack.

'OK, you can't go back out in this, why don't you stay here tonight,' Roo said.

Theo arched an eyebrow at her.

'You can put that eyebrow back down. Even if I wanted to throw my cautious heart out of the window, I haven't got the energy to get up to any shenanigans. But I'm sure we can share a bed like two sensible adults.'

'We can. But just to be clear, I don't have any spare clothes here and I doubt you have anything that will fit me. So I will be topless, as all of this is soaked.'

'I'm sure I can restrain myself. You're not that hot.'

He laughed loudly.

She went upstairs. Who was she kidding? She'd always thought he was beautiful but now he was very much a man and not a boy, he was impossibly even more attractive. And he was so muscular, she'd felt that the night before. She was probably going to have to lie on her hands all night to stop herself from stroking his bare chest, or worse, licking it.

She snorted at the idea.

'Something funny?' Theo said, following her up the stairs.

'The idea of me restraining myself.'

'Well if you have a momentary lapse, I won't hold it against you.'

'Good to know.'

She grabbed her pyjamas and scurried off to the bathroom to get changed. She quickly washed and cleaned her teeth and came back out to the bedroom to find Theo standing there almost completely naked apart from his tight black boxer shorts.

The noise she made was nothing short of a moan and he had the audacity to grin at her. He knew very well what he was doing but she knew there wasn't an alternative, he couldn't exactly sleep in wet clothes.

'Would it be OK if I used your toothbrush?' Theo said.

She could hardly say no. His mouth had been everywhere on her body the night before as he had explored her in the most intimate way possible. She couldn't exactly complain about sharing a toothbrush now.

'Go for it.'

He disappeared into the bathroom, and she got into bed. The storm was still raging outside.

Theo came back into the bedroom and got into bed next to her. They both lay on their back, staring at the ceiling. It was weird as hell, especially after what had happened here the night before. What she really wanted to do was cuddle up to him and fall asleep in his arms but was that appropriate for two people that were just going to be friends?

Before she could think more about it or talk herself out of it, she rolled over and placed her head on his chest, her arm around his waist. Immediately he wrapped his arms around her and she liked that he didn't question it when she was the one that said she just wanted to be friends.

He kissed her on the forehead. 'Goodnight, Roo.'

She looked up at him, his gentle eyes watching her with warmth and affection. She reached up and gave him a brief kiss on the lips. 'Goodnight.'

He smiled and reached out to turn off the light and then wrapped his arms round her again.

She knew she was blurring the lines here, but this just felt so right. She belonged here and she couldn't help smiling as she drifted off to sleep.

CHAPTER EIGHT

Theo woke up early the next morning and carefully slipped from the bed. He threw on his clothes which had been on the heated towel rail all night and gave Roo a kiss on the head. 'I have to go, beautiful.'

She smiled and opened one eye sleepily. She stroked his face before drifting back off to sleep again.

He left the hut and ran straight into Shay again.

'Why are you always lurking around like a bad smell?' Theo said.

'I work here, remember. So things are going well with Roo? I'm happy for you. You two were always made for each other.'

'It's not like that. I mean it was and then it definitely wasn't and now I think it's a maybe.' He smiled as he remembered cuddling up to her the night before. 'Anyway, I got a call out last night and she helped me with it. On the way back, we got caught in the rain and I ended up staying the night, platonically.'

Shay's eyes widened. 'She helped you?'

'With some fox cubs,' Theo said, meaningfully.

Shay let out a sigh of relief. 'But did you tell her?'

Theo stared at him. 'Have I told her about my highly illegal dealings? Have I told her that the cute, wholesome wildlife rescue centre is actually a front for something much darker and seedier?'

'I wouldn't say dark and seedy. I certainly don't lose any sleep over my involvement with it.'

'Neither do I, but it's illegal however you want to paint it. And it's a very divisive topic for some.'

'You don't trust her to keep quiet?'

'Oh I do, I just don't want her to think badly of me. I'm enjoying the way she looks at me right now. I'm not sure how she will look at me once she learns what I'm up to.'

'Well, if things turn serious between you and you two end up getting married, she'll need to know what she's marrying into. The Lucas family are a bunch of criminals.'

Theo laughed. 'We'll have to initiate her into our ways.'

'Look, it's no big deal. We'll just be really careful around her until you do tell her.'

'Yeah I'd appreciate that. I was going to ask her around for dinner with the family tonight, so keep schtum. I will tell her, but we have other things with our relationship to navigate first.'

Shay mimed zipping his lips shut.

'I have to go, see you tonight.'

Shay waved and Theo ran off down the hill.

Roo was just finishing getting ready for work when there was a knock on the door of her beach hut. She rushed to answer it, wondering if Theo had come back. She noticed it was a woman and she couldn't help smiling when she realised it was Carrie.

She opened it and straight away Carrie wrapped her in a big hug.

'Roo, it's so wonderful to see you again.'

Roo smiled and wrapped her arms around her. 'It's good to see you again too.'

Carrie stepped back, holding Roo at arm's length. 'You've grown into a beautiful young woman.'

Roo blushed. 'Thank you. And you haven't aged a day.'

'I have a hot boyfriend who is keeping me very active. It turns out great sex is the key to eternal youth.'

Roo laughed.

'Look I won't keep you, I know you're off out to work, I just came by to give you one of my breakfast muffins, there's bacon, egg, tomatoes and mushrooms in it. I brought one for Theo as well. He's probably worked up an appetite.' Carrie clapped a hand over her mouth. 'I didn't mean doing *that*. I meant because he's always working so hard, not because he spent the night finding the secret of eternal youth himself. Shay said he stayed over here last night but that was platonic, wasn't it? Oh you don't need to tell me, it's none of my business. Unless you want to tell me of course. No, no, ignore me. I brought one for Charlie too, because he's always working so hard and I don't know anything about his sex life, nor do I need to know.'

Roo couldn't help the smile from spreading across her face at Carrie's little monologue, although she didn't know which part she should address first.

She cleared her throat. 'Thank you for the muffins, that was very kind. I'm sure Charlie and Theo will appreciate it too.'

Carrie let out a sigh of relief, probably because Roo had bypassed the embarrassing parts of what Carrie had said.

'And will you come for dinner tonight? Shay and Fern will be there and I'm sure they will love to see you again.'

'I would love that, thank you.'

'Oh good. Shall we say seven?'

Roo nodded.

'Right, I'll let you get on, make sure Theo and Charlie get their muffins.'

'I will.'

Carrie gave her a wave and hurried off down the hill.

Roo smiled and shook her head. Dinner was definitely going to be interesting.

Theo walked into Charlie's office and closed the door.

'I need to talk to you,' Theo said, sitting down.

'This sounds serious,' Charlie said, closing his laptop.

'Ginny phoned me last night.'

Charlie frowned. 'What? Why? Is she OK?'

'It was work-related.'

'She shouldn't be phoning you about work, she knows better than that. Why didn't she come to me?'

'Because it concerns you. Sally has been up to her old tricks again. She was telling Roo, I mean Aurora, all about how you and Beth were having sex in your office when she was working here.'

Charlie stared at him. It was clear he was furious. 'You are joking. Please tell me this hasn't reared its ugly head again.'

'Ginny heard her talking to Aurora. I saw Aurora last night and she confirmed it was true.'

'You shouldn't be dealing with work matters outside of work either. This needs to be dealt with professionally, not in the pub or the gym or anywhere else.'

Theo raised his hands in defence. 'Me and Aurora are friends, I bumped into her and we were chatting when Ginny called. She overheard what Ginny was saying and confirmed it. I wasn't gossiping about it in the pub.'

Charlie sighed. 'Sorry. We just need to handle this properly. I need to talk to HR and see where we stand on this. She was on her last warning so I don't know where we go from here. We can't let this continue. Beth would be horrified if she knew about this.'

'I need to be really clear about this. I want her sacked. She is ruining your reputation and Beth's and she isn't even here to defend herself. Sally has been warned multiple times and it makes no difference. If you need to go through HR and do this formally and professionally, that's fine, but I want her gone by the end of the day.'

Charlie nodded. 'OK.'

'And if you need further ammunition, Sally was gossiping about other members of staff too. She told Aurora about who is sleeping with who. You and Beth aside, that isn't appropriate behaviour either. Aurora ended up putting her headphones in so she wouldn't have to listen to it.'

'OK, that will help, a lot. We'll have to interview the members of the design team today, including Aurora and Ginny so we can build a case. I'll speak to Annabel and get the ball rolling today.'

Charlie lifted the phone to call HR and Theo stood up to leave. 'Let me know what you need from me.'

Charlie nodded.

'By the way, are there any changes to my diary this week that I should know about?'

Charlie shook his head, clearly distracted. 'Not that I know of.'

'OK, good.' Theo gave him a wave and walked out.

Roo opened the door to Orla's café and although it was quite full with people who had evidently been swimming as they all had wet hair and were wrapped in dry robes, they were all eating their breakfast and the counter was empty.

Orla was waiting for her, a big smile on her face. 'How's things with the loved-up couple?'

Roo smiled. 'Well, it's not as smooth sailing as I was

hoping it would be. I started at my new job yesterday and guess who's the CEO?'

Orla's smile slipped from her face. 'Oh no. You're working for Pet Protagonist?'

'Yes.'

'Oh crap, I didn't make the connection when you said you were working for a small publishing company. I bet that was awkward.'

'Yeah, you could say that, the managing director showed me round and then introduced me to the CEO and there he was,' Roo sighed. 'We talked about it privately and I decided that we shouldn't continue seeing each other, people will be judging him for sleeping with the new girl and looking at me and thinking I only got the job because I'm sleeping with the boss. But I've kind of regretted it ever since and I know part of me backing out is because I'm scared of getting involved with him.'

'Why? You know Theo.'

'I think that's the point, we have so much history, this thing could get serious very quickly and I worry about what will happen when it ends.'

'Why would it end?'

'All my relationships end and Theo isn't known for his long-term relationships.'

'Maybe that's because you two have never been with the right person before. I firmly believe that everyone has their one, the person they're supposed to be with. Maybe you were meant to come back here and find each other.'

'I'd love to believe that's true. And there's a big part of me that thinks I should give us a chance. We had a lovely night last night, I had dinner at his and then I found out he works with the local wildlife hospital when he got a call-out and I ended up helping him.'

Orla's eyes widened slightly. 'Oh, what animal did you have to help?'

'Three abandoned fox cubs,' Roo said.

'Oh that's good.'

'Good?'

'I meant good that you were able to help them. What drink did you want?'

Roo looked at her in confusion. She was blatantly trying to change the subject. 'Umm, chai latte please.'

Orla set about making the drink and then rang it through the till. 'So you helped him with the fox cubs?'

Roo paid. 'Yes, there was no sign of Mum and there was that big storm last night so we had to take them in. But it was just so lovely working with him, he's the kindest, most wonderful man, I know I could very easily fall in love with him.'

'And that makes it more scary,' Orla said, sympathetically.

Roo nodded.

'I get it, I really do. I once told a man I loved him and he ran for the hills.'

'Oh no, Orla.'

She waved it away. 'It was a long time ago and I was very young, just seventeen but I do understand the fear of putting your heart out there and getting it broken. But when something like that happens it doesn't destroy us, although it hurts pretty bad at the time, it makes us

127

stronger, we pick more wisely who to give our hearts to, we don't wrap our hearts in bubble wrap and lock them away for ever.'

Roo nodded. 'You're right. But now I need to know who broke your heart so I can do bad things to them.'

Orla laughed. 'Like what?'

Roo thought about it. 'I could give them evil looks every time I saw them.'

'I don't think he deserves that, it wasn't his fault he didn't feel the same way, and he had his own emotional baggage to deal with. But as I said, it was a long time ago, so no need to go to battle on my behalf.'

The door opened behind Roo and she glanced around to see a huge Bernese Mountain dog come barging in, tail in the air, big smile on his face. At the other end of the lead was a very heavily pregnant woman who Roo realised was Theo's little sister, Fern.

'Fern, hi.'

'Roo, oh my god, I heard you were back,' Fern said, moving forward to give her a hug. 'How are you?'

'I'm good, how are you?'

'I've eaten too many cakes as you can see,' Fern stroked her large belly affectionately.

Roo laughed. 'Congratulations, and I hear you've married a wonderful man.'

'I have, Fletcher is the most amazing man I've ever met.'

'And who is this handsome boy?' Roo asked, stroking the soft velvety head of the Bernese.

'This is my beloved Bones.'

'Hello Bones.'

The dog wagged his tail excitedly.

'And I hear you and Theo are—'

'Friends,' Roo interrupted. 'For now at least.'

'Oh that's not what I heard.' Fern laughed.

Roo looked at Orla.

'Don't look at me, I haven't told anyone. This has the markings of Carrie. Although Shay has seen Theo coming out of your hut twice now, so it might have been him.'

'So there is something to tell?'

'Oh is that the time?' Roo said, quickly changing the subject, she grabbed her drink from the counter. 'I must go.'

Fern laughed. 'Why don't you come to dinner tonight at Carrie's house.'

'I've already been invited and I stupidly said yes, so I guess you can all give me the third degree tonight.'

'I look forward to it.'

Roo gave them both a wave and walked out.

Roo walked into the office and was surprised by how many people were already here. She had deliberately got in early to make up for the later start the day before, but half the office was already filled with people busily working away. She wondered if there was some kind of flexi-hours arrangement available so people could come in early and leave early. Either that or some people really loved their jobs.

She sat down next to Danielle again and noticed there was a laptop open on the far side of her desk, next to Sally.

'Hey,' Danielle said, cheerfully. 'You're going to be working on your own today.' She gestured to the laptop. 'But I'm here to help if you need me. I'll be working on a calico cat on my computer. But I thought you might enjoy working on an Appaloosa.'

'An Appaloosa? Isn't that a horse.'

'Yes. If you log in and go to your inbox you'll see the photos for the horse, she's called Sprinkles.'

Roo logged in. At least working on a horse would be a bit different to working on a freckly English Setter. She clicked on the file with the photos of Sprinkles and her heart sank. Sprinkles was a predominantly white horse covered in hundreds of brown freckles. She was going to go crazy if she had to deal with freckles on a variety of animals for the next month.

'Ooh what's in the bag?' Sally said, gesturing to the bulging bag of delicious breakfast muffins that Carrie had given her.

'Oh they're not mine, they're for Theo and Charlie.'

Sally snorted, 'You brought cakes in for the bosses?'

Roo's eyes widened in alarm, suddenly realising how this would look. 'No, not me. I bumped into Theo's mum on the way into work and she gave them to me to give to them.'

'You know Theo's mum?' Danielle asked.

'Knew. I knew her when I lived here fourteen years ago. I've just bumped into her again for the first time.'

There, that was completely truthful. She didn't need to mention the invite to dinner that night.

'A lot of people are going to find it a bit weird that you've brought cakes in for Charlie and Theo. Some might say you're trying to get preferential treatment,' Sally said.

'A lot of people don't actually need to know. They're just breakfast muffins from Theo's mum, it's hardly the seedy gossip you're desperately looking for,' Roo snapped.

Sally stared at her in shock and Roo knew she'd said too much.

Just then a message popped up on her screen and she realised it was another message from Betty, the office manager. She opened it, wondering whose mug had been stolen now.

from: officemanager@petprotagonist.com
to: everyone@petprotagonist.com

Please be advised the management will be talking to all members of the design team today, individually. There is no need for concern.

Please do not use office milk for your breakfast cereal, you should be eating breakfast at home.

Please do not leave used teabags in the sink.

Remember, if you cause a jam in the photocopier, please sort it out and don't leave it for the next person to deal with.

Regards

Betty Dimble - Office Manager

"No need for concern," Danielle scoffed, realising Roo had seen the message that had probably gone out earlier. 'As soon as everyone saw that message this morning, everyone has been concerned. Why would they need to speak to us all individually? Something is going on.'

'I think they're making redundancies,' Sally said.

'I doubt it,' Roo said. 'From what I gather, the business is a huge success. They are publishing in multiple languages and are selling copies all over the world.'

'That sounds like management speak. Someone's been talking to Theo,' Sally said.

Roo sighed. 'Those are the things Charlie told me when he hired me. I know you'd really like there to be some exciting gossip about me and Theo because we knew each other in our teens but there really is nothing more to it than that. We're friends, that's it. And there definitely won't be any preferential treatment, with or without these muffins.'

She hated confrontation but Sally was really bringing out the worst in her. Or maybe the best. Maybe it was time she stuck up for herself.

Just then another message popped up on the screen and her heart leapt to see it was a message from Theo.

from: theo@petprotagonist.com
to: everyone@petprotagonist.com

A big welcome to our newest member of staff, Aurora Clarke, who joins us as lead designer. We were all very impressed with her design portfolio which can be viewed via the link at the end of this message, and her wealth of experience in many design areas and across multiple design programs. Aurora has been working in design for over fourteen years. I'm looking forward to working with her on *A Knight's Tail* tomorrow after she's had a couple of days to settle in.

Theo

Roo cursed under her breath. She didn't know if that had come from Charlie or whether Theo had decided to do that without consulting Charlie first. If it had come from Charlie, then that was a very sudden U-turn, and why would he do that unless Theo had said something to him? And what would happen if she didn't start on *A Knight's Tail* tomorrow? It would look like Charlie didn't think she was ready and that wouldn't look good to the rest of the design team.

'No preferential treatment, eh? You've been here one

day and already you've been promoted to lead designer. We can all see that's because you and Theo are friends or probably friends with benefits,' Sally said, loudly.

'This isn't preferential treatment. Charlie hired me as lead designer weeks before I even knew Theo was here. When we discussed my job he said I would be in charge of creating the illustrations for the new book. That was always the plan but Charlie wanted me to settle in for a few days first.'

'That hardly seems fair. Some people have been here since the beginning, they should be promoted to lead designer, not you. Even Nate worked here for six months before he was given a promotion,' Sally said.

Roo rubbed her hand across her face. 'I think it comes down to experience and skills. If you look at my design portfolio on that link, you'll see the kind of things I've worked on in the last fourteen years.'

'Are you saying I'm not experienced or skilled enough to be lead designer?' Sally said.

This was going from bad to worse. 'I think Charlie saw something in my work that he really loved. I have quite a unique style and he obviously wanted that for the story illustrations.'

'Are you really a lead designer?' Danielle said.

'Yes.'

'Then me showing you how to do the freckles yesterday is something you can do in your sleep?'

'But I don't know this program, it's been really useful getting to know the software.'

'You must have found the whole thing really patronising.'

'Not at all, you've been wonderful to work with, very patient.'

Danielle grunted her disapproval and even Sally turned away from her to get on with her work for once.

Roo dragged the laptop closer to her so no one would see what she was doing, then opened up the internal messaging system. This would act like an instant message rather than the internal emails that seemed to do the rounds addressed to everyone.

She opened a new message to Theo.

ROO:

Why did you do that?

Theo's reply was instant.

THEO:

Do what? I always send a welcome message to all new employees, telling our current employees a little about them. This is no different.

ROO:

You deliberately mentioned about me being a lead designer.

THEO:

Because you are. And continuing pretending you're not is going to be worse for you when you do take up that role.

ROO:

But you said I'll be working on A Knight's
Tail tomorrow.

THEO:

That's what my diary says. No one has
told me differently.

Theo sent a snapshot of his diary that clearly showed
he was supposed to be working with her on *A Knight's Tail*
from Wednesday onwards.

ROO:

You've made things very difficult for me.
Sally thinks I've been promoted over her
because me and you know each other.
Danielle is insulted that I've been on
freckle duty which she now thinks is
beneath me.

THEO:

And this was exactly what I was trying to
avoid further down the line. Charlie should
have made it clear to everyone what you
had been hired to do. He's got you here
on false pretences if he intends for you to
work on every design department before
moving you up. I'm not sure what he's
playing at and if this was anyone else but
you, I'd be asking him about it by now.
But I'm not supposed to know anything
about this so I'm carrying on as normal.

She sighed. Theo was right. All of this could have been avoided if Charlie had told everyone she was a lead designer but she couldn't help feeling annoyed that Theo had done this when she had asked him not to.

THEO:

It wasn't my intention to upset anyone down there, especially not you. I just wanted everyone to know what you were hired to do, so even if you are moving around the design department for the next few weeks, they will all know it's only temporary. I'm going to have to go. Charlie has just walked into my office, he looks pissed off too.

Roo sighed. What a mess.

'Why did you send that message?' Charlie asked.

Theo sighed, he really was going to get it in the neck today. The only thing he could do was play innocent.

'What was wrong with the message? I always send the welcome message to new employees. You told me it looks good if it comes from the CEO. You gave me a template to follow and all my welcome messages follow the same format, what job they will be doing, what experience they have. What did I do wrong?'

'I was going to circle Aurora around the different roles in the design team for a few months first.'

'Well you never told me that. I have it in my diary that I was starting the designs for *A Knight's Tail* with her as from tomorrow. I even asked you this morning if there were any diary changes and you said no.'

'I thought I'd start her off easy for a few months. I want her to get used to the software. Besides, all the roles in the design department are important and she should learn them all.'

Theo knew Roo didn't want him to talk to Charlie about this but now the subject had been brought up he couldn't let it go and he knew he would do the same if this was anyone else that Charlie had hired.

'But you hired her as a lead designer,' Theo said, in confusion. 'Why would you not want her to do that? You were so excited when you headhunted her, you showed me everything that she'd been doing and we knew we had to get her on board. You even told her she would be creating the illustrations for the new book, that's not fair on her to change the job description after she comes here.'

'Well yes, but Sally said that some of the designers aren't happy that I'm bringing in a new lead designer when some of them have been there for months or years, especially when some of those designers, who are getting paid less than Aurora, then have to show her how to use some of the tools.'

'Are you really going to take advice on how to run your company from Sally? Someone who was so bitter and twisted about you promoting Beth over her, that she spread malicious lies about the two of you and is still doing that now.'

Charlie sighed and Theo knew he had hit the mark with that.

'What if the other designers are upset with us bringing someone in from outside the company?'

'That's just how business works sometimes. Roo's credentials are incredible. She has more qualifications than the whole design team put together. And you're using her to put freckles on a dog? You're not using her to her full potential.'

'I think we need to give her some time to get comfortable with the software and get to know how everything works,' Charlie said.

'Yes for a few days, maybe even a week, not a few months. If you do that you're undermining her by showing the rest of the design team that she isn't capable of the job she was hired to do. And how do you think she feels about this?'

Charlie sat down, running his hand through his hair.

Theo leaned forward. 'Mate, you're my best friend, the company has grown to be as successful as it is today because of you. And even when you've made decisions I didn't agree with, I've always trusted you. If this is the way you want to go, I trust you. But if you want my opinion, if she's on bloody freckle duty for a month, I think she'll walk.'

'When have I made decisions you haven't agreed with?'

Theo sighed that Charlie would focus on that.

'Lots of times, but what the hell do I know, you're the one with a business management degree.'

'We're a team, I would hope you'd tell me when you didn't agree with what I was doing. What didn't you agree with?' Charlie said.

Theo had clearly opened a massive can of worms with this.

'OK, let's look at Sally. You should have sacked her for all those rumours she was spreading about you and Beth. She told everyone you two were shagging in your office every day when you two were creating a new book. And you were dating Beth, you should have protected her. She doesn't even want to come back to work now because Sally is still here.'

'She's happy staying at home with Hope.'

'Look I don't want to get between you and Beth on this one, but you need to have a talk with her because from what I can see, she's going out of her mind with boredom.'

Charlie shook his head. 'I couldn't sack Sally. It felt like it was too personal, like I was getting her back for Beth. I wanted to remain professional.'

'I could have sacked her. There was nothing personal between us but you insisted we couldn't. That we had to give her a warning. I trusted you on that yet she's still here spreading those lies. Thankfully we'll be getting rid of her for good after today but we should have done that last year.'

'Yes, I'll be relieved once that is over. But I'm sorry if I do things you don't like.'

'Mate, you're amazing, the company is where it is now because of you.'

'I don't agree with that. It was your idea, your program.'

'And I don't have the first idea about running a business, I still don't and we've been doing it for over two years. It's all you. In an ideal world, you'd be CEO and I would be working in the basement as a software developer. I don't have any complaints about the way you run our company. Never have.'

'Apart from Aurora.'

'I don't want to lose her. She's a brilliant asset to the company.'

'OK, OK, duly noted.'

'Just talk to Aurora, see if she's happy.'

'I will.' He looked at his watch. 'Interviews with the design team start in fifteen minutes. Shall we do it in my office?'

'Yes that's fine.'

Charlie nodded and walked out. Theo let out a heavy sigh. He just had to hope what he'd said was enough.

CHAPTER NINE

Roo was just finishing the freckles on the Appaloosa on the second page when she was approached by Betty, the office manager.

'Aurora we'd like to see you upstairs now.'

'Oh sure,' Roo said.

'Don't forget your favouritism muffins,' Sally said, giving her a fake sarcastic smile.

Roo ignored her but grabbed the muffins anyway.

A few others, including Ginny, had already been taken up. But thankfully no one was saying anything to anyone else about it, regardless that the ones that hadn't gone upstairs were desperate to know.

She followed Betty upstairs to Charlie's office where Charlie, Theo and another lady called Annabel, who Roo knew worked in HR, were sitting around Charlie's desk. Betty joined them and Roo sat down on the opposite side before remembering her muffins.

'Oh before we start, Theo, I um… bumped into your mum this morning, she gave me these muffins for you and Charlie.'

Charlie's face lit up as he reached for the bag. 'Are these Carrie's famous breakfast muffins?'

'They are.'

Charlie let out a moan of appreciation. He took a big bite of one of the muffins before passing the bag to Theo.

'You saw my mum,' Theo said, taking a sniff of the bag. 'She came to my hut.'

Theo smiled and rolled his eyes. 'Of course she did.'

Roo glanced at Betty and Annabel. 'Sorry I don't have muffins for you.'

Annabel didn't seem to mind but Betty had adopted the suck a lemon look that she'd worn the first day when she'd caught Roo listening outside Theo's door.

'I don't think muffins are appropriate at a meeting like this,' Betty said.

'Well, I didn't know what kind of meeting it was,' Roo lied, knowing full well this was about Sally. 'There were no details on the message about what the meeting was about so I didn't know that muffins were inappropriate.'

Theo smirked and Charlie quickly took one more bite, then wrapped the rest of the muffin in its greaseproof paper and put it in his top drawer.

'Let's get down to business,' Annabel said, straightening her papers on the desk. 'There has been a formal complaint about one of the members of staff gossiping about Charlie and telling lies about inappropriate behaviour. This has been corroborated by two other members of staff. Do you know who we're talking about?'

Roo straightened her face because this was a serious matter. 'Sally.'

'That's correct. The witnesses all said that Sally was talking to you about Charlie and Beth. Would you be willing to share with us what was said?'

Roo explained everything that Sally had said and while it felt a bit underhand to go behind Sally's back like this, at least she wasn't the only one to confirm Ginny's complaint. Besides as guilty as she felt, what Sally had done was far worse than what she was doing. She told them that Sally had also gossiped about other members of staff too.

'Thank you for that,' Annabel said, making notes.

'We don't condone any kind of gossip in the office, especially not lies,' Betty said. 'Did you do anything to deter her actions?'

'To be fair, it was Aurora's first day yesterday,' Theo said. 'And it really isn't her place to try to stop unacceptable behaviour in the office. That's kind of your job.'

Betty clearly bristled at this.

'I'm afraid I didn't,' Roo said, suppressing a smirk. 'It was really uncomfortable to listen to, even before I knew it was lies. But I didn't feel like I could tell her to stop talking when it was my first day and I was hoping to make a good impression. I put my headphones in so I wouldn't have to listen to it, but even that upset her as she thought I was being rude.'

Annabel nodded. 'Thank you for your time and your

honesty. We'd appreciate your discretion in not telling anyone about the contents of this meeting, especially not Sally.'

Roo nodded and stood up to leave.

'Aurora, just a second,' Charlie said. 'I just wanted to check if you were happy with the current work situation and the plan to move you around all the different design areas.'

She stared at him in alarm. She glanced at Theo who was clearly willing her to say something. But she couldn't say anything in front of Betty or Annabel. She didn't even want to say something to Charlie but she knew she had to at some point, just not now.

'Yes of course.' She plastered on a bright smile to prove it and she saw Theo's shoulders slump in disappointment.

'OK, thanks Aurora,' Charlie said.

She started to walk out but she couldn't bear the thought of disappointing Theo. She knew she had to be brave, fight for herself, fight for the things she wanted.

She turned back. 'Actually, Charlie I'm not. When you approached me to offer me a job, you said you wanted me as lead designer, you told me if I came to work for you I would be creating the illustrations for the new book. My written offer of employment and employment contract also confirmed this is what I would be doing and I came to work for you based on that. I appreciate I need a few days to get to know the software but my skills and experience in multiple design programs over many years means I can adapt easily to any design software. If you feel I need to shadow someone, that someone should be Nate, so I can see what his job of lead designer entails day to day. It shouldn't be learning how to put freckles on a dog which is where I would imagine someone with no design experience would start. I am a team player and I'm always happy to cover someone's desk if they are on holiday or sick but again, I will be able to adapt easily without the need to shadow every area of design for the next few months.'

Her heart was racing in her chest. She didn't want to be the woman that caused trouble in her first week but continuing with the plan to circle her around all the design areas was undermining her in front of all the other designers. It would also drive her crazy.

She glanced at Theo and he had the biggest smile on his face.

Charlie stared at her with wide eyes. 'OK, we'll have you report to Nate this afternoon.'

'What's going on?' Annabel said.

He cleared his throat. 'I thought it might be best to circle Aurora around all the design departments first to give her experience but also so not to upset the current designers because she has come in as lead designer and not been promoted to it as Nate and Beth were.'

'I do appreciate the reason behind it,' Roo said. 'But I presume you have managers here that that were brought in as managers and weren't promoted to that position.'

'That's true,' Charlie said.

'This is no different.'

'Whatever your reasons, this should have been communicated to Aurora before she accepted the posi-

146

tion. Changing your mind now would be a breach of contract,' Annabel said.

Charlie nodded. 'My apologies, Aurora, it wasn't my intention to upset you with this. You'll be starting the illustrations for *A Knight's Tail* with Theo this afternoon once we've finished these interviews and when you're not with him you'll be with Nate, at least for the next week.'

'Thank you. And if it helps ease your conscience a little, the person that was shouting the loudest after Theo sent his welcome message this morning was Sally, no one else seemed to mind.'

Charlie smiled. 'That does help, thank you.'

'And while I'm here, I had an idea to help with personalising the different animal characters.'

'Aurora, we do have other people to see,' Betty said. 'This is not the time to air all your problems.'

'No, it's OK, we are always open to new ideas,' Charlie said, he nodded for Roo to continue.

'Avatars are very big right now and people love doing them. On social media you can create your own avatar, choose the hair colour, hair style, eye colour, mouth shape, face shape, the shape of the body, even the clothes. There are websites where you can make yourself into a Disney character or apply the Disney treatment to your pet. People love doing it and will happily spend a few hours creating the perfect avatar for themselves or their pet. We could offer the same thing so our clients design the character that will feature in our books, they will choose where the freckles go and what shade of brown the freckles are. They can even add accessories if they wish like a pair of glasses or a hat. Obviously, we can still offer the same personalisation we offer now for those clients who don't want to spend hours perfecting their dog or cat character or for those that are not technologically minded but my guess is that a lot of people would love to design their own and that will save us a lot of work and will ensure they get a character they love.'

'I love this idea,' Theo said.

'I do too,' Charlie said. He looked at Theo. 'Can it be done?'

'Yes, it's a bit of work, but yes. This is a brilliant idea thank you, Aurora.'

She smiled and before she could upset Betty any further, she hurried out.

Roo looked up as Nate, the last member of the design team to go for his interview returned to his desk. Everyone had gone up apart from Sally. So the management team were obviously now making a decision based on all the evidence. She wasn't sure what the outcome would be, but she couldn't help thinking how her life would be a tiny bit easier if Sally was no longer there.

Roo had finished the Appaloosa as quickly as she could without cutting corners. She still wanted it to be perfect but she wanted to finish it so she could start *A Knight's Tail* that afternoon without it hanging over her head.

She turned to Danielle, who had barely said a word to her since she came back down from seeing Theo and

Charlie. She really didn't want it to be awkward. 'I've finished Sprinkles the horse, can I help you with your calico cat?'

'I don't need help thank you,' Danielle said.

Yep, definitely awkward.

'Well I'll be working with Theo this afternoon, starting on *A Knight's Tail* and shadowing Nate when I'm not working with Theo. So if there's nothing else you need help with, I might go and sit with Nate for a bit until Theo needs me.'

Danielle shrugged.

'I still can't believe you've been promoted after one day, just because you and Theo used to date.' Sally sneered, loud enough for the other members of the design team to hear.

'Oh so that's why you got the job?' Danielle said.

'I got the job because I am qualified for it. I had no idea Theo worked here until I walked in here yesterday,' Roo said, knowing she was flogging a dead horse getting them to believe it, even if it was the truth. 'Also, Theo and I were friends in the past, we never dated. And I haven't been promoted. Charlie hired me as lead designer.'

Sally scoffed and Danielle didn't say anything.

'Well, thanks for showing me around the software yesterday. I'm going to go and see Nate.'

Nate looked up at the mention of his name, grinned and waved at her which might be the only friendly face she'd see for the rest of the day.

Roo sighed and walked over to where Nate was sitting.

He patted the chair next to him. 'Don't worry about them. They're just jealous that we're the elite.'

'That's probably not helping,' Roo muttered.

'My husband says, if I don't blow my own trumpet, then no one else will do it for me.'

'Well, that's probably true.'

'And from what I hear you're the dog's bollocks, honey, so you got to flaunt it.'

She smirked. She was going to like working with Nate.

'So I'm working on finalising the background design for *A Wizard's Tail*. It's about a dog wizard that goes to wizard school and has to stop a bad dog wizard.'

'Now that sounds familiar,' Roo laughed.

'It's legally different,' Nate winked. 'Besides, it turns out the bad dog wizard is just misunderstood and they become best friends.'

'That's nice.'

'A lot of the stories we started with here were based on traditional or well-known stories. And that works really well as people kind of know what to expect but with some added twists. But some of the newer ones that are coming out later this year are much more original, that's why they've hired the story writers to come up with something new and unique.'

'I like that they are branching out; new stories will appeal to new readers. So what have you done with *A Wizard's Tail?*'

'All of it really, not the story or the typesetting, but all the design work so far. I've had a lot of fun making this as magical looking as possible. I've worked closely with

Charlie and Theo on getting their ideas onto the page but I've largely had free rein to represent the story as I see fit. I've even added a ginger cat and fluffy brown owl as friends for our hero dog. Once it's approved, then I can add more detail, bricks to the castle, lights on in the windows, sunlight on the clouds, blades of grass nor just swathes of green, which is where I'm at now. I love it. I see each page as a little work of art.'

'I love this, the pictures are so detailed and I love the little sparkles of magic on each page.'

'I do love sparkles,' Nate said.

She grinned.

'I got a message that you'll be working with Theo later today, when he's not in meetings. You'll go through the new story, *A Knight's Tail*, and come up with ideas together to portray that. Then you'll start putting together a very rough draft for him to approve. He is very much a perfectionist and he'll come back with a hundred improvements or things he'd like to change. You'll go away and make those changes and then once he has approved that you can add all the finer detail, like I'm doing here.'

'So I'll be doing most of the work down here,' Roo said. She really didn't want people to start gossiping about the amount of time she was spending in Theo's office, just like they had done with Charlie and Beth. Already, with the knowledge that she knew Theo, people were starting to assume her job had merely come about through nepotism.

'Well, the first few days you'll be upstairs with Theo as you thrash out the story but after that you'll be back down here. He likes to be very hands-on with every new book. Both he and Charlie do.'

Roo let out a little sigh, there was no getting away with it.

Nate glanced over at Sally. 'Did you really used to date Theo?'

'No, we were friends in our teens. We never dated in the past. Not so much as a kiss.'

That was mostly true. They had never kissed *in the past.*

'We haven't spoken in fourteen years and I had no idea he was working here when I agreed to come here. I barely know him.'

Although she knew him well enough to let him trail his tongue and mouth over every inch of her body.

'We've reconnected since I've come back, but we're just friends.'

Well that was a grey area. Friends who had slept together, twice, and shared a bed together the night before. But obviously, she couldn't share those details.

'Damn girl, he is hot,' Nate said, fanning himself. 'You have to tell me if that friendship turns into something more. I need to live vicariously through you.'

'I don't think that will happen. Theo doesn't date anyone from work. And we're friends. I don't see him that way.'

Theo walked into the office and her heart betrayed those words by thundering against her chest just at the sight of him. He walked straight over to her. Everyone was now leaning up, peering over their computers to see what he would do. Did they expect him to scoop her up and carry her out the office like in *An Officer and a Gentleman?* And why did her stupid heart speed up at that thought?

'I'm ready to start work on *A Knight's Tail* now, if you'd like to come upstairs,' Theo said.

Roo nodded and stood up. She started following him out the room and glanced back at Nate to see him giving her two big, exaggerated thumbs up and a wink. She looked around the room and everyone was watching her go.

Christ, this was exactly what she wanted to avoid.

She let the office doors close behind her and she heard excited chatter start the second it did. She sighed. It didn't matter if it was true or not, the possibility that she and Theo were dating was the most exciting thing that had happened for these people all week, or perhaps all year.

'Are you OK?' Theo asked softly, as they walked up the stairs.

'Yeah, apart from everyone thinks we're definitely doing it.'

'Why do they think that?'

'Because I've been promoted after one day, or so they see it, and because they know we're friends, which Sally has twisted and told everyone we used to date.'

Theo sighed. 'That's why I sent that message this morning, emphasising that you were hired as lead designer, I didn't want anyone to think you were being promoted in a few weeks' time. And Sally knows that, Charlie went to her last week and asked if you could shadow her for a few days, and she said no because she felt really uncomfortable teaching someone who was getting paid a hell of a lot more than her. That's when Charlie panicked about what the other designers would think about you coming in as lead designer instead of realising the protest was coming from someone who is just bitter and twisted.'

'So what, she's just stirring it up for fun?'

'Mainly because she thinks she should have been promoted to lead designer and because she's a malicious, nasty piece of work. No one likes Sally. I'm sure there will be a lot of people happy to see the back of her.'

'You're sacking her?'

'Yes. She'll be told just before she leaves to go home today. And I never told you that.'

She zipped her lips closed.

'And as for the other thing. Have you heard the expression, you might as well be hung for a sheep as for a lamb?'

'Are you suggesting that if people are going to gossip about us doing it when we aren't, we might as well do it?' Roo laughed at the audacity.

'I would never do that,' Theo said, innocently.

She smirked and rolled her eyes.

They reached the top floor and bumped into Charlie as he was coming out of his office.

'Aurora, I want to thank you for being honest about what Sally said to you, I know that can't have been easy, especially on your first week. I also want to reiterate that the rumour about Beth and me is categorically not true. Whenever I worked with Beth in my office, the door was always left open, so I'm not sure how anyone could possibly believe it, but they did.'

'You don't need to explain yourself to me. But for what it's worth, I believe you. Sally gossiping to me yesterday made me feel really uncomfortable. It was completely inappropriate and very unkind.'

'Well thank you.'

Roo smiled. 'And thank you for the opportunity to work on your new book. I'm excited about working on it.'

'You won't be saying that after a few hours of working with this one. He's a complete perfectionist.'

'As every good designer should be.'

'Well, I'll leave you two to it.'

Charlie walked off and Theo gestured for her to go ahead into his office which was at the very end of the corridor.

She walked in and noticed the view for the first time – the last time she had been in here, all she'd seen was Theo. She could see the whole of Apple Hill Bay from up here, the cute little cottages, in many different colours, the shops, the harbour and the coast that stretched as far as the eye could see.

'Wow that's an impressive sight.'

'Being CEO has some perks.'

She turned to look at him and he was standing by the door. 'Charlie has suggested I leave the door open too just in case people get the wrong idea and think that I'm secretly ravishing you on my giant desk.'

She gave the desk a pat trying not to imagine what that would look like if he did ravish her on it.

'People will think that anyway thanks to Sally. They know I know you, so that obviously means shagging each other's brains out.'

'Well in that case we should definitely shut the door, really give them something to talk about.'

She laughed. 'They'd probably all run outside to try and see us through the windows.'

'It's one-way glass, so they'd have a job. By the way, before we get started. I was wondering if you wanted to come for dinner tonight at my mum's house. Fern and Shay will be there. Fern's husband Fletcher and Mum's boyfriend Antonio will be there too.'

She grinned. 'Your mum already invited me. And your sister.'

He smirked and rolled his eyes. 'Why am I not surprised? OK, let's make a start,' Theo picked up a tablet, swiped the screen a few times and handed it to her. 'That's the story of *A Knight's Tail*. Do you want to have a little read and then we can throw around some ideas?'

She took it and went and sat on the sofa, curling her legs up under her as she started to read. It was laid out on the tablet like a giant picture book with just a few lines at the top of each page and a big blank space that was going to be filled with her ideas and images. She had to flick through each page to read the whole thing. The story was sweet, funny and heart-warming which was a lot considering how short the story was. She scrolled back through and read it again.

'OK, so set in medieval times, we definitely need to open on the first double page spread with the castle and the kingdom on this blank page, to establish the setting,' Roo said. 'We can have lots of beautiful countryside and trees. Maybe the coast in the distance. Then we can have our hero on this page, maybe looking over at the kingdom, a knapsack on his back.'

She looked up at Theo and he was watching her with a big smile on his face.

'OK, this is normally the part where I tell the designer what I want.'

'Oh God, sorry. Why don't you tell me what you want?'

He rubbed his hand across his face. 'You know what. Why don't you do some sketches of what you envisage each page will look like and we can take it from there?' He handed her a big art pad and a pot of pens.

'Are you sure? I know you love this part.'

'Yeah, but I'm too much of a control freak when it comes to the books we produce. But maybe I should trust the designers to do the job we hired them to do.'

She stood up and took the paper. 'Shall I go back downstairs and work on this?'

'No, do it here.' He gestured to his desk.

'But don't you have work to do?'

'No, I'm all yours.'

She sat down at his desk. It really was huge. There was definitely room for her and Theo to ravish each other on it. She shook her head. She needed to stop thinking like that. She started sketching out ideas for each page, referring to the text and trying to incorporate that into her designs. She got lost in it, creating this medieval world.

She glanced up and saw Theo watching her.

'What are you doing?'

'Enjoying watching you create a masterpiece.'

'I'd hardly say that, these drawings are very rough.'

'But I can see you're excited about it. I remember that feeling.'

'Look, we can do this together. I don't want to take this away from you.'

'It's fine, I'll be a big pain in the arse later when I get you to change everything. Have fun with it.'

'OK, but it's a bit weird having you watch me like this.'

'Would it be weird if I told you I really want to kiss you right now,' he said, quietly.

She stopped and stared at him. She glanced at the door which was still open but he'd said it quietly enough so no one would hear.

She swallowed. 'Would it be weird if I told you I keep thinking about ravishing you on this desk?'

He smirked. 'I have condoms in my top desk drawer.'

She gasped. 'Oh my God, why?'

'Because ever since you mentioned it yesterday, I've been thinking about it too, so I thought I'd put them there just in case one day you'll let me.'

Holy shit, it had just got a lot hotter in here and Roo didn't think it was the dodgy air conditioning.

She chewed on the end of her pen for a moment, she couldn't take her eyes off him. His eyes went dark as he watched her roll her pen across her lips.

'I'd love to say to hell with it, let's try this desk on for size, but I don't know if I'm brave enough for that. I'd be scared someone would walk in on us.'

'I didn't mean now. You mean too much to me to want to risk your reputation like that. But there are many nights that I work late and it's just me in the building. If it's something you really want, it can easily be arranged.'

God, she couldn't deny how much she wanted that. Not just sex on the desk. She wanted him, in every way possible. But could she risk her heart for some fun with Theo?

She sighed. 'We're not very good at the just-friends thing, are we?'

'I'm trying really hard to be respectful of that and I certainly don't want to do anything that could risk our friendship but I'm finding it harder and harder to keep my thoughts strictly platonic, especially when we cuddle in bed or have conversations like this. I'm not going to lie, I want you and not just sexually. I want more than that, so much more. But I will try to keep my thoughts squeaky clean if you don't want that.'

'I do want that. I'm just scared of getting hurt. If we get involved it will mean more than any other relationship I've ever had before, because it's you. And I can try telling myself it's just sex, or just for fun, but it won't be that. At least not for me.'

'Not for me either,' Theo said, not taking his eyes off her. 'But I'm not scared of it. I've never felt this way before and I'm excited about what might happen between us. I have a feeling we will be amazing together. But if you need more time, I'm happy to wait.'

She bit her lip. She knew she needed to be brave, because if she walked away from him she'd regret it for the rest of her life. She just couldn't bring herself to take that step.

'Look, I'm not going to say anything more about this,' Theo said. 'You know where I stand but I'm not going to keep hassling you about this. Now back to work. When you've worked here for a few days, you'll soon realise I'm a hard taskmaster. I expect those rough sketches to be on my desk in an hour.'

She laughed, relieved the topic had moved on, at least for now.

Roo came back downstairs just before five. Most of the people had gone but those that were left were all aflutter with something that had just happened. A few people were standing in huddles or whispering to each other at their desk.

She went back over to Nate, who was closing down his computer and getting ready to leave.

'What's going on?'

'Sally was sacked.' His eyes were alight with what was seemingly the most exciting gossip he'd seen and heard this year.

She knew she had to act surprised and not like Theo had told her everything.

'Oh my God.'

Nate nodded. 'She was called upstairs to see Charlie and Annabel just before she left and while she was up there, Betty came and collected her things and shut down her computer. Imogen asked what was going on and Betty said that Sally wouldn't be back. They then took her down in the lift and escorted her out of the building, she didn't even get a chance to say goodbye.'

'Oh wow.'

Roo was secretly relieved she hadn't had a chance to leave with a parting shot – she was sure Sally would have found some way to blame Roo for this.

'Everyone heard her gossiping to you about Charlie yesterday, which she's done several times before. But when people started hearing her gossiping, really unkindly, about others in the office, people got pissed off. When they were called upstairs this morning, a lot of people didn't hold back. Although no one seems to know who made the official complaint to get the ball rolling. Was it you?'

Roo blinked. 'No of course not. It was only my first day yesterday, I'm really not the sort of person who likes to put the cat amongst the pigeons. I'm more the sort that keeps my head down and hopes everyone will like me.'

'Well likeability is overrated in my opinion, you're never going to be everyone's cup of tea, so just be yourself and you'll find your people.'

Roo smiled at that.

Just then Theo and Charlie walked out together and Roo wondered if they would address the whole Sally debacle to the few that were left behind, or whether it would just go out in some kind of message to everyone the next day along with an update on Kevin's missing coffee mug.

'Goodnight everyone,' Charlie said, as if he hadn't just sacked someone for spreading malicious lies.

Theo gave a wave but didn't say anything. In fact, he didn't even look at her and she knew he did that so as not to reinforce any gossip, but it still felt a little weird, especially after the lovely afternoon they'd spent together laughing and chatting over the design of the new book. She inwardly berated herself for being silly, she couldn't have it both ways. And she knew she'd see him later anyway when they went to Carrie's for dinner.

'I kind of expected them to address it,' Nate said, as Charlie and Theo disappeared through the doors.

'I suspect they'll send a formal message tomorrow when everyone is here. Either that or just hope everyone will forget if they don't mention it.'

Nate laughed. 'That's the most exciting thing that's happened here for a long time, people are unlikely to forget it. The only thing that would have made it better was if we'd seen her being dragged from here, kicking and screaming.'

'I'm sure it was a lot more civilised than that.'

'You don't know Sally.'

Roo laughed. At least if people were talking about this for the next few days, they might forget about her and Theo.

She grabbed her stuff.

'Any plans tonight?' Nate said.

'Yes, I'm having dinner with an old friend,' she said, truthfully.

'Oh nice.'

'What about you?'

'My husband is taking me out to dinner, somewhere romantic apparently. He's not really the romantic type, so I'll be surprised if it's something more than fish and chips, but I'm just happy to go on a date for once rather than being stuck at home.'

Roo thought about that as she put her jacket on. If she did decide to take a chance with Theo, their dates would always revolve around his house or hers as they couldn't take the risk of going out to a restaurant and someone from work seeing them. Although she didn't need big romantic dates or gestures, she'd always be happy with fish and chips. Sitting on Theo's balcony overlooking the sea as the sun was setting, it didn't get more romantic than that. Keeping their relationship a secret wouldn't be easy or fun. But maybe some things were worth the risk.

CHAPTER TEN

Theo watched as Charlie took his knight with his queen, which had been lurking at the back completely unused until this point. Charlie was always the kind to plan ahead, while Theo always lived in the here and now. Hope babbled on his lap and banged the table making the chess pieces shudder.

'I see your game,' Theo said, jiggling his goddaughter with his legs. 'You distract me with this beautiful monster and then you swoop in and take all my pieces.' Theo moved his bishop.

'You would still lose even if she wasn't there,' Charlie said, moving his rook to a place where he could take Theo's bishop.

Beth placed a plate of cookies on the table and sat down between the two of them, taking a cookie and curling her leg up to her chin as she pondered the board.

'So tell me about the new girl, Aurora, is it? Charlie thinks there's something going on between you two.'

Theo smiled as he made his move. 'Why would he think that?'

'He said when he brought Aurora in to see you on her first day, the looks between you were explosive. He first thought it was anger but later he thought it was something more.'

Theo looked across at his friend. 'Is that right?'

'Something's going on,' Charlie took Theo's rook. 'My Spidey senses are tingling when it comes to you two.'

'Your Spidey senses are wrong this time. There is nothing going on between me and Roo.'

'You see, you keep calling her Roo, which is quite a cutesy name for someone who is just your colleague.'

'We were friends, best friends in our late teens and I always knew her as Roo then. I'm not afraid to admit I was completely in love with her back then, but nothing ever happened between us. She moved to Chicago when she was nineteen and after a few months we lost contact. I haven't seen or spoken to her in fourteen years. I was shocked to see her again and I'm happy she's back, but we're just friends.'

He didn't feel the need to share what had happened on Sunday night before her first day. And it was the truth to say nothing was going on as right now, they were just friends. Although there was flirting and Roo was trying to decide whether she wanted a relationship with him, she might never be brave enough to take that step with him. They might always be just friends.

'But how did you not recognise her name when Charlie told you she was coming to work for you?' Beth asked.

'She had a different name growing up. I never knew her as Aurora Clarke, just Roo Butler. Her mum never took her dad's name when they got married and Roo had her mum's name too but when her mum and dad got divorced, Roo changed her name to her dad's surname after that.'

'So, nothing's going to happen between you?' Charlie asked.

Theo went to move his queen, but Beth cleared her throat dramatically. He glanced at her and she shook her head. He checked the board again and realised in doing that he was risking his king. He glanced around at his few remaining pieces. He touched the bishop and looked at her and she nodded. He made his move.

'I can't promise that nothing will happen, we get on very well. It's possible it might develop into something more, but I do know how inappropriate that would be as CEO.'

Beth scoffed. 'Being managing director didn't stop this one pursuing me.'

Charlie smiled as he moved his knight. 'I have no regrets there.'

Beth's eyes lit up, grabbed Theo's queen and moved it towards the top of the board. 'Checkmate.'

Charlie groaned and Theo laughed, even Hope clapped her hands together excitedly.

'Apart from finding out I married a chess genius,' Charlie said.

Roo walked over the hill with Theo towards Carrie's house. Theo took her hand and she smiled up at him.

She saw Fern looking through the window at them and pretending not to look as she quickly darted away, but she was only to be replaced with Carrie, peering round the side of the window.

'They're going to get a big kick out of us being together, even if we technically aren't. Shay has caught me coming out of yours early in the morning twice now. I'm sure my mum has practically married us off already. So I apologise now if she starts talking about wedding venues or dresses.'

Roo laughed. 'I don't mind. It's nice that they are excited for you. They love you and care about you. They just want you to be happy.'

'Hmm. I think I'd be slightly happier if they didn't interfere. But you're right and I do love them for caring.'

The kitchen door was flung open as they drew close and Carrie came barrelling out, her arms outstretched as she pulled Roo into a big bear hug.

'Roo, it's so lovely to see you.'

Roo smiled and hugged her back, feeling a big lump in her throat. She had missed Carrie too, and she hadn't realised how much. But Carrie had always been more of a mum to her than her own mum had.

'It's good to see you again,' Roo said.

'Come in, come in, let me introduce you to everyone, our little gang has got a little bit bigger since the last time you came to dinner,' Carrie took her hand and pulled her in.

Roo glanced back at Theo, who was smiling and shaking his head.

'This is Antonio, my other half,' Carrie gestured to a tall, handsome man who was at the stove stirring a pot. He smiled and waved his spoon.

'This is Fletcher, Fern's husband,' Carrie went on, indicating a great big bear of a man with gentle eyes.

'Hello,' Fletcher said, softly.

'Hi.'

Bones barged towards her, wagging his tail and sniffing her. 'That is Bones, my grandpup, and Fern and Fletcher's dog. And this is my grandchild,' Carrie stroked Fern's large belly proudly as if she had done something in the making of it. 'And of course, you know Fern and Shay.'

Fern came over and gave her a big hug. 'Roo, it's good to see you again. It's lovely to have you here. So you and Theo are together? You were a bit vague about it this morning. I'm so excited. I always thought you were made for each other.'

'We're not technically together,' Roo said.

'But you were holding hands walking up here,' Fern said.

'And I've seen Theo coming out of your hut twice,' Shay said, giving her a hug too.

'And Mum said—' Fern started.

'I didn't say anything,' Carrie said, meaningfully.

'We're... working on it,' Roo said. 'This is new for us and we're... I'm just getting used to the idea.'

They all stared at her as if she was speaking Greek.

Carrie recovered herself first. 'Well, let's sit down. Dinner will be another half an hour so we have time to chat. Theo said you're working at Pet Protagonist.'

'Oh that's why,' Fern said, sitting down. 'If you're together, it would be weird at work.'

'Would it really?' Carrie said. 'Millions of people meet their husbands and wives at work.'

'Look at poor Charlie and Beth. They got lambasted when they got together,' Fern said. 'People love to gossip. And if it's not true, they embellish, make it more juicy. The CEO romantically involved with the new girl would be a hot potato of gossip. I understand why you're being cautious.'

'I think people would get over it very quickly,' Carrie said to Fern, although it was obviously directed at Roo. 'You can't let what other people think interfere with matters of the heart. Some people only fall in love once in their life, you don't want to miss out on that. I think you need to be bold and courageous when it comes to love, don't let anyone stand in your way.'

'I think,' Shay said, meaningfully. 'That Roo has only been back a few days and it's probably a bit early to talk about love and maybe we should leave them to work it out for themselves without us interfering.'

'I agree,' Theo said, firmly. He took Roo's hand under the table and gave it a squeeze.

She smiled at him.

'I hear you were helping Theo with some fox cubs last night,' Shay said, helpfully changing the subject.

'I did, I know I'm not supposed to be happy about orphaned fox cubs because that part is really sad. And I know their best chance of survival is in the wild, not as a tame fox, but I did love getting to feed them last night. It felt like an incredible privilege. I'd really like to help out some more.'

There was an awkward silence then, as if she'd said the wrong thing.

Shay cleared his throat. 'Well, there are always baby hedgehogs being brought to the centre.'

'Yes,' Antonio quickly jumped in. 'And lots of baby birds at this time of year. A lot of birds are bad parents, or the baby birds fall out of the nest before they are ready to fly.'

'Baby rabbits too,' Fletcher said. 'We get a lot of them.'

Roo narrowed her eyes. Why did it feel like they were covering up for something?

She glanced at Theo and he had his head in hands, shaking his head. He groaned and looked up. 'You guys would make terrible spies, they would know you were lying as soon as they looked at you. What happened to being subtle?'

They all looked sheepish.

'What's going on?' Roo asked.

'OK, we need to tell you something about Little Paws,' Theo sighed. 'It's highly illegal, so if you don't want to get involved in something dodgy, we will totally understand. But if you do want to help with Little Paws, then I don't want to be creeping around behind your back and lying to you, so it's your call, walk away now and keep your shiny reputation intact, or get involved in a seedy, dark underworld.'

'It's not that big a deal,' Fern said.

'I think you're overselling the dark side of it,' Fletcher said. 'I feel pretty good about my involvement in this. There's certainly nothing seedy about it.'

'But it's not legal,' Theo said.

Fletcher shrugged. 'I don't think anyone has ever gone to prison for it.'

'I've done far worse things in my life than this,' Shay said.

'I was a bit concerned myself when I first found out,' Carrie said. 'I was worried about how it might affect my business here if people found out I was involved, but the alternative is just horrible, so I had to help.'

'What is going on?' Roo said, in alarm.

'In all seriousness, Little Paws could get shut down if anyone finds out,' Antonio said. 'There are even some staff members who don't know anything about this because the fewer people that know the better. So if you really want to know, you have to promise not to tell anyone. Even if you choose not to get involved because of the risk of getting fined or getting some criminal charge against your name, you can't ever tell anyone.'

Roo looked around at the very serious faces of Theo's extended family. Something very weird was going on here. 'I think I need to know all the facts here so I can make an informed decision.'

Theo took a deep breath. 'Squirrels.'

She looked at him in confusion. Of all the possibilities that had gone through her mind of what they could be up to, she hadn't expected him to come out with that. 'What?'

'It is illegal to rescue, rehabilitate and release grey squirrels. It is also illegal to keep them in captivity.'

Pennies started to drop into place. 'So what happens if someone brings you an injured or orphaned squirrel?'

'Technically and legally, we're supposed to end the animal's suffering,' Theo said.

She looked around the table and Antonio mimed dying with his tongue sticking out.

Roo gasped. 'No!'

'It's horrible isn't it?' Fern said.

'Why?' Roo said.

'They aren't native to the UK, so many people, including the government, believe they should be eradicated,' Fletcher said.

'Apparently, they damage a lot of trees by stripping the bark and this is having a huge financial impact on the forestry and timber industry,' Shay said. 'But even if the greys were completely eradicated and the red squirrels, which are native, were able to flourish again, the forestry industry would still have the same problem as red squirrels strip the bark on the trees too, but people would be up in arms if they tried to cull them.'

'Grey squirrels get a lot of bad press,' Carrie said. 'Most people will say, oh the greys killed all the reds, but it isn't true. There is some evidence that the American greys brought diseases over that the reds were not immune to, but red squirrels had their own squirrel pox in areas where there were no greys for them to catch it from. And reds are on the decline mainly because of man. We hunted them almost to extinction in the past just like we did with the wolves and the beavers. We've chopped down their natural habitats and they can't live without the conifer trees. Reds and greys live side by side in America, they don't kill each other off.'

'People say they aren't native, they don't belong here,' Antonio said. 'But neither are domestic cats and they kill millions of birds every year – some of them are endangered too.'

'We brought these grey squirrels to the UK around two hundred years ago and they were kept as pets or in private collections or in zoos,' Theo said. 'Some escaped, some were let go as actually squirrels don't always make the best pets, they can be aggressive or just complete assholes. There were loads of recorded, official releases in the early 1900s, from zoos and wildlife parks because a new law was imminent stating that squirrels were no longer allowed to be kept in captivity so there were hundreds released in the years prior to that. The grey squirrels are our responsibility, we brought them here so we should look after them. They are wonderfully intelligent, brilliant characters and hugely adaptable to different environments.'

'So we can't do anything to help them?'

'There are a couple of licensed squirrel rehabbers in

the south-west that are allowed to keep them in captivity but they can't release them. We don't have any near here and any rehabbers normally only take squirrels from their immediate area. We can't get a licence for Little Paws as the government have made a rule that they won't issue any new licences, so we're a bit stuck with what to do with them.'

'That's where The Secret Squirrel Society comes in,' Fern said, her grin spreading across her face.

'That's my sister's lame name for us, but it works,' Theo said, smiling fondly at Fern.

'So what is it that you do?' Roo asked.

'Lizzie, the badass octogenarian I was telling you about? Her sister, Violet, runs Little Paws and her niece, Eloise, is the vet there as well as Eloise's husband, Jack. In theory, when people drop off a squirrel, we tell them that we will transport them to a local licensed squirrel rehabber. In reality, we smuggle them to Lizzie late at night.'

Roo felt the smile spread across her face. 'You're squirrel smugglers.'

Theo nodded. 'Lizzie owns a massive old farm. She doesn't have farm animals anymore, she stopped doing that years ago, sold off most of the land too, but she does have several huge barns. She has large indoor enclosures inside her barns. No one knows the squirrels are there. She looks after them until they are fit enough to be released in to the wild and then late at night, one of us will collect them and take them back to the area they were found. If that is unknown, she releases them into the woods at the bottom of her farm. We don't have any forests or woods nearby that are used by the timber industry so it's unlikely that the small number of squirrels we do release back into the wild every year are having any impact on them. There are no red squirrels locally so they can't be affected either, so I don't feel remotely guilty about what we do.'

'I want to be involved,' Roo said, eagerly, she waved an imaginary placard in the air, 'Save our squirrels.'

'I just want to reiterate that it is illegal. Little Paws would most certainly be closed down if anyone knew of their involvement. I'm not sure what actions the police would take against individuals, whether it would be a fine or whether we could be looking at a prison sentence, but the government have passed these laws in an attempt to eradicate the squirrel problem. I don't think anyone in authority would take kindly to what we do if they knew.'

'I don't care, I want to help.'

Theo smiled at her. 'You can't tell anyone what we do here. Not least because it's a very divisive topic among the public. Some love squirrels, some absolutely hate them.'

'My lips are sealed. Can I be a member of The Secret Squirrel Society?'

She looked around the table and everyone nodded.

The timer went off on the oven and Antonio stood up. 'Dinner is ready.'

Carrie and Fletcher stood up to help him.

Fern grinned. 'Welcome to the gang.'

Roo closed the door to Carrie's house after hugging everyone goodbye and looked at Theo who was waiting for her.

'I love your family.'

'They love you.' He took her hand and they started walking up the hill towards her little hut. It was a beautiful, clear night, thousands of stars sparkling above the sea.

She looked up at Theo. He was a good man and hearing tonight how he was prepared to risk it all to save the squirrels had ensured he'd captured another little bit of her heart. In fact, she knew if she wasn't careful, she could very easily hand over the whole thing to him. And while that was scary, she'd also started feeling excited about it too. He made her feel so happy. She wanted more from him. She didn't want to hold back from him anymore. If he could risk it all for a squirrel, his reputation, his freedom, she could damn well risk her heart to be with this wonderful, kind, generous man.

They reached her little beach hut, and she opened the door and then turned to face him.

'I've been thinking about us.'

He smiled. 'I'd be lying if I said it wasn't constantly on my mind too.'

'I want to take a chance on us, I want there to be an us. You are the most incredible man I've ever met and I've jumped into relationships with men far less worthy than you are. But I think that was the problem, I knew dating you wasn't going to be like dating any other man, it was going to mean more, so it had the potential to hurt more. But love is a risk and I want to take it with you.'

He stepped closer and wrapped his arms around her. 'You don't know how happy that makes me. You make me want something I've never wanted before.'

He kissed her. She melted into him, feeling with every fibre of her being that this was where she was meant to be. She stroked her hands down his back and round his neck and he moaned against her lips. He held her tighter against him, but it wasn't enough, she wanted to feel his skin against hers. But just as the kiss started to change into something more, he stepped back.

She looked at him in confusion.

He cleared his throat, seemingly trying to focus on what he wanted to say. 'We can take it slow. We don't have to jump straight into bed with each other, just because we're together. I want this to work more than anything. If you want to take some time before we connect in that way... Before we *reconnect* in that way, that's totally fine.'

She reached out and grabbed his shirt, pulling him back to her, she kissed him again. 'This mouth has been over every inch of my body. I think we've bypassed taking it slow. And I'm more than OK with that. Our connection won't get stronger because we deprive ourselves of making love to each other, part of our connection is from that incredible night. I want to be intimate with you. I want to be with you in every way.'

He kissed her hard and shuffled her back through the door. 'I don't need to be persuaded, Roo. I'm yours, however you want me.'

He kissed her again and kicked the door closed behind him. Clothes came off very quickly and he lifted her. She wrapped her arms and legs around him but he just held her there, kissing her, slowly, leisurely as if he had all night when she was desperate to be with him again.

He moved to the sofa and sat down with her still wrapped around him. She pulled back slightly to look at him and he smiled as he stroked her hair from her shoulders. 'You are spectacular, Aurora Clarke.'

She smiled and kissed him again. His hands caressed her skin like a whisper, he was so reverential as he touched her, making her feel adored. His hot mouth wandered across her neck as his fingers stroked across her breasts making her gasp. When his mouth replaced his fingers, she cried out. Her body was humming with need. He slipped his hand between her legs and she felt that need building, tingling through her body until it ripped through her so hard and fast that it left her breathless.

She lifted his head and kissed him hard. He pulled back slightly, grabbed his jeans and yanked a condom from the pocket, then slid it on. She knelt up and with his hands at her hips, he guided her down on top of him. She stared at him, stroking his face, loving the adoration he had for her in his eyes. She kissed him gently, moving against him as he stroked up and down her back. She ran her hands over his chest and shoulders, feeling the rock-hard muscles there. He slid his hands down her back to her hips and pulled her tighter against him and she let out a groan at the feel of him inside her.

That sensation started to build again. Her need for him, her feelings for him, his touch, his tenderness, it was all too much. But as his hands tightened at her hips, as his breath caught on her lips, as he moaned against her kiss, she knew she was having the same effect on him too. And then she was falling, taking him with her, grabbing at his shoulders, calling out his name. As she came down from her high, her breath shaky, he kissed her gently and she knew she'd just given him another piece of her heart.

CHAPTER ELEVEN

Theo had just finished laying out breakfast on the table on the decking when Roo appeared, sleepily rubbing her eyes and wrapped in a bath robe. Her hair was a tangle of curls and she looked absolutely adorable.

'Hey,' she said.

He walked over and kissed her, stroking her face. 'Good morning, beautiful.'

She smiled against his lips. 'Morning. No early morning meeting to rush off to?'

'Not today,' Theo said. 'Most of this week was blocked out to sort out the designs for *A Knight's Tail*. So I'm going to phone Charlie shortly and say we are working on them at home until lunch and then we'll go in then.'

'Wait, we can't do that.'

He smiled at the frown and he leaned forward and kissed it in an attempt to make it disappear. It lessened slightly but it didn't go away.

'Come and have breakfast,' Theo said. 'I bought bacon rolls from Orla's café. They are magical. And I'm sure they're the main reason why my brother is completely in love with her.'

He sat down and as she moved past him, he took her hand and pulled her onto his lap, wrapping her in a blanket to protect her from the cool air of the early summer morning.

He kissed her on the nose and passed her a bacon roll. Everything seemed better when he had eaten, he was hoping she wouldn't be frowning so much after tasting the amazing bacon rolls.

She took a bite and closed her eyes. 'These are incredible. What does she do to them to make them taste so good?'

'No idea but there are always queues first thing in the morning to get them. Now tell me, why we can't take the morning off to work on the designs from here or my house?'

'It's only my third day, I'm still trying to make a good impression.'

'You've made a very good impression on the CEO.'

She smiled and shook her head. 'It's not just you, I want Charlie to think he made a good decision hiring me. I want the others in my department to see I'm a hard worker and not slacking off in my first week. They need to know I was hired for my skills and experience in design, not just because I know the boss.'

'Some will think that anyway, especially when they find out we're dating.'

'Then I need to prove them wrong and I'm not planning on announcing our relationship status to the whole office.'

Theo took a bite from his own roll. There was a part of him that didn't want to hide what they had. His first proper relationship and he was excited about it. People would judge him too, just like they had when Charlie had dated Beth, although he didn't care about that. But he did understand that his position in the company afforded him the security that Roo didn't have, and he did appreciate he wasn't down in the main office dealing with the jokes and comments all day. He knew he had to protect what they had and her somehow. If she wanted to be discreet, he would do that for her, despite wanting to shout about it from the rooftops.

'How many designers or story writers have you worked with at your house?'

He chewed on his sandwich. She probably had a point about that. There had been the odd occasion when he or Charlie had worked from home, when they weren't feeling a hundred per cent or in Charlie's case when his daughter hadn't been well and he wanted to keep an eye on her, but Theo had never had meetings with anyone at his house. He liked to keep work and his home separate. Home was his haven where he didn't have to think about work. It was funny he hadn't thought about keeping them separate when he'd had this bright idea this morning. It wouldn't be a chore talking about work in his house with Roo.

'I want things to stay professional between us at work,'

Roo went on, clearly interpreting his silence for an answer.

'I wasn't planning on pinning you to the desk in the middle of the design department, or mauling you on the stairs.'

'What were you planning on doing with our morning off work?' Roo said.

'Well first I thought we could have hot shower sex, then I thought we'd spend a few hours actually looking at the designs, maybe sat here like this, and then I thought I'd ravish you again, maybe on the breakfast table before we went off to work.'

She grinned. 'As tempting and as lovely as that sounds, it doesn't sound particularly professional.'

'I can keep my tie on if that helps.'

She burst out laughing, stroked his face and kissed him. God, she tasted delicious, salty from the bacon, but sweet too. He could kiss her all day and never tire of it. He arranged the blanket over her waist so no one could see what he was going to do next and as he continued to kiss her, he slid his hand up the inside of her thigh. He was delighted to find that she wasn't wearing anything under that robe. She gasped against his lips as he touched her there and she pulled back and looked around.

There was no one in sight; it was too early for that, and no one could see what he was doing even if there was anyone nearby.

She kissed him again and arched against his hand. He smiled against her lips as he touched her. She moaned softly and it made his stomach clench with need and desire.

'We need to take this back inside,' Theo said.

'Why?'

'Because I need to hear you scream.'

She checked her watch. 'We've probably got time for hot shower sex if you're quick.'

'I can't promise I'll be quick, but we do have flexi-hours at Pet Protagonist, you arrive late, you leave late.'

'That works for me.'

She stood up, took his hand and led him back inside.

By the time Roo arrived at work, it was getting close to ten. Theo had said she didn't need to call anyone, lots of people started and finished at different times during the week without notifying anyone first. Apparently when they logged into the computer it would log their start time and log off time anyway, to automatically keep track of the hours they worked. She intended to make sure she worked until at least six to make up for it.

Theo had gone home to get changed, which she was thankful for. She didn't think it would look too good if she walked into work late hand in hand with her boss. Even just arriving at the same time would raise some eyebrows.

She smiled and waved at a few people as she walked through the office and sat down next to Nate.

'Hey, sorry I'm late, I was at the dentist. But I'll work late tonight to make up for it.'

'The dentist, eh?' Nate nudged her playfully. 'When you and Theo both didn't show for work this morning, we all assumed you were doing the horizontal fandango.'

She felt her cheeks heat.

'Oh my darling, you are practically glowing,' Nate said. 'I was only joking, but did you really do the wild thing with our CEO?'

'Of course not. I'm blushing because you all think we did. I was at the dentist I have no idea what he is doing. My relationship with Theo is strictly professional.'

Nate looked unconvinced.

'Honey, you look like someone who just had the best sex of their entire life. If it wasn't Theo, I want to know who it was who put that huge smile there.'

She smirked.

'There is someone,' Nate gasped.

She knew she had to throw him a fragment of a bone or she'd never get on with any work.

'Yes, I had a hot date last night and yes it was magnificent and no it wasn't anyone from work and no I'm not sharing any more details than that. And I really was at the dentist this morning. But as I'm already late today, I'd really like to crack on with the designs for *A Knight's Tail*.'

Nate grinned. 'OK, OK. I'll let it drop for now. But I will need to know more details. Why not show me what you've got?'

She pulled the big sketch pad out of her bag and turned to the first page.

'What's this you're using? I haven't seen this kind of technology before.'

She laughed. 'It's called pen and paper.'

'It will never catch on.' Nate studied her sketches. 'You have a lovely style, I like this.'

Nate's screen beeped with an incoming message and Roo saw it was a message from Betty.

'I wonder if this is about Sally,' Nate said, clicking into it.

from: officemanager@petprotagonist.com
      to: everyone@petprotagonist.com

Please remember that waste paper goes in the green recycling bin, card goes in the brown recycling bin.

Please do not put your lunch in the recycling bins.

Please be advised whoever keeps stealing the milk with the purple top is drinking expressed breast milk.

Sally Jenkins was terminated yesterday due to inappropriate behaviour.

Regards

Betty Dimble - Office Manager

Nate snorted. 'Did they kill Sally? I know her gossiping was bad, but termination seems a little harsh. Although no one saw her leave so maybe they did.'

Roo laughed at the choice of words in the email. 'I also feel like it deserves more of a mention than being tagged onto the end after the stolen breast milk.'

'Right? Surely it deserved to be first place in the message, unless they are trying to downplay it. Not give her the attention she so sorely wanted.'

'Maybe.'

Just then Theo walked into the office and Roo couldn't help but watch him as he walked across the room. He was wearing a smart, grey waistcoat today over a white shirt with his sleeves rolled up to the elbows. He looked hot as hell. And he was whistling.

'Well someone looks happy,' Nate said, following her gaze. 'He looks like someone who had a great night of hot sex too.'

She felt herself blushing again and she knew Nate had seen it.

Theo walked straight up to her and she couldn't help notice how many people were watching them.

'Hey, Theo,' Nate said. 'Roo was just telling me about the magnificent time she had with her mystery man on her hot date last night.'

Roo felt herself flushing even more but Theo didn't bat an eye.

'Is that right? Well Miss Clarke, when you've finished gossiping, perhaps you can join me upstairs to do the job you're paid to do. And while we're up there, we can have a conversation about what's appropriate to talk about in the workplace.'

With that Theo turned and walked out of the office.

Roo stared after him in confusion.

'Shit, he's pissed off,' Nate said. 'Are you two really not together?'

'No.'

'Then he's angry you went out with someone else last night.'

'Or he's angry that I'm busy gossiping with you and not doing my job,' Roo said.

'Or that,' Nate said. 'I've never seen him angry before. He's probably sensitive to gossip after sacking Sally yesterday.'

'I'd better go and try and smooth things over with my lovely drawings.'

'It might take more than that.'

She picked up her pad and hurried upstairs. Theo was probably mad because she'd said she didn't want anyone to know about them and then gossiped with Nate about it.

Theo was standing inside his office, with his arms crossed as he waited for her.

'Close the door behind you, Miss Clarke.'

She did as she was asked and as soon as the door was closed, Theo broke into a huge grin.

'How was that? Thought that might throw them off the scent a little.'

She laughed. 'You're not mad?'

'Of course not.'

'Apparently, everyone thinks we were at it this morning because both of us were late.'

'Well they were right.'

'And I said I'd been at the dentist but Nate said I had a post-amazing-sex glow. So I told him I had a hot date last night.'

'That was magnificent, let's not forget about that part.'

She moved forward and wrapped her arms around him. 'It was magnificent. It was the most incredible sex I've ever had.'

He cupped her face and kissed her. 'For me too.'

'Did you want to talk to me about appropriate conversations for the workplace?'

'Mmm,' he kissed her. 'Is this appropriate?'

She smiled against his lips. 'Probably not.'

He trailed his mouth down her neck, following the collar of her shirt dress down across her chest. 'How about this?'

She gasped softly. 'Definitely not, especially if you want me to concentrate on work today.'

'Damn it. Fine we'll get on with some work, but you can make it up to me tonight.'

'How will I do that?' Roo asked innocently.

'Oh I have some ideas.'

It was getting close to six o'clock and Roo was working at her desk, or rather, Nate's. Most people had already left for the day, including Nate, although there were a few stragglers still working away.

All the sketches for *A Knight's Tail* had been approved or improved on and she was now drawing those sketches digitally onto the blank page templates of the book. Theo had to deal with a call from one of the translators, so she had come down here to finish off the first stage of designing the book.

She was aware of Theo as soon as he walked into the office and while she tried to be subtle, she couldn't take her eyes off him. How was she supposed to work alongside this man every day? It had been almost impossible to sit at his desk today and concentrate on work.

He came straight over to her desk.

'Thank you for your work today,' Theo said formally as he slid a piece of paper onto her desk. 'The book is really looking good. I'll see you tomorrow.'

With that he walked off. She carried on working on her computer for a minute just in case anyone was watching and after a while she casually opened the paper.

We're on SSS duty tonight. Meet me at my house in an hour.

Underneath was a doodle of a squirrel just in case she'd forgotten what SSS stood for. Her heart leapt. She was excited about being involved in this, being a secret undercover agent for the Secret Squirrel Society was thrilling, and she was doing something worthwhile. And spending time with Theo was never a chore.

She finished off the sketch she was doing and a little after six, she logged off and waved goodbye to the stragglers.

It was still daylight outside but the sky was already turning a plum and blueberry colour. She hurried up the hill to her little beach hut and quickly got changed, choosing something black for her evening of incognito top-secret activity. She bit her lip as she thought and just for a joke she grabbed her black mascara and wiped the wand across her cheeks in two stripes so she looked like she worked for special ops or the SAS. She knew Theo would get a big kick out of it.

She left her hut and hurried across the hilltop and then down the cliff path to Theo's cottage. She knocked on the door and after a few moments Theo answered it.

He burst out laughing when he saw her and took her into his arms. 'You look amazing and I love you for doing this but our undercover operation works better when we don't look like we're about to steal a priceless work of art.'

She laughed. 'So I won't be needing the balaclava?'

He kissed her forehead. 'Sadly not.'

'OK, OK, I'll just wash my face.'

He watched her as she moved to the sink and rinsed her face.

'I think it was your silly sense of humour that first attracted me to you when we were younger. We had a lot in common, our love of wildlife, skateboarding, went to the same school. But it was you always making me laugh so much that I found so attractive. You were sunshine after years of rain. I always expected the unexpected with you and I loved that.'

She turned to face him, patting her face dry with some kitchen towel. 'A lot has changed in fourteen years. I'm a bit more sensible now.'

'I don't know. I never expected you to turn up at my house tonight dressed for combat.'

'I just wanted to make you smile.'

'Well you did that.' He moved towards her, cupped her face and kissed her.

'We have two squirrels to help tonight,' Theo said as he drove to Little Paws. 'There is a baby, Tilly, we will be transporting to Lizzie's farm for her to look after until she is released. And a juvenile, Barney, who probably shouldn't have been brought to us in the first place.'

'Oh no,' Roo said.

Theo nodded. 'Actually there's a really good chance Tilly shouldn't have been brought in either. Lizzie may take her back tomorrow to where she was found, wrapped up in a basket and see if the mum comes back for her. They sometimes do, the mums are very good parents.'

'So you don't think Tilly was abandoned?' Roo asked.

'It's possible. Squirrels get hit by cars all the time, and sometimes they fall out of trees and can get injured. Of course there are predators, foxes and birds of prey that will kill squirrels, domestic cats too. So there could be any number of reasons why the mum has not been able to come back to look after her baby. But squirrel mums are doting and don't tend to just leave the babies alone. Babies do sometimes fall out of their nests though. Our advice when people find a baby is to try and put it back in the tree and Mum will normally come down and collect it. If you observe the baby for a few hours or come back later and the baby is still there, there's a good chance the baby has been abandoned. But I think most of them that come to us don't need us because Mum is around somewhere and it breaks my heart a little knowing there's probably some distraught mum squirrel out there searching for her baby.'

'That's so sad.'

Theo nodded. There was so much he loved about working in wildlife rescue but there were times when it did hurt.

'We get so many young animals brought in by caring and well-meaning members of the public who just don't understand wildlife. We always encourage the public to call us before they bring any animals in, we have that message right next to our contact telephone number so we can advise them accordingly and half the time our advice would be to leave the animal alone because Mum is probably very nearby. We also like to know exactly where the animal was rescued so we can release wild animals in the same place and sometimes we go back to see if we can find Mum. Just saying, we found it in Apple Hill Woods, isn't enough, we really want to know which tree, so we ask the public to mark it somehow or take photos of the tree. But a lot of times, the first we'll know about a rescued animal will be when they turn up at our door with the animal in a box. I do understand that people care and worry about our wildlife. And I would rather people brought animals in if they are worried than leave them. But it's a fine line between rescuing an animal that needs our help and one that doesn't.'

'Yeah I get that. So what happened with Barney?'

'He approached a member of the public yesterday in Morgy Hill Woods and even climbed her leg. This is really common in popular areas. People picnic regularly up in the woods and the squirrels up there will have long associated humans with food. They will approach the picnic tables and of course people think it's cute and feed them. Barney's mum will probably have shown him how to get food from humans in this way. It's not something we encourage but it happens regardless. A lot of people will encourage squirrels in their gardens in the same way.'

Roo nodded. 'I've seen a lot of videos on social media of people handfeeding squirrels in their garden, or setting up obstacle courses for them.'

He smiled. 'Yes me too. They are super-intelligent creatures and it's wonderful to see them work out something like that to get the food. Although we don't condone anything that would make a wild animal tame, we worry less about the squirrels than other animals as they are largely at ease with humans anyway. But people worry that the squirrels are coming up to them for help. Our caring member of the public brought him in because he was obviously a baby that had been abandoned. That was their words. Barney is a perfectly healthy juvenile and a really good weight. He's approximately ten to twelve weeks old and would have recently left the nest or the drey and is finding his way in the world. Mum would still probably be nearby and while Barney doesn't rely on her for food anymore, she might teach him and be near to guide him and watch over him. Juvenile squirrels tend to stay near the drey for around two years.'

'I bet he's still quite small though. How do you tell the difference between a baby and a juvenile?'

'Mainly their tails. A baby squirrel, depending on its age will have a thin tail, it's like a rat or mouse tail in many ways, but a bit fatter and with very short hair. A juvenile will have a fluffed-out tail like the adults. You'll see the difference tonight. But if you find a small squirrel with a fluffed-out tail, it's a juvenile and unless it has an obvious injury, it should be left alone.'

'Good to know.'

She was silent for a while and he looked over at her.

'You really are passionate about this, aren't you?'

'Yeah, I am.' He thought about it for a while. 'I've always had an interest in wildlife, always loved watching it but I think growing up being told I was worthless I have always wanted to prove I was worth something, that the life I lived was worthwhile. And that doesn't mean a big, successful company or fast cars, it means doing something good with my life.'

He paused before he carried on. He never talked about this. After he was adopted by Carrie at thirteen and then brought to Apple Hill Bay a few years later, it was easier to pretend that life prior to Carrie never existed rather than telling people about his painful past and how no one wanted him. Apple Hill Bay had been a new beginning for him, a chance to move on from the past without everyone knowing every little detail about his life. Although living in a small town, word soon got around that he was adopted, but Theo never told anyone the reason why. Even with Roo, he'd never wanted her to think he was weak so he'd kept it all buried away. But now they were adults, it felt safe. He trusted her.

'No one wanted me as a child. My birth mum hated me just for being born. She was trying to make it as an actor, and I got in the way of that. She would often leave me with my nan and she didn't want me there either. When I was with my birth mum she would hit me and slap me because I ruined her life. I was eventually taken into care after the school saw the bruises and no other member of my family wanted me. I was seven years old and I spent the next six years in a thousand different foster homes.'

'Oh, Theo.' Roo put her hand on his leg and he wrapped his hand around hers. 'You've never spoken about this before. I obviously knew you grew up in foster care but not the reasons why. I never wanted to push you for an explanation. This is horrible. I'm so sorry.'

He stared out the windscreen as he drove. 'I'm not telling you this for sympathy. I just feel some empathy for the squirrels. They are born in a country where half the population would like to see them dead or want to kill them just for being born. People hate them, consider them a nuisance, they try to hurt them. I want to give them a chance. They didn't ask to be brought here or be born here but they deserve to be here as much as the reds. They deserve to be here as much as I do. I didn't deserve to be treated that way as a child and the squirrels don't deserve to be hated either. It just makes me want to fight for them, like someone should have fought for me.'

She reached up and stroked his face and he leaned into her hand slightly.

He pulled up outside the rescue centre and Theo could see the lights were on inside. Eloise, the vet, was waiting for them.

'Wait, before we go in, I need to say something,' Roo said. 'You are the most incredible man I've ever met. And I know you've had a life of feeling worthless but you are worth something to me. You were made to feel like you shouldn't be here, told you weren't wanted but I have always been grateful to have you in my life, I feel so very lucky to know you.'

She leaned forward and kissed him. He swallowed the lump of emotion in his throat as he kissed her back. She had always seen him, seen more of him than he'd ever seen in himself. Why hadn't he realised that before?

She pulled back and stroked his face. 'Come on, we have some squirrels to save.'

She got out of the car and he followed her. He opened the door for her to go inside and he smiled at Eloise who was feeding one of the fox cubs, Storm, if he remembered correctly.

He waved hello but didn't say anything, they always

tried to keep talking to a minimum while there were wild animals being treated.

Eloise finished feeding and took the cub out of the room to its cage before returning.

'Hey, this is Roo, a new member of the SSS. Roo, this is our vet, Eloise.'

'Hello,' Eloise said.

'Hi, how are the cubs doing?' Roo said.

'Good actually. They're really healthy. I think they miss their mum. One of our team took them back up to the old mine today and left the box out for a few hours to see if Mum would come back for them but there was no sign of her. So they'll be with us for a few months. But they are eating really well. We'll probably be able to start transitioning them onto solid foods really soon.'

'That's good. I mean good that they are healthy and eating. It's not so good that they've been separated from their mum.'

'No it isn't, but these little guys are strong. They will survive.'

'When life is hard, you come out the other side so much stronger,' Roo squeezed his hand.

'Yeah, you're right,' Eloise said. 'OK, here's your box.'

She gestured to a box file, the kind that you store documents in. The more incognito the better. They never carried squirrels out of there in a pet carrier. The box would be well lined with straw or shredded paper and probably some blankets or old clothes. The baby squirrel would definitely be comfortable.

He picked it up carefully.

'She's been fed but will need feeding again in four hours. Here's her file. Lizzie will give you Barney when you get there and all his details of his release site.'

'Great thanks.'

Eloise smiled and waved goodbye as she walked back out of the room, probably to deal with another animal before she went home.

They went back outside and got in the car. Theo placed the box on Roo's lap.

'Can I have a peek?'

'Yes but let's get out of here first, so no one walks past the car and sees what you have in the box.'

He drove off.

'The box is very small.'

'Tilly is very small. She won't be squashed in there.'

He hit the country road that led up to Lizzie's farm and gave her the nod to open the box.

She peered inside and gave a little squeak of excitement when she saw Tilly.

'She's so tiny.'

He leaned over to look. 'Christ, she is. She's probably only a few days old.'

'Will she survive?'

'Hopefully. If she feeds OK then she stands a really good chance. The formula milk we use will be good at helping her to put on weight.'

He carried on driving as she put the lid back on. 'You're doing a wonderful thing.'

He glanced over at her.

'The SSS. You are doing something incredible.'

'It feels good,' Theo said. 'When I see Tilly, blind and completely helpless, I do wonder how anyone can possibly hate something so small and cute. And when you drill down into why, a lot of it is based on misconceptions such as killing off the reds. But we did that ourselves by hunting them and chopping down their trees. They repopulated the UK with red squirrels from Scandinavia, so most of them aren't native either. The greys are just a lot hardier than the reds. They are born to survive, to adapt, to thrive and now they are being punished for it.'

'But you save them.'

She was looking at him like some kind of hero and that made him feel things he'd never felt before. It was hard to describe but Roo made him feel whole. All his life he felt broken. A square peg in a round hole, but she didn't look at him like that. She looked at him like he was someone. As if he was special.

It wasn't long before they reached Lizzie's farm, which had a keycode entry and a huge electric gate. He leaned out the window and typed in the code and the gate slowly slid open.

'She takes security very seriously,' Roo said.

'She has to because of the squirrels. She doesn't want anyone driving in and seeing them. Most of the younger ones are in indoor enclosures to start with, but the older ones tend to be kept outside. She always comes down to the gate for deliveries so the only people that go inside the grounds are part of the SSS or at least in the circle of trust. No one will ever know what we do here.'

He drove round the back of the farmhouse and waved at Lizzie, who was coming out to greet them.

Theo took the box off her. 'Come on, I'll show you around the whole undercover operation.'

Roo got out of the car and smiled at the woman who looked a lot younger than her eighty-three years. Her long hair was up in a high ponytail and she was wearing flowery denim dungarees and a bright pink t-shirt.

'Lizzie this is Roo, the newest member of our team. This is Lizzie, our fearless leader.'

'Hello, I—'

Roo was interrupted by Lizzie embracing her in a giant bear hug. She smiled and hugged her back.

'Thank you for being a part of this,' Lizzie said. 'It's a big responsibility and I'm always so very grateful to anyone who wants to get involved.'

'Oh, how could I not?' Roo said.

'Would you mind showing her around?' Theo said.

'Of course.' Lizzie linked arms with her and escorted her back into the farmhouse. 'Theo has never brought a girl here before, are you two together?'

'Yes, we were friends a long time ago and now we're together.'

'He's a bit hot, isn't he?'

Roo giggled. 'I think so.'

'But such a gentle soul.'

'Yes he is.'

'I am here you know,' Theo said, following them in with his precious cargo.

'I've just never seen you with a woman before and I never knew why, you're quite the catch,' Lizzie said.

'Maybe I was always waiting for the right woman,' Theo said and Roo grinned at him over her shoulder.

'Well, let me show you the nursery. I have it in my old dining room as I have to be up throughout the night to feed them every four hours. I'm not traipsing out to the barn in the middle of the night so I had it converted. It's not like I ever used it anyway. I always eat in the kitchen.'

Lizzie opened a door off the kitchen and Roo saw a long room with cages up one side. The floor had been tiled and there was a stainless-steel bench on the opposite side. There was also a comfy-looking rocking chair in one corner, which was at odds with the medical facility Lizzie had going on here. Roo wondered if Lizzie sat in it as she fed the babies.

'I have ten cages in here. But I can take two or three babies in the same cage if I need to. Squirrels are very sociable. The cages at that end are bigger for once they start growing a bit. But once they are fully weaned, I move them to the enclosures in the barn. It's a bit early in the season to have lots of babies, but these will fill up in a few weeks. I have one other at the moment, Belle is over there. I might put Tilly in with her, they can cuddle together for warmth. Let's have a look at her then.'

Theo put the box down on the counter and opened the lid. They all peered inside. Tilly was half bald, her eyes closed, snuggled up inside what looked like an old fleecy hat.

'Oh she's very young,' Lizzie said, scooping up the hat so she wasn't handling Tilly directly, she opened a glass cage and carefully placed her inside another ball of fleece and clothes, presumably with Belle the other baby. 'These are heated cages to keep the really little ones warm. They'll probably be in here until they are about eight weeks, moving to the bigger cages at the end of the room, we have low things for them to climb on in there, we don't want them to fall and hurt themselves while they are learning to climb.'

She shut the door.

'Here's all her paperwork. Eloise has just fed her, she says she'll need feeding in four hours,' Theo said.

'I'll be feeding Belle then too so that works for me,' Lizzie said. 'Come on, I'll show you the juvenile enclosure.'

They followed her outside to a large barn. She opened the door and ushered them in to an entrance room with another door. She shut the outside door.

'We always shut one door before opening the other because the juveniles are crafty about getting out. I have two in here that are a bit younger than Barney, but very healthy and happy. I'll get a few more as the season progresses.'

She opened the door and they stepped inside the barn.

Roo looked around and smiled in wonder at what a brilliant enclosure Lizzie had created for the squirrels. There were ropes everywhere, netting, perches and several nest boxes dotted around the room. There were vines stretched across the walls and ceiling too. The floor was covered in a thick layer of straw and hay. There was also lots of bags of nuts hanging from various parts of the room. Two squirrels were having the time of their lives, chasing each other over the ropes, climbing up the netting and across the vines. They were clearly well entertained.

'This is amazing.'

'I try to create an environment that replicates the outdoors so they can learn their skills. These guys will be moved to an outdoor enclosure soon with the same kind of facilities and they'll be in there until their release.'

'I love it; their every need is catered for.'

'They are such intelligent animals, I like to provide things that will stimulate them.'

'You've certainly done that,' Roo said, as she spotted the large hamster wheels dotted around the place too.

Lizzie smiled as one of the squirrels hung upside down to eat some nuts. It was clear she adored her little charges.

'Right, Barney isn't going with you tonight I'm afraid. About an hour ago he started limping. He's been absolutely fine for the last twenty-four hours, eating, drinking and playing. He'd been in here and they all seemed happy enough but I wonder if one of the others has bit him. It happens sometimes, they can be a bit territorial, so I've separated him and we'll keep an eye on him for the next few days. He might just have caught his claw while playing. There's nothing I can see that's wrong with him so I'm not too worried.'

Just then Lizzie's phone beeped with a notification and

she fished it out of her pocket. 'Oh, it's a message from Violet.'

Roo remembered that was Lizzie's sister and the owner of Little Paws.

Lizzie took a few moments to read it. 'Oh no.'

'Is everything OK?' Theo said.

Lizzie looked up and she looked so upset, like the spark had just gone out.

'Adam has just served Violet with notice on Little Paws. When the lease comes to an end later this year, he wants us gone. We have five months to pack up and leave.'

Theo swore.

'Violet is calling an emergency meeting tomorrow night for all the staff and everyone involved. Although she doesn't yet have a venue big enough. She doesn't want to do it at Little Paws as that many people will disturb the animals and we can't have it here as many of the staff don't know about the SSS.'

'You can hold it at Pet Protagonist,' Theo said. 'If it's after six, most if not all of the staff would have left by then. We have a big meeting room upstairs that can hold fifty people if we set up the room correctly. And some of my staff might want to come along for support too, as many of them enjoyed working there. We just have to make sure there is no mention of the squirrels.'

'I'll let Violet know. Thank you.'

'Of course.'

'I don't know what will happen if we have to leave. We've made all those changes to specifically cater for the different animals. The place is perfect for all our needs. If we came here, we couldn't look after half the animals we look after now. And we'd have to get rid of the squirrel enclosures as we couldn't keep that secret with all the volunteers and staff coming and going.'

Roo watched Theo put a hand on her shoulder. 'We'll fix this. Try not to worry.'

Lizzie nodded. 'Everyone has worked so hard to get that place up and running, including Adam's grandad. Poor Joseph would be horrified to know his grandson is ousting us after all this time.'

'It might not come to that,' Roo said. 'Maybe we can talk to Adam?'

Theo shrugged. 'That's not a bad idea. He was always very close with his grandad. It couldn't hurt to try. Let's see what Violet wants to do tomorrow night and go from there. Don't give up hope, Lizzie. We have five months to sort something out so let's not worry just yet.'

'You're right of course. Maybe we can raise some money and buy the land off him. Hold a few charity events.'

'That's the spirit,' Roo said.

Theo leaned down to give Lizzie a hug. 'We'll see you tomorrow.'

They walked out and got back in the car and Theo was quiet as they drove out.

'Are you OK?' Roo put her hand on his leg.

'Yeah. I just feel so sad for Violet and Lizzie and for all the animals.'

'Hey, what happened to "don't give up hope" and "let's not worry just yet" and "we'll fix this"?'

'I said that for her. I'm not sure what we can do. The only reason Adam would want us out is so he can sell the land and I don't think we can compete with that. I know he has had money worries himself, like most people. Raising money with a cake sale, or any other charitable event isn't going to scratch the surface of the amount we'd need to buy the land off him. And more people have less to give to charity when they can barely scrape together enough money to pay their own bills.'

'Could Pet Protagonist help?' Roo said.

Theo shook his head. 'Not with the kind of money Little Paws would need.'

She looked out the window watching the twilight change to darkness as she thought. 'How big is the land?'

'I think it's around twenty acres.'

She pulled out her phone and started scrolling through Rightmove, looking at land for sale in Devon and Cornwall; she skimmed past the ones with planning permission. As Theo had said before, land with planning permission was worth millions. 'There's twenty-one acres of pasture land for sale, in Devon, near to the sea for just over two hundred thousand. I mean we won't raise that kind of money from a cake sale, but that figure feels sort of doable.'

'If he sells it for two hundred thousand, I could probably buy it off him myself,' Theo said.

'Would you? That's a lot of money to lose with no chance of ever getting it back.'

'I would do it in a heartbeat,' Theo said, without any hesitation. 'And I wouldn't consider it losing. It would be an investment in something wonderful and worthwhile. And an investment in my happiness. I love working at Little Paws, feeding the animals, rehabilitating them, releasing them into the wild. There's no greater feeling than that.'

She smiled knowing that another piece of her heart had just been given to him.

She returned her attention to the phone and carried on scrolling through the properties. Then her heart leapt as she saw a listing.

'Adam has put the land up for sale already,' Roo said, quietly.

'What?'

'It's here, on Rightmove.'

'We only just got notice today.'

'I guess he thinks the sale will take a few months to go through anyway, by which time the lease will be up.'

'How much is he asking?'

Roo sighed. '£1.7 million.'

'That's ridiculous. It's not worth that. Wait, does the listing mention anything about planning permission?'

She clicked into it and scanned through. 'It mentions that it would be the perfect place for residential dwellings subject to the proper planning permission but nothing to say that permission has been requested or approved.'

'Then where the hell did he get that price from? Without planning permission, it wouldn't even be worth a quarter of that.'

'Maybe he's just chancing his luck.'

Theo shook his head angrily. 'That's just pure greed.'

They sat in silence as they drove back towards The Little Beach Hut Hotel and she didn't know what to say. If the land was up for sale already, there didn't seem any chance of talking Adam round. And for that price there was no chance of raising the money to buy it off him.

Theo parked the car and they got out. He reached for her hand as they started walking over the hill. The moon was glittering over a mirror calm sea, the stars sparkling like crystals above them.

They arrived at her hut. He gathered her in his arms and kissed her. Then he stepped back. 'I'm in a horrible mood. I'm just going to go home and be alone.'

'Theo, if you want to stomp around and be angry you can do that. If you want to sit and fester in your own anger and not talk to anyone, you can do that too, but I'm not leaving you alone, even if that means we don't say a word for the rest of the night. So do you want to be angry here or at your place? Either is fine with me but I'm staying with you.'

He smiled. 'Let's go to mine. I can cook us some dinner and then I can hold you while I sleep.'

'That sounds good to me.'

Roo was sitting on Theo's lap, her back to his chest as they sat on his balcony looking out over a moonlit sea. His arms were wrapped around her and the radio was playing softly in the background. They'd had dinner but Theo hadn't spoken much and she knew he was trying to figure out a way to save Little Paws.

'All of Me' by John Legend came on the radio and she stood up and offered out her hand. 'Dance with me.'

He stared at her for a moment and she wondered if he would say no. But he took her hand and got up. 'It would be my pleasure.'

She wrapped her arms round his neck and he held her close against him as they started to move around slowly to the music and the way he was staring at her, she knew he wasn't thinking about Little Paws any more.

He bent his head and kissed her and she pressed herself tighter against him. He pulled back slightly and stroked her face.

'Thank you for being here tonight. This can't be much fun for you. If you need me to take you home—'

She placed a finger over his lips. 'I'm right where I need to be, here with you.'

He kissed her again and they carried on dancing, moving around slowly.

'We'll find a way to fix this,' Roo said. 'We have our meeting tomorrow night and someone will have a suggestion that we haven't thought of.'

'I hope so.'

She stopped dancing. 'You will find a way. I know it because you have a tenacity and determination and dogged perseverance to succeed. As a teen, I watched you create all these little businesses and money-making schemes. You were creating websites for local business when you were sixteen because you had the confidence to walk into their workplace and tell them you'd create something amazing for them and you did. You got knock-backs, things didn't work but you never gave up. You'd tweak things, change things, try something new, but you were determined to forge your own path in life, do it your way. I admired that so much.'

He frowned. 'You've always seen things in me that I never saw myself. I felt like such a failure in school and after. I was never academic like you, I always struggled with almost every subject apart from IT and art. Failed most of my exams. I felt so worthless back then.'

'I never saw that, I saw a boy that worked so hard at school to understand, took extra classes at lunch and after school to try to better yourself. That work ethic still hasn't changed even though you're in a job you don't even enjoy anymore. You go in for early morning meetings, stay late for phone calls from people across the globe, you work your arse off to make it work and I know you will apply the same ethic to sorting this out.'

He smiled. 'Your faith in me makes me feel like I could take on the world. You make me stronger.'

'You are strong, I've always seen that. And knowing what you went through as a child, well, you had to have strength to endure that.'

'I wish I'd known then what you saw in me, maybe I would have had the confidence to tell you I loved you and maybe you'd never have left.'

'Maybe we needed this time apart to grow so we could be together now? I can't imagine having such open and honest conversations with you back then. But I'm here now.' She fingered the buttons on his shirt. 'What are you going to do with me now I'm here?'

He bent his head and kissed her and without taking his mouth from hers, he scooped her up in his arms, kicked the patio doors closed behind them and carried her upstairs.

CHAPTER TWELVE

Theo walked towards Orla's café the next morning, holding Roo's hand. The sun was shining brightly over the turquoise sea, the flowers dancing in a gentle sea breeze and with this wonderful woman in his life, it didn't feel like the sky was falling today. He had a new determination – he wasn't going to let Little Paws go without a fight.

He opened the door for Roo and then took her hand again as they walked inside. His mum was at the counter chatting to Orla and for a second he thought about dropping Roo's hand so his mum wouldn't know about them, but she had her ways of finding out and he wouldn't be surprised if somehow she already knew. Besides, he'd held Roo's hand the other night when he'd had dinner at his mum's and they weren't together then so maybe they'd get away without the third degree about their relationship and whether they were going to get married soon.

Carrie turned around and smiled to see them, her eyes

lighting up and he could see the question on her lips. He glanced at Orla and she must have read him loud and clear.

'We were just talking about Little Paws,' Orla blurted out, saving them from an interrogation. 'I can't believe Adam is going to sell it.'

'Or trying to, though I can't see anyone buying it for £1.7 million,' Theo said. 'A lot of the land at Little Paws is waterlogged and the rest of it is up a steep slope, what on earth would they do with it?'

Roo went to the counter and ordered their drinks.

'What can we do?' Carrie said. 'I'm good friends with Councillor Bishop, maybe she can help? I don't know how these things work but could the council put some kind of preservation order on the land?'

'That's a brilliant idea but I'm pretty sure that just applies to trees, not land as such,' Theo said. 'But we do have several old trees on the land, maybe we can preserve them. It would mean they couldn't build on it which would mean that Adam would be unlikely to be able to sell it or at least might be persuaded to sell it at a more reasonable price.'

'It can apply to entire woods too,' Roo said. 'I did some temping work for a local council in London when I came back to the UK. I was just typing up letters and admin stuff but I worked in a department that dealt with this kind of thing. It's not just individual trees, although that tends to be the norm. You have to prove the woods or trees are a local amenity, which means they are a benefit to the public or its important as part of nature conservation. If you can prove the trees are needed as part of your animal rehabilitation, then that could help massively.'

'We have dens built under the trees in the foxes' enclosure. We also have trees as part of our hedgerows and the hedgehogs live in there,' Theo said.

'I'll have a word with Councillor Bishop, see what we can do,' Carrie said. Rooting around in her bag for a notebook and pen, she started jotting down a few things.

'From what I can remember, these things do take time to come about,' Roo said. 'But they can do temporary tree preservation orders if a threat is imminent.'

'Well, if a preservation order is out of the question, maybe Councillor Bishop would agree to some kind of grant to help us buy the land ourselves,' Theo said.

'She might. She's always saying the council have no money, but then they pay out to have new signs in the park saying, 'Welcome to Apple Hill Park'. Why do we need that? Everyone knows it's Apple Hill Park. You have so much support for all the good work you do up at Little Paws. I don't think it would be hard to get people to rally behind you.'

'We're holding a meeting tonight at Pet Protagonist, six o'clock, everyone is welcome.'

'I'll be there,' Carrie said. 'And Councillor Bishop will be too if I have anything to do with it.'

'I'll be there,' Orla said, handing over their drinks.

'Just no one mention the SSS,' Theo said.

Carrie and Orla mimed zipping their lips closed.

He took his drink and Roo's hand, said his goodbyes and walked out before Carrie could change the subject.

'Right, we should say goodbye here,' Theo said.

They had walked to the Pet Protagonist office along the river path, which was always quiet at this time of the morning. It was Theo's suggestion they took that route to work as apart from the odd jogger or dog walker, no one else used it. He knew how much she wanted to keep their relationship a secret and he was trying his best to protect it. Roo was grateful for that. He couldn't protect her from the looks and little comments from people about them, convinced they were together even before they were. He caused a stir every time he came and spoke to her in the main office. There was nothing he could do about that, but she knew he was making her work up in his office a lot more than was necessary so she wouldn't have to hear it.

Right here, they were sheltered from view of the office by a clump of overhanging trees, so she reached up and kissed him, stroking his face as he wrapped his arms around her.

She pulled back. 'I'll see you in there.'

He smiled. 'You can count on it.'

She went up the steps to the square in front of the office that had a large fountain shaped like a whale. Currently there was a dog splashing around in the pool of it. She joined a few others who were also heading into the building. She went upstairs and joined Nate at his desk, logging on to her laptop.

'You look happy,' Nate said. 'I presume your hot dates with your mystery man are going well.'

'Very well,' Roo said.

A few other people arrived and logged in at their computers. She loved the flexibility here, that you could just turn up whenever you wanted as long as you put the hours in and did the work.

'I remember those days, the hot, passionate early days of love,' Nate said.

'I wouldn't go so far as to say it's love. It's a bit too early for that.'

'Trust me, I've seen that look before – you're in love with him.'

She stared at her screen. That was a revelation she wasn't expecting so early in the morning. Was she in love with Theo? She knew she was slowly falling for him but had she already fallen?

'Who are you in love with?' Meryl asked, eating a stinky over-ripe banana as she sat next to her. She wondered if Betty would send an email about stinky bananas.

'No one,' Roo said.

'Not our CEO then?'

'Why would you think it was him just because we work together?'

'I see the way you look at him, all doe-eyed and as if you'd like to do rude things with him. I'm trying to decide whether it's completely one-sided and you just have some silly schoolgirl crush on him or whether you two are secretly doing the frickle-frackle on his desk.'

Roo glanced around the design team to see if anyone was listening in to this conversation. Danielle was watching it all unfold and Ginny looked appalled by the way this conversation was going.

'The what?'

'You know, the jingle-jangle, the hibbety-jibbety, doing the monster mash.'

'OK, OK, I know what you mean, I've just never heard it called that before. And I can categorically promise we've never done anything on his desk other than design the illustrations for the new book.'

'Really?' Brooke said, from the other side of Meryl. 'You two aren't together?'

Roo let out an audible sigh. Were these kinds of conversations going to be a permanent thing?

'I saw Theo in town last night with another woman, a redhead,' Nate said. 'If anyone was about to do the schnoodle-canoodle, it was those two. They couldn't keep their hands off each other. They were heading off towards Theo's love shack, so no guesses what they were going to do.'

Knowing that wasn't remotely true, she flashed Nate a grateful smile for trying to divert attention away from her.

'I knew it!' Meryl said, triumphantly. 'I knew it was one-sided. Theo barely ever looks at you when he walks through here. And he has too much integrity to start sleeping with women from the office. He's the CEO, he knows that everyone respects him and that there's certain standards to uphold in that position. He's never even looked at a woman from the office in that way before, so there's no way he'd start with *you*.'

Wow, that was a thinly veiled insult if ever Roo heard one.

She glanced over at Ginny again who was shaking her head in disbelief.

'Jesus, Meryl, say what you really mean,' Nate said.

'I'm just saying she's not really his type, it's not a criticism.'

'Well what's his type?'

'Redheads evidently, and women not from the office. And realistically a man like Theo could get any woman he wanted. He's not going to go for someone like Roo. Or someone like me or Brooke,' Meryl quickly tagged onto the end, obviously realising how bad that sounded. 'He would go out with someone who is model-perfect. And I think you're setting yourself up for a huge disappointment if you're hoping that after a few weeks of working with him, he'll take you to the summer ball.'

'I think she's exactly Theo's type,' Nate snapped, defensively. 'She's pretty, smart, funny. If I wasn't gay and happily married, I'd be asking her to the ball myself.'

She smiled at Nate for saying that. But this was getting ridiculous.

'See, you are exactly Roo's type, aside from being gay. I think you two are much more suited than Roo and Theo.'

The sad thing was that she had believed this when she was a teenager, that there was no way that Theo would ever be interested in someone like her. But she was a different woman now, the kind of woman that had spent the night having her body worshipped and adored by Theo Lucas. She felt really smug about that.

'I think they are doing it,' Brooke said. 'The freckle-frickle or whatever you called it. Maybe not on his desk but in his house or hers. The chemistry between them almost crackles, they arrive at work at almost the same time and I saw them the other night, well I think it was them. I was walking the dog over by the Little Beach Hut Hotel, well it was dark and I was quite far away, but I saw this couple holding hands and I'm pretty sure it was them. Then it started raining and they ran for one of the huts, they both went inside, the light came on upstairs and then off again a short while later and he didn't come back out.'

Roo's heart leapt at that very close call. It was highly likely that was her and Theo but Brooke didn't know for sure.

'Well that's the kind of evidence that would stand up in a court of law,' Nate said, sarcastically.

Just then Theo arrived, whistling happily to himself as he walked across the office floor and then disappeared to the upstairs offices.

'See, they arrived at the same time,' Brooke giggled.

'Oh for goodness sake, at least five other people arrived here just after me, I suppose I'm shagging all of them too. I don't know who the couple was that you saw when it rained the other night, but it definitely wasn't me. I was tucked up in bed watching Pirates of the Caribbean on TV. And can you please stop talking about me as if I'm not here and talking about my love life like it's the latest bit of seedy celebrity gossip you might find in a trashy magazine.'

Brooke and Meryl stared at her in shock and then turned their attention back to their laptops. That had stopped them, at least for now.

She turned to Nate, who offered out his hand for a discreet high five under the desk and she took it.

A private message from Ginny popped up on her screen.

GINNY:

> Brilliantly done. More people should stand up to them. What they are doing is horribly inappropriate. I'm sorry you've had to put up with this in your first week.

Roo sent a quick reply.

ROO:

> Thank you. It is wearing thin. But I'm sure they will find something else to gossip about soon.

They all worked in silence for a while and then a message flashed up on all their screens.

from: theo@petprotagonist.com
to: everyone@petprotagonist.com

As I'm sure many of you are aware, our charity partner is Little Paws, a wildlife rescue hospital. Many of you spent some time up there helping to care for the sick, injured and abandoned animals when we first partnered with them last year. I have worked there in my spare time ever since and know the importance of the work Little Paws does.

Unfortunately, the landowner has now given Little Paws five months' notice to leave the property with a view of selling the land for property development. Everyone involved with Little Paws is deeply upset by this news. We will have a meeting here in the conference room at six o'clock tonight to discuss how we move forward from here.

If you would like to come, you'd be very welcome to join us, but of course it's not obligatory to attend.

Thanks

Theo

'Oh no.' Nate said. 'They can't close down the wildlife hospital. They help so many animals.'

'It's awful,' Roo said, pretending this was the first she'd heard of the news too. 'When I came here and heard about Little Paws, I looked them up on Instagram and they are always posting pictures of the animals they rescue. Can you imagine them not being there to help anymore?'

Another message popped through.

from: officemanager@petprotagonist.com
    to: everyone@petprotagonist.com

Please can I ask all staff to check their drawers, bags, lunch boxes, or anywhere on their desk for any stray teaspoons. I bought a box of a hundred a few weeks ago and they have all gone from the staffroom already.

Kevin's mug is still missing.

Do not bring fans from home they are a fire hazard.

Naked Chris Hemsworth photos are not appropriate for desktop backgrounds.

Regards

Betty Dimble - Office Manager

'Damn! Who has naked Chris Hemsworth photos on their computer?' Nate said, looking around the office.

Betty's timing was terrible. Theo's serious message was

being completely overshadowed by the ridiculousness of messages about naked Chris Hemsworth and missing mugs and spoons.

A private message popped through on her screen from Theo.

THEO:

Aurora, please come to my office so we can continue working on A Knight's Tail.

She gathered her stuff up, gave Nate a wave and headed upstairs. She walked into Theo's office and shut the door.

He immediately cupped her face and kissed her and she couldn't help smiling against his lips.

'How's it going down there today?' he asked.

'Well, Brooke thinks she might have seen us together outside my hut the night of the storm, but she's not sure as it was very dark.'

'Oh crap.'

'Don't worry, as Nate says, it's very flimsy evidence. However, the fact that we've arrived at work at similar times twice now is irrefutable in her eyes and our crackling chemistry.'

'Crackling chemistry? I am nothing but professional with you down there.'

'Oh but that's all a ruse in her eyes and she is right about that. Meryl thinks we might be doing the frickle-frackle on your desk because I'm all doe-eyed when I look at you, but she's pretty convinced it's one-sided and you wouldn't stoop so low as to go out with me.'

His face darkened. 'What?'

'To be fair to her, she lumped her and Brooke into the 'wouldn't go out with' pile too. I don't think she meant it as an insult. It was more that you could have any woman you wanted so you'd have someone perfect.'

'Which is why I wanted you, because you're perfect for me. You're the best god damn thing that's ever happened to me and the most beautiful and incredible woman I've ever met. And how is that not an insult to say I wouldn't be interested in you because you're not perfect enough? Who is she to say who is good enough for me? Only I get to decide that. And why is it she's thinking about whether you're good enough for me and not if I'm good enough for you? How dare she say that?'

'Hey, I'm telling you this as my boyfriend, not my boss.'

His face softened. 'Your boyfriend?'

'Well, what else am I going to call you, my lover?'

'No I like boyfriend. I've never been someone's boyfriend before.'

'Well you better hold on to me because Meryl thinks Nate is more my kind of man.'

'Nate is gay.'

'I know but me and him are much more suited than me and you apparently.'

'Not in my eyes.'

She smiled and stroked his face. 'And you don't know how smug I feel listening to how you wouldn't be interested in me, knowing that I spent the night wrapped in your arms.'

'I'd love to take you to the ball next week and show them all how happy you make me.'

'I'd love to do that too,' she said regretfully, knowing they really couldn't do that.

He sighed. 'And what the hell is a frickle-frackle?'

'Exactly.'

'Good God, it's like being back at school. I'm so sorry you have to put up with this.'

'It's OK, because after dealing with them, I get to come up here and be with you and all the frustration and anger goes away when I'm with you.'

'It's really not OK. What can I do?'

'I don't want you to do anything. I feel like it would just make things worse.'

'It's not appropriate. We just sacked Sally for gossiping and inappropriate behaviour.'

'You sacked Sally because she was spreading malicious lies about Charlie and Beth and had been warned about it multiple times. You can't go sacking anyone else just because they think we're doing the humpity dumpity.'

He burst out laughing. 'The what?'

'I know. What happened to just calling it sex?'

'We've never had sex, Roo, I've only ever made love to you.'

She smiled at that. 'Come on, let's get on with some work.'

Theo stood up and stretched as he looked out of the window on the pretty harbour below him and the boats bobbing about in a gentle sea breeze.

Roo had gone out to get some lunch with the promise she'd bring something back for him. It was frustrating that he couldn't just go out to lunch with her without everyone losing their minds about how exciting it was. He and Charlie would often go out to lunch together without anyone batting an eye. He'd even gone out for lunch with Nate a few times when they were working together on the designs for a new book. Why did it mean something different when it was him and Roo?

He also knew that while he would do everything he could to keep her happy and keep their relationship secret, this secrecy wasn't going to work long term. He understood why she wanted to keep it secret. The gossip and comments about them was already too much and no one even knew they were together. At some point, someone would find out or they would have to come clean and Roo would have to deal with the fall out of that. If she continued lying about it, then that would reflect badly on her when she finally told the truth. He wanted to protect her from all of this, especially the mean comments, but he had no idea what he could do.

He sighed. He couldn't even talk to Charlie about this as no one at work was supposed to know and he didn't want Charlie to think that any conversations about Roo were biased in some way. If he said he loved Roo's illustrations, for example, he didn't want Charlie to think he was just blowing his girlfriend's trumpet.

He wandered across the hall to Charlie's office opposite his but it was empty. He went down the hall a little way only to find him in the empty office next to Theo's, looking out of the window.

'Hey.' Theo said.

Charlie turned and smiled. 'Hey. Listen, I'm sorry to hear about Little Paws. We'll do everything we can to save it.'

'Thank you. We have a few ideas but Adam is currently asking for £1.7 million for the land so I'm not sure what we can do. Hopefully we can come up with a plan tonight.'

'I'll be there.'

'Thank you.' He looked around. 'What are you doing in here?'

'Just wondering what we could do with this office.'

Theo looked around in surprise. It obviously used to be a secretary's office for the previous CEO who worked in this building before Pet Protagonist took it over as there was an interconnecting door between his office and here. Theo didn't have his own secretary or assistant so it had stayed empty. Charlie had an identical room next to his office, although that room had become more of a storeroom and dumping ground.

'Why do you want to do something with it?'

'Because Betty said she wanted it.'

'Oh hell no. I really don't want that woman in the office next to me. She'll be coming in to see me all the time telling me about missing spoons and how the staff use too much toilet paper.'

'Yeah, I didn't think you'd be enthralled with that idea.

She has her own office on the main floor downstairs and as office manager I feel like she needs to be down there with most of the staff not up here. Not just for our own sanity but for the approachability factor for the staff. Right now they feel like they can just pop their head round her door at any time they have an issue, not come upstairs among the managers. Coming up here would feel more like a formal complaint than a minor issue with someone eating an egg sandwich. But I didn't want to say no, so I told her I had plans for these two offices and I was going to move some staff around for a better work environment.'

Theo laughed. 'So now you have to do something with them.'

'Ideally, but all the managers up here have their own office so I'm not sure what to do.'

Theo looked around. It was a big room, easily big enough for two or three people. Suddenly he had an idea and the more he thought about it, the more it made sense. It would kill two birds with one stone.

'We could move some people from the main office up here.'

'Like who?'

'Roo and Nate for starters. The lead designers work so closely with us on the illustrations of the new books that they are always backwards and forwards coming up here and back down there again. It kind of makes sense to have them up here permanently. And really they aren't part of the design team in the sense of all the little design jobs that the rest of them undertake down there, they are our illustrators so perhaps they should have their own room, with a giant desk just here in the middle like I have, to lay out all the pages of the book and see the bigger picture. That way they can help each other with the different illustrations too and not have to take over the whole design desk downstairs to do it.'

Charlie nodded, taking it in as he studied the area.

'And in your spare office over there, once we've cleared out all the crap, we could put the story-writing team,' Theo went on. 'It's so noisy in that main office with the marketing team shouting over each other and the design team chatting away, plus the noise from the printing room that drifts upstairs. Every time I walk through there, the story team have their headphones on. Writing a story is hard and requires silence, concentration and no interruptions or distractions. They can have the peace and quiet they need up here. Having their own office space will really benefit both teams, so it feels like a win-win all round.'

'I think that's a brilliant idea. It does make sense. I never even thought about how noisy that office is for the story-writing team. But I know myself when I have to write an important email how much I need quiet to do that. And it would be better to have our illustrators up here too, for us and for them.'

'We could sort this room out next week. We have spare desks in our storage room, we could grab four or six of them to create a big working area for the illustrators in here, at least until we can order a proper large desk like mine. We can get some help to clear out your spare office for the story-writers next week too.'

'Great idea, I'll start the ball rolling.' Charlie walked out the office. Theo loved that he was a man of action.

He chewed his lip and looked out the window for a moment. What he had suggested was going to be beneficial to both teams and he knew the story-writing team would appreciate it, as would Nate, but he couldn't deny bringing Roo up here would have the added benefit that she wouldn't have to deal with the petty gossip anymore. The rest of the design team would continue to talk about their relationship or have opinions on it, but Roo wouldn't have to listen to any of it and she wouldn't have to keep lying all the time. He just hoped Roo would be happy with the news too, because once Charlie got the ball rolling on something, there was no stopping him.

CHAPTER THIRTEEN

Roo walked back into the office and headed straight upstairs to Theo's office so she wouldn't have to hear any more gossip and comments about her and Theo. It was a shame because it cast a shadow over what was otherwise a wonderful job. She had loved working on *A Knight's Tail* over the last few days. But surely the gossip would die down soon, especially if they didn't give them any more ammunition. It would just become old news.

She could see Theo was alone in his office so she walked straight in.

'I got you lunch.' She held up a bag from the nearby café. 'Chicken and bacon mayo in a roll the size of my head.'

Theo laughed. 'Thank you.' He moved to take it off her and then shut the door. He cupped her face and kissed her briefly. 'I need to talk to you about something.'

She looked at him suspiciously. 'Why do I feel like I won't like this?'

'You might.'

She saw the hope in his eyes.

'Go on.'

'I umm... got you your own office up here, the empty one next to mine.'

She stepped back from him in shock. 'What? Why would you do that? That isn't going to solve anything. They already think I've got this job because of you, my own office will add to people thinking I'm getting preferential treatment. And the office next to you? That will just make things worse.'

He held his hands out in defence. 'Let me explain. When I said your own office, I meant you and Nate will be sharing the office as our lead designers and illustrators. We always work so closely with the lead designer on the illustrations in a new book, it makes sense to be able to have you both up here so we can liaise with you two more efficiently. We're going to get you two a giant desk like mine so you can spread out all the pages of the book and help each other. We're also moving the story-writing team up here, they will be in the room next to Charlie so they can have some peace and quiet away from the main office. It actually makes sense to do this for both you two and the story-writers, but yes I suggested it partly to try and protect you from all the gossip.'

She sighed and moved back to him, wrapping her arms around him. 'I do love you for trying to help me but you should have checked with me first.'

He hugged her too. 'It kills me that you are having to sit down there and hear comments like you're not good enough for me, when nothing could be further from the truth. I hate that their obsession with our relationship is causing you so much stress when I can see how much you love your job. And Charlie wanted ideas for using these two rooms because Betty wanted to move up here and he didn't want to just say no to her. The idea came to me and it seemed like the perfect solution for everyone. And you have to admit, from a professional point of view, it actually does make sense. And from a personal point of view, moving you, Nate and the story team up here doesn't make it look like it's singling you out.'

She sighed. 'It does kind of make sense, professionally. We don't have a ton of space down there and we're looking at our illustrations on a small computer or laptop screen. It would be a good idea to have a big desk to work at.'

He gave her a cautious smile.

'I just hope they don't think I got my own office because we're doing the jingle-jangle.'

He smirked. 'Was that from Meryl too?'

'Yes.'

She bit her lip. Maybe having an office with Nate would be the best way to deal with this. The rest of them could gossip and bitch about her and she wouldn't ever have to hear it. This thing was never going to go away and when they finally outed themselves it would just get worse.

She'd never really made friends in her working life;

she'd moved on too many times to make any lasting bonds. She'd hoped here things would be different but having a relationship with the CEO was never going to make a good impression on people.

Maybe ignorance was bliss.

'When can I move in?'

'Really, you're OK with it?'

'They can't possibly say it's me getting preferential treatment if there's four other people benefitting from it. And if they do, I won't be there to hear it.'

'I'm relieved I can do this for you. I can't stop it, other than if I sack everyone, but at least you might get some peace up here. It will probably be towards the end of next week. We have the publication of the new book on Monday and the first few days of a new release are always manic, but I'll try and get it ready for you as soon as I can.'

She nodded, feeling a small sense of relief. 'Thank you.'

Theo was pleased to see that the meeting room was packed. All the staff and volunteers from Little Paws were there, as were his family and other members of the SSS. He liked that several members of the Pet Protagonist staff were there too, including Charlie, Ginny and Nate. The rescue centre was important to lots of people. He was also pleased to see his mum's friend, Councillor Bishop. Maybe the idea of getting a tree preservation order had some legs.

Despite all the support, Theo still had no idea what

they could do to save Little Paws. How could they even begin to raise £1.7 million?

Violet was chatting to a few people while she waited for the last few people to arrive, but when the last person came in, she stood up and moved to the front of the room. She looked confident and bold as she stood there, as if she could take on the world. Only a few people would really know how upset and shaken she was by this news.

'Thank you all for coming. As most of you know, Little Paws received notice from the landowner that we need to leave when the lease is up in five months' time. We don't have an alternative location and even if we did we wouldn't have the money to adapt it for our needs with the different animals' enclosures. Adam Larch, the landowner, intends to sell the land, and already there is a listing on Rightmove for it. My sources at the council confirm he applied for planning permission to build a hundred residential properties on the land. The application and subsequent appeal were rejected, which makes the £1.7 million price-tag baffling. No one will buy land they can't build on for that kind of money. I feel like he would be open to offers, something that would reflect the kind of land it really is. So I'm looking for some suggestions for how to raise the capital to buy the land outright.'

Danielle raised her hand. 'Could we ask large companies to donate big prizes that could be auctioned off?'

'We could try,' Violet said. 'It would depend what kind of prizes we get. The bigger the prize, the higher people would be willing to bid.'

'Could we ask people to sponsor an enclosure?' Roo said. 'The doctors could sponsor the foxes for example, or the opticians could sponsor the otter enclosure.'

'I like that idea,' Violet said. 'A whole year's worth of sponsorship would give us a big lump of cash up-front.'

'I think we need to be practical,' Shay said. 'I know Adam has been having money problems, so he's going to sell it for the most amount of money he can get. It might be easier to find a new location and use the money we're trying to raise now to adapt it to our needs, rather than wasting time trying to stay where we are. We only have five months. In that time we could have built new enclosures at a different location so we can just move out of one and straight into another when the lease comes to an end.'

'You make it sound so simple,' Violet said. 'Land without planning permission is fairly hard to come by, especially the right kind of land with hedges, woods, and rivers to accommodate the different animals. And if we were to buy land outright that would cost a lot of money.'

'No more so than the money you would need to buy the land off Adam,' Shay said.

'But then we would need more money to build the enclosures and develop the land,' Violet said. 'Lizzie sold most of her farm to pay for the development of Little Paws. We don't have that kind of money to spend again. If we were to rent the new land, I don't think we would find anything we could afford. The arrangement we had with Joseph was very cheap.'

'If you're talking about raising two or three hundred

grand to buy the land at Little Paws, which would be a fair offer for Adam, then you can use that money to pay the rent or buy the new place. If you put posts out on social media asking for volunteers to help develop the land, lots of people would come forward. They could donate their time or the tools needed. Some people are far happier to donate time than money,' Shay said.

'I think that's a fair point,' Charlie said. 'If Adam has put the land up for sale for £1.7 million, I can't see that he will come down as low as two-hundred thousand, if we could even raise that much. What's a fair offer for us and for him will probably be two different things. I think we should at least look at different options and locations while we are fundraising.'

'I think you're right,' Lizzie said. 'We have to accept we might lose Little Paws. And at the very least we need a back-up plan. It won't hurt to look around and do some research into locations and prices.'

Violet let out an audible sigh. 'Fine. Shay, would you mind looking into new locations?'

'Sure.'

It was clear Violet had hoped that people would rally behind Little Paws, fight for its survival, not just give up and move on. Theo couldn't help but feel sorry for her, but he knew Shay had a point.

'I'd like to talk to Adam,' Theo said. 'Maybe pull on the heartstrings a little. If anyone has any photos of Joseph working at Little Paws, especially with the animals, I could take those along and see if we can get Adam to honour his grandad's memory. Even if we can't persuade him not to sell, it might help persuade him to take a smaller offer.'

'I have plenty of photos of him at the rescue centre,' Violet said, fondly. 'Joseph loved the animals.'

'That will be great,' Theo said.

'A lot of big companies will do donation matching,' Roo said. 'Either they match the amount an employee has donated or match an amount that a team of their employees raises.'

'We'd be happy to do that here,' Charlie said. 'We can set up a fundraising page here at Pet Protagonist and we will match every donation made by an employee.'

He quickly looked at Theo to see if he approved and Theo smiled and nodded.

'We'll do the same at the Little Beach Hut Hotel,' Carrie said. 'Not employees as we don't have that many of those but guests, for every pound donated by one of the guests, we will match it. At this time of year, with guests staying weekends and for a few weeks at a time, we have on average over a hundred different guests a week. If they all donate a pound each, we'd soon have a few thousand pounds with our matching promise.'

'Thank you, both of you, that's very kind,' Violet said.

'I think we should try crowdfunding too,' Roo said. 'I can set up a fundraising page and share it on social media in the local area and further afield. The beauty of crowd-funding is you don't need people to make big donations, you ask for tiny amounts like a pound or two but you target thousands of people. There are over five hundred thousand people living in Cornwall; if all of them donated just fifty pence we'd have a quarter of a million pounds. Of course, not everyone will, but a little donation can go a long way if we target enough people.'

'Anything anyone can do to help will be great,' Violet said. 'If we fundraise in multiple ways, even small events like a tea party, or a cake sale, every little will help.'

'We could involve the local news too,' Orla said. 'The more people that know about it the better.'

'Good idea,' Violet said. 'Councillor Bishop. Did you want to say something?'

'Yes. I'm afraid I only heard of Adam's intentions to sell the land today. I knew he'd applied for planning permission and part of the reason we rejected it was because of the occupancy of Little Paws and we recognise the important work you do for wildlife conservation. But part of the reason it was rejected was the unsuitable land at Little Paws. It's very steep in parts and logistically developing the land for residential use would be very hard. However, the land he owns on the other side of the river is flat and we do need more houses in the town, especially affordable homes for the locals. If he was to apply for planning permission solely for that land and not yours, it's likely he would get it, but of course there are many factors that go into our decisions regarding granting planning permission. Maybe if he did that and he was able to sell that land with planning permission, he would leave Little Paws alone as he'd get a decent amount of money for that other land. Although of course there is no guarantee that he wouldn't then come after the land at Little Paws again at a later stage.'

'You say that you recognise the important work we do for wildlife conservation; is there a way the council would see fit to help us financially?' Violet asked, boldly.

Councillor Bishop didn't even bat an eye. She was obviously used to being asked for money all the time.

'As I said, I was only made aware of your predicament today, so I have prioritised it as a point of discussion in tomorrow's meeting. Knowing our current financial situation, I doubt we would be able to offer anything more than a small grant, if we could even afford that. But it was suggested by one of my constituents that we could issue a tree preservation order on the trees on your land or rather Adam's land. This will be another point of discussion at tomorrow's meeting, because that is normally given to trees on public land and benefit all members of the community. That obviously doesn't apply here as the land is private use. But if my colleagues agree we could issue it on the basis of conservation.'

'Forgive me, but we need a bit more help than just preserving a few trees,' Violet said.

'If the trees are preserved there can be no cutting down or any other damage to the trees ever again. It means that Adam won't be able to build on the land and therefore would find it hard to sell it.'

'Oh,' Violet said, perking up. 'That could work.'

'Of course, if he couldn't sell and he still needed the money, there's nothing to stop him from charging an exorbitant rent.'

'Oh,' Violet visibly deflated. 'Well, thank you all for any help you can give.' She turned back to the rest of the room

'I don't want to keep you all any longer, you have families and your lives to get back to, but if anyone else has any fundraising ideas, please do email or phone me. I've printed out some cards with my contact details on, if any of you want to discuss it further, please do get in touch. We will fight this and with all your help I feel sure we can beat it.'

There was a polite round of applause and people got up to leave. Some chatted to Violet briefly before they left. Theo's family came over to say goodbye to Theo and Roo before they left and then only a few stragglers remained: Violet, Lizzie, Eloise, her husband Jack, Roo and Charlie.

Charlie approached Violet. 'As our charity partner we will do everything we can to save Little Paws. You have my word on that. But if you have to move somewhere else, we will help you start again.'

'Thank you, Charlie,' Violet said.

Charlie turned back to Theo. 'I'd better go, I want to give Hope her bath before she goes to bed. We'll talk some more about this tomorrow.'

Theo smiled and clapped him on the back. 'Thanks mate.'

Charlie left and Violet sighed and sat down, suddenly showing her age. 'I'm too old to start again. I haven't got the energy to build new enclosures, to dismantle and pack up everything at Little Paws.'

'But you have lots of people willing to help you do all that. No one is expecting you to lift a finger,' Roo said. 'People care about Little Paws, tonight's meeting is testament to that. They might not have the money to save it, but as Charlie said, people will donate their time. How many calls do you get from members of the public every week wanting help for a sick, injured or abandoned animal? Most people want to help animals as much as you do. Everyone will pull together for this, whether at Little Paws or somewhere new.'

Violet looked at her. 'It just feels like giving up. Me and Joseph, all of us here, we worked so hard to build Little Paws. If we were to pack up and leave it feels like all of that was for nothing.'

'It's only giving up if you walk away completely and give up on the animals that need your help every single day,' Roo said. 'And it wasn't for nothing. You have built a successful charity, rehabilitated and released thousands of animals. That is something incredible. And yes, it will be sad to move on somewhere else, but you can still do incredible things somewhere new. Make it bigger and better, do all the things you would have done differently the first time. Knowing now that hedgehogs seem to be the animal you have to help the most, you can ensure there are more hedgehog enclosures to cater for them. We will help you, everyone here tonight and many more people will help too.'

Theo watched Roo as she spoke and he couldn't help but smile. He knew he was falling in love with this brilliant, kind and wonderful woman.

He nodded. 'Roo's right, you can't give up now, not after you've achieved so much. And we'll help you no matter how the cards fall.'

'Thank you,' she nodded, sadly. 'I'm going to go home

and feel sorry for myself. I'll be fine tomorrow.'

'Come to us for dinner, Mum,' Eloise said. 'You can wallow there just as easy as you can at home.'

Violet nodded. 'Sounds perfect.'

They all said their goodbyes and everyone left leaving Theo and Roo alone.

Theo wrapped his arms around her and kissed her forehead. She hugged him back and he felt some of the tension ebb away.

'It's such a mess,' Theo said. 'It's not just the animals who will suffer because of this, it's Violet, Lizzie, and all the other staff and volunteers too.'

'I know but we will find a way to fight this, even if that does mean starting over, we'll make it work.'

He smiled and cupped her face. 'I love your positivity. I feel it spread through me when I'm near you. I feel like I could take on the world when I'm with you.'

'You don't need me for that, your passion for this is fierce and strong and insanely attractive.'

He laughed.

She looked up at him. 'You didn't tell Violet about your intention to buy the place.'

'I don't know if it's possible. I don't know if Adam will reduce the price to something I can afford or that I could afford to buy new land either. I don't want to get her hopes up if it's not viable. I need to look into what I could realistically afford too. I'll talk to Adam and then we'll go from there.'

'I get it. We'll find a way.'

'I know, let's go home.'

CHAPTER FOURTEEN

A few days later, Roo and Theo were feeding the fox cubs at Little Paws when the doorbell rang at the reception. It was Sunday afternoon, the sun was shining brightly and it had been noticeably quiet all day. Eloise was down in the otter enclosure dealing with an eye infection and the fox cubs were seemingly getting bigger and stronger every single day.

She knew Theo would want to put the cubs away first before bringing any other animals into the room, so she went to the intercom and told the person waiting they'd be out in a minute.

Theo finished feeding Storm before popping her back in the box and carried them back to their cage. They always tried to keep talking to a minimum when they were handling the animals and surprisingly she was OK with not filling the air with conversation. She felt so at ease with Theo that it was peaceful just focusing on feeding the animals.

He came back into the room. 'Right, let's see what's waiting for us out there. We've not had any phone calls so it could be anyone's guess.'

She followed him out to the reception and could see a very distressed woman carrying a shoe box.

'Hello,' Theo said, warmly. 'How can I help?'

'I found her in my garden,' the woman thrust out the shoe box. 'I think my cat might have got her. She's still alive, but there's a lot of blood.'

Theo carefully opened the box and pulled a face. He showed the box to Roo and she let out a little gasp. There cowering in the corner was a small mole, its little pink nose was sniffing the air, and its large hand-like claws spread out to the side. She'd never seen one before outside of pictures and on TV so it was a wonderful yet sad surprise to suddenly see one this close. There were a few tea towels in the box around and under it but there were several patches of blood on the towels.

Theo handed the box to Roo and turned back to the woman.

'You did the right thing in bringing it here, can I just take some details from you?'

Theo took her name and address. 'You say you found the mole in your garden? If we are able to help it and rehabilitate it ready for release, will you be happy for us to do that in your garden? We always like to release a wild animal where it was found.'

'Yes of course, but I'd be worried my bloody cat would hurt it again.'

'They mostly stay underground out of the way, your cat most likely spotted it when it was clearing out its tunnels. But it might be best to release it somewhere else nearby. I'll discuss it with our animal-care manager and get back in touch with you if we decide to go ahead with your garden.'

'Will you be able to help her?' the woman said.

'I don't know. Cat injuries can be quite severe and there is quite a bit of blood. We do have a vet onsite today so she will do her very best to save her or him. Do you want to give it a name?'

'Oh, I hadn't thought of that. Let's call her Bluebell as that's where I found her, under the bluebells.'

'Great name. Please do give us a call tomorrow to check up on her.'

The woman nodded and left.

'She didn't give a donation,' Roo said.

'Most people don't,' Theo said. 'They've done their good deed by bringing the animal in, they don't think about the expense of food or medication the animal will need after. Most of our donations come in after we've done a social media post, sharing a photo of a new arrival, especially the babies. Or we'll put an appeal out asking for stuff off our wish list. The local greengrocer donates all the bruised or over-ripe fruit and veg that he can't or won't sell and that keeps a lot of the animals happy. But we still need money for medication and of course rent and utilities.'

'I launched the 'Save Little Paws' crowdfunding donation page yesterday and there's links on the Little Paws website. Even if we only ask for a pound every time someone comes in, it will all help. And in my experience of crowdfunding, you ask for a pound and most people give more than that. We need to pull on the heartstrings, tell them if we don't get enough donations, there will be nowhere left to bring animals like Bluebell.'

'Good idea, I've never been great at asking people to donate. Violet is a lot more brazen about it. But we definitely need to start asking people when they come here.'

Theo looked inside the box again and sighed.

'What are her chances?'

'It depends on how bad the damage is. Moles are quite hardy creatures but cats are little shits when it comes to killing wildlife. I'll go and get Eloise and she can take a look.'

'It is small, isn't it? Is it definitely a girl?'

Theo grinned. 'Moles are one of the creatures that its quite hard to tell. Females have male genitalia.'

'What?'

'Just one of the many quirks of nature. Let's bring Bluebell back to the examination room and I'll go and grab Eloise.'

Roo put the lid back on the box and carefully carried her into the examination room.

Theo disappeared off to go and find Eloise and Roo sat down, pulling her tablet from her bag so she could reply to any comments on the crowdfunding page. So far everyone was very supportive and she was surprised at how quickly the pot had started to grow in less than twenty-four hours since it had launched.

She'd only been working on it for a few minutes when the doorbell rang again. She got up and went out to reception and was surprised to see a man in a suit and another man that looked like he'd walked off a construction site. Maybe they had come from the old mine development where she and Theo had collected the fox cubs. Maybe they had disturbed some more animals.

'Hello, how can I help you.'

'I'm Quentin Lambert from Lambert and Sons, the estate agent selling this property, and this is Mr Fenton. We're here for a viewing.'

Roo narrowed her eyes. 'Did you inform Violet there would be a viewing today?'

'We spoke to Adam and he said it would be fine.'

'Adam Larch is our landlord but we are the tenants and as such we have rights, as you are well aware, Mr Lambert.'

Quentin had the good grace to look embarrassed and she knew she'd hit the nail on the head. She had no idea what those rights were but she knew they couldn't just turn up whenever they wanted to have a look around.

'What are those rights, Mr Lambert?' Roo asked, in a way that said she knew exactly what those rights were.

'We have to contact you twenty-four hours before the viewing to ask your permission.'

'Anything else?'

'It has to be at a reasonable time.'

'I'm not sure Sunday afternoon could be considered a

reasonable time but I suppose that is subjective. However, you have not sought permission from us for this viewing so you will need to contact Violet and come back at a time that is reasonable to us.'

'Well, we're here now so…'

She arched an eyebrow at him. 'We are a working wildlife hospital. There are sick and injured animals here and we can't have them disturbed by people walking around the enclosures. The whole point of our operation is to rehabilitate the animals back into the wild and we do that with as little exposure to humans as possible, and that includes them hearing us too. Anyone brought here must be made aware that talking must be kept to a minimum and when you do talk it must be very quiet. You will not be allowed in the animal enclosures so you'll only be able to view those parts from the outside. Mr Fenton, I'm sorry you've had a wasted trip today but I'm sure you can understand our position.'

Mr Fenton didn't look happy at all. 'I don't see how me having a quick look around could harm any of your precious animals.'

Suddenly Roo was aware of Theo standing next to her.

'My colleague has clearly explained why we need notice and why this isn't reasonable. We have work to do here so we'd appreciate you not taking up any more of our time.'

'I'm sure your landlord won't be happy about this,' Quentin said.

'Our landlord fully understands our rights too,' Roo said.

The two men looked at each other, clearly realising they weren't going to get what they wanted, and left.

She turned to Theo and he was grinning. 'I love this change in you. You don't take any bullshit, do you? You have this steely, big-balled, take no prisoners attitude and I love it.'

She laughed. 'The audacity of just showing up and expecting us to let them in.'

'Well they certainly got that message loud and clear.' He gathered her in his arms and kissed her. 'You surprise me every single day and every day I feel another piece of my heart being handed to you.'

She looked at him in surprise, her heart suddenly racing in her chest. 'Theo, I—'

'Look I know it's early days for us and of course I'm not expecting you to feel the same way but I'm falling for you.'

He kissed her and she pressed herself against him, stroking his face. But they were interrupted by raised voices outside. They pulled apart to see Mr Fenton letting Quentin know exactly what he thought about the non-viewing today.

Theo sighed. 'I need to talk to Adam. What happened today was not acceptable and I need to see if he would be open to offers. And if he thinks Sunday afternoon is a reasonable time for a viewing then it can also be a reasonable time for a little chat.'

'You're going now?'

'Yes.' Theo stepped back and grabbed a small photo album that Violet had dug out for him.

Roo sighed. She wanted the chance to talk to him about what he'd just said, to tell him she felt the same, but now clearly was not the time. 'Shall I come with you?'

He shook his head. 'I know Adam. I can probably talk to him easier if it's just the two of us.'

She grinned. 'You mean my big-balled, take-no-prisoners attitude won't help in this situation?'

He smiled and kissed her. 'Probably not but I won't be long. Are you OK here for a while?'

'Sure, I need to take some of this fruit down to the various enclosures anyway.' She spotted Eloise through the door, working on Bluebell. 'How's our mole friend?'

'Eloise is hopeful it's just surface wounds. We'll see how she goes in a few days. If I'm not back and you want to go, head back to mine if you want and I'll cook us some dinner. There's a spare key underneath the gnome. Feel free to let yourself in.'

'Sounds good.'

He kissed her again and then walked out.

Theo knocked on Adam's door and after a few moments a very harassed and damp-looking Adam answered.

'Oh God, Theo I haven't got time to deal with this now, I'm dealing with a very leaky sink.'

'Can I help?'

'Do you know anything about replacing a U-bend?'

'A little. I renovated my house and did most of the work myself. I can certainly give it a go.'

Adam gestured for him to come in and Theo followed him down to the kitchen to see water all over the floor.

'Have you turned the water off at the mains?'

'What?'

'I'll take that as a no. Any idea where the mains tap is?'

'I have no idea. Honestly, this practical stuff is beyond me. I can barely put up a shelf straight.'

Theo put the photo album down on the table and looked under the sink but there was no sign of it there. He opened a few kitchen cupboards but couldn't see it. 'Do you have a downstairs toilet or an airing cupboard with a boiler in it?'

'The toilet is the first door on the left back there. The boiler is upstairs.'

Theo went to the toilet and sure enough found a little tap to the side of the sink. He quickly turned it off and went back into the kitchen.

'For future reference, it's next to the sink in there.' He knelt down, getting his knees instantly wet. The pipes under the sink were soaking, there was no wonder Adam hadn't been able to remove the U-bend.

'Do you have a dry bit of rag, I need to get rid of some of this water.'

Adam passed him one and Theo started drying.

'What are you doing here, anyway?' Theo asked. 'Living in an old farmhouse doesn't exactly seem up your street.'

'You're right, it's not.' Adam sighed. 'I just have so many fond memories of the place, growing up here, hanging out with Grandad. When he died it seemed like a good idea to move out of my rented flat and move into here. But the place is a mess. There is so much that needs repairing. I fix one thing and something else goes wrong and I have no money to do anything big. The roof needs completely redoing but that kind of thing costs thousands. That's why I've decided to let it all go, sell the lot, Little Paws, this house, the land across the river. I just can't afford to keep it. Grandad always used to do his own repairs. He was always tinkering around the house, even a few days before he died he was up on the roof. Silly old fool.'

'He loved this place,' Theo said, unscrewing the old U-bend and catching the remnant water in the rag.

'I know he did,' Adam said, softly. 'But maybe selling it will give someone else the chance to love it too. Right now, it feels like a millstone around my neck.'

'I didn't realise you were selling the house and the rest of your land too.' Theo chewed his lip. He should have had a look at the listing. The £1.7 million-price tag actually made a lot more sense now. This was a large five-bedroom house, and despite the much-needed renovations, the house alone would be worth close to a million. There were thirty-odd acres of land on the other side of the river and it was a lot flatter there too. The chances of being able to develop that land was much higher than using the land at Little Paws which was hilly and very wet, even Councillor Bishop had said as much.

'Yeah, it makes sense to just start over somewhere else. I had a man come and look at the land over the river this morning. He feels quite confident he could get planning permission there. Although you'll be pleased to know he wasn't too impressed with what he could see of Little Paws.'

Theo sat back on his heels. 'What's the ideal here? If the house was perfect, would you stay here, make a home here?'

Adam sighed. 'Marilyn is pregnant.'

'Oh congratulations.'

'In a perfect world, I would love to raise my child here. Even without the land, the garden gives us so much space and it's quiet and peaceful here. I go outside and talk to the donkey every morning while I have my breakfast. He seems to like the company and I love the views. There are loads of rabbits here and I love seeing them. But the house is in such a state that Marilyn has gone to stay with her mum as she thinks it's too damp to stay here anymore.'

'So why not separate it into two or three lots? Lot one being over the river which is much more attractive to potential buyers. That would be your cash cow as it has much more potential to develop into houses. Lot two will be the land at Little Paws, you sell that for what it is, grazing or arable land. No one is ever going to be able to build on that. There's rivers and marshland and great big holes in the ground thanks to your grandad helping to build artificial dens for the foxes and badgers. We've adapted the rivers to make our own lakes for the otters. And none of it is level; some of it is very steep. It would take a lot of work to get that into a sellable condition and could put some buyers off if they have to buy that too. With the money you get from lot one, you could rent a house to live in for the next year and pay someone to do this place up for you so you have somewhere wonderful to raise your child, complete with a donkey. And if after you've done it all up you still didn't want to live here anymore, you could sell the house separately.'

'I can do that? Sell them separately?'

'Yes, it's a little bit of a faff with Land Registry to separate them but nothing a good lawyer couldn't help you with.'

Adam sighed and looked around. 'I really do like it here. I don't know if Marilyn is that keen but right now she can't see past the leaky roof and everything falling apart. But I know it has so much potential. We could have a nursery and a walk-in wardrobe for Marilyn, she's always wanted one of those.'

'If you were to sell the land at Little Paws for a fair price, for what it would be worth as grazing land, I'd buy it off you in a heartbeat.'

'You would?'

'Little Paws is important and it meant the world to your grandad. I'd like to carry on what he started.'

Adam looked around as he thought and Theo picked up the new U-bend and screwed it into place, then wiped the area clean and dry.

'What would I get for it if I was to sell it as grazing land?'

'It varies, depending on the quality of the land but somewhere around one eighty or one ninety.'

'One hundred and ninety is nice but 1.7 million is much nicer.'

Theo sighed and rolled his eyes. He stood up. 'You have the chance to get what you really want out of this; a home you love for you and your family and some decent money in the bank even after all the renovations. Don't be greedy and lose it all. The chances of anyone buying a crappy bit of land and a leaky dilapidated old farmhouse just to get that land over the river is very slim. And I think your grandad would be disappointed in you if he saw you selling Little Paws after all the time he spent there building the place.'

'Well thankfully the sentimental old fool isn't here anymore to judge me on how I cope with the mess he left behind,' Adam snapped. 'And I've had a lifetime of disappointing people so now will be no different.'

Theo knew instantly he'd said the wrong thing. 'Adam, I—'

'Thanks for your help with the U-bend, but if you don't mind I've got work to do,' Adam gestured to the door.

Theo nodded and walked out. Maybe he could try again in a few days when Adam had calmed down a little.

'997!' someone from the marketing team cheered.

Roo looked up at the rolling total screen in the middle of the office. It was publication day for *Captain Pet's Name and the Search for the Lost Treasure,* and everyone was getting very excited about how many copies they had sold so far. It was released officially at midnight although those that had signed up to the weekly newsletter were able to pre-order their copy and they'd got a fair few pre-orders over the weekend. And when she'd got into work that morning there had already been a number of sales from Australia, New Zealand and lots from Europe. The marketing team were getting very excited and everyone was waiting for the rolling total to hit one thousand.

And while Roo was of course happy that this book was doing well, she was more interested in the crowdfunding total to save Little Paws. There had been no word from the council about whether they were going to get a grant or how much it might be; there had been no movement on the tree preservation order either. Theo's chat with Adam hadn't ended well, so they really did need to focus on raising as much money as they could, either to help with buying Adam out or for the buying and development of the new land. The crowdfunding donation page had been launched on Saturday and it had been shared by a lot of people on social media. What had started off as a slow trickle of incoming funds was now moving quite quickly. There was already over £7000 in the pot and she was hopeful they might have raised over £10,000 by the end of the day.

She minimised the donation page and turned her attention back to the illustrations she was doing for *A Knight's Tail*, adding in all the tiny details to make the book shine.

A message from Charlie appeared on her screen.

from: charlie@petprotagonist.com

to: everyone@petprotagonist.com

Congratulations everyone on another successful publication day. This has probably been our most successful launch yet, it's not even ten in the morning and we're about to hit a thousand sales so far. This is all down to everyone here and all your hard work, so a massive thank you from me, Theo and the rest of the team.

As you know we are not the type to sit back on our laurels, we are launching *A Wizard's Tail* in just six weeks. After that we are aiming to release *A Knight's Tail* six weeks later. The plan is to release a new book every six weeks until the end of the year.

To that end, we are moving some staff around to maximise efficiency and provide a more productive working environment. By the end of the week, or the beginning of next week, the story-writing team and our lead designers will have an office upstairs. We are doing this to create a quiet working environment for our story team and a place for our lead designers to be able to work together on our story illustrations. We will be liaising with these teams over the next few days to get an idea of what they need in order to create the best space for them.

**Don't forget, today is the last day to buy your tickets
for the ball.**

Thanks,
    Charlie

'Oh my god, we're going up in the world,' Nate said, standing up and doing a little dance, with his hands raised in the air. 'Our own office, baby.'

He held his hands out for a double high five and Roo felt embarrassed when she slapped his hands in return. What would everyone else on the design team think? Although the story-writing team were clearly as overjoyed as Nate was by this news. Billie was even hugging Grace, she was so happy.

The marketing team let out another whoop of joy as the rolling total reached 998. Roo could understand why Billie was so happy, it could get very noisy in here at times.

'See, I told you they were doing the freckle-friggle,' Brooke said to Meryl. 'It's funny they never moved Nate upstairs before Roo arrived here, now she gets a fancy-ass office. Theo clearly wants her closer. Oh, I bet she'll be in the room next to him. That's empty right now and it has an interconnecting door. She can sneak in there for a quick fraggle-froggle.'

She heard Ginny on the other side of the desk mutter loudly, 'Oh for God's sake.' She'd clearly had enough of this too.

Roo sighed. 'I'll be sharing an office with Nate. I could hardly sneak off for any kind of extracurricular activity with Theo when Nate is a few metres away and Charlie's across the hall.'

'So you're not denying there is extracurricular activity,' Brooke said, her eyes alight as if Roo had just admitted it.

'I'm saying that the reason for this move is clearly professional, so Nate and I can spread our illustrations out across the office and help each other not so Theo can have not so secret sex with the new girl. Unless you think he's sleeping with Billie, Grace, Daniel and Nate too, I'm not seeing the preferential treatment here.'

Nate choked on his drink.

'You've got to admit that you being here one week and now getting your own office is a bit weird,' Meryl said.

'You said we weren't doing the frickle-frackle, that it was completely one-sided because he wouldn't stoop so low as to go out with me,' Roo said in exasperation.

'It's just a little odd.'

'And is it odd that Grace, Billie, Daniel and Nate are moving up there too?'

'No but—' she trailed off.

Roo waited to see if there was any more evidence to prove she and Theo were together, but this felt as flimsy as Brooke maybe, possibly seeing them together in the rain and dark the week before.

'I think it's brilliant,' Nate said. 'And I don't care the reasons why.'

Roo saw Theo coming across the office towards her.

'Why don't we ask Theo?' Roo said, her patience wearing thin.

Meryl and Brooke looked at her in alarm.

'Ask me what?' Theo said as he drew near.

'The reason why we're getting our own office.'

Theo looked at her in confusion and then at Brooke and Meryl. 'I have no idea. What you have to understand is that as CEO, many of these tiny, insignificant decisions don't cross my desk. The first I heard about this office change was when I read Charlie's message five minutes ago. This came from him and I presume, as with everything that Charlie does, there is no underlying reason for this, but it's as he says, to increase productivity and efficiency. I do know the story team struggle to concentrate in this noisy environment, so it's good for them to be moved somewhere quieter and Charlie and I liaise with the lead designers so much regarding the illustrations it makes sense to have them closer. But if you have any issues with this decision, please feel free to discuss this with Charlie.'

'We don't have an issue with it,' Brooke said, quickly.

'We were just curious,' Meryl said. 'But we understand now.'

Theo nodded. 'Aurora, can I have a quick word.'

'Sure,' Roo stood up.

'It won't take long, let's just use the meeting room back here.' Theo gestured to the small meeting room at the back of the office, and she followed him in there. He closed the door behind them. 'I've just had a message from Violet, and I have some good news and bad news.'

'Oh, hit me with the good news, I really could do with some of that this morning.'

'Well, the council have agreed to give Little Paws a £10,000 grant towards its survival.'

'Oh, that's wonderful.'

'And they are moving forward with the tree preservation order.'

'Oh wow. Does that mean that Adam won't be able to sell it?'

'It just means he can't build on the land, or at least if he does, he can't do anything to affect the trees. And it means the council will be very unlikely to give any planning permission for it. He can still sell it as arable and grazing land. As that's quite hard to come by, he may still get some decent money for that, not 1.7 million, but a few hundred thousand. I think it will put people off from buying it though if a tree preservation order is in place.'

'That's great. So, what's the bad news?'

Theo let out a heavy sigh. 'Well, that's what I brought you in here for. I wanted you to know before Violet puts it out on social media, but Bluebell died this morning.'

Roo let out a gasp. 'Our little mole?'

'Yeah, her injuries were just too severe. She was so small, she didn't stand a chance against a cat.'

Roo felt tears prick her eyes. It was silly to get upset over the death of a mole, but she'd held that tiny creature in her hands yesterday as she was helping Eloise tend to her wounds and now she was gone.

'Hey, come here,' Theo said, wrapping his arms around her and kissing her forehead. 'Working in wildlife rescue can really suck sometimes, it's hard and horrible but the good far outweighs the bad. There was nothing anyone could do for Bluebell, but at least we tried.'

She hugged him back as the tears fell down her cheeks. 'Sorry, it's just a bit of a shock. Bluebell seemed to be OK yesterday when we put her in her cage, burying into the bedding we put in there for her. I thought if she was able to do that then she'd be OK.'

Theo stroked her hair but just then Charlie walked into the room with Billie and Grace, from the story department.

They leapt apart as if they'd been doing something bad but not before Charlie and Billie had seen them, maybe even Grace too.

Charlie looked furious.

'Sorry, I just had some bad news and Theo was—' Roo started.

'I can see quite clearly what Theo was doing,' Charlie said.

Roo felt her cheeks heat.

Charlie turned to the two women. 'Can we put a pin in our meeting for half an hour, I have something else to deal with first.'

Grace and Billie stared between Charlie and Theo with wide eyes, and they nodded.

'Theo, can I have a word?' Charlie said.

Theo swore under his breath and followed Charlie out of the meeting room. Roo cringed inside, quickly wiping the tears from her cheeks. Grace and Billie gathered round her, letting the door shut behind them.

'Are you OK?' Grace said.

Roo couldn't even tell them that she'd been upset by the death of a mole, they wouldn't even begin to understand. 'I just had some bad news.'

'And Theo was comforting you,' Billie said, her eyes alight with the prospect of juicy gossip.

'He was just being nice. I really need to get back to work.'

She hurried out and back to her desk. She was pretty sure that lovely bit of gossip would be around the whole office by lunchtime. She bit her lip as she looked towards the door to the upstairs offices. What was Charlie saying to Theo?

CHAPTER FIFTEEN

Charlie opened the door to his office and Theo walked in waiting for all hell to break loose. And Charlie was right to be angry; being found with his arms round an employee was not acceptable. Theo had always been one hundred per cent professional with his staff before. Even a few months before when Cara had come to work crying because she'd lost her mum, he'd brought her into the meeting room so she could cry in private and he'd brought her cups of tea and got a box of tissues. He'd even got one of her close friends at work to sit with her before calling her a taxi to take her home with two weeks' compassionate leave. But he'd never hugged her.

But Cara was not the woman he was falling in love with and it had killed him to see Roo upset over Bluebell's death.

Charlie shut the door. 'What the hell was that? You've

just been caught in a compromising position with an employee.'

'It was a hug, Charlie.' But Theo knew he couldn't dismiss it.

'People are going to talk about this, it reflects badly on you and the company. And Aurora could slap a sexual harassment charge on you.'

'Charlie, we're together.'

That took the wind out of his sails. 'What?'

'Dating, seeing each other, spending every night wrapped in each other's arms. I'm not sure what you want me to call it.'

Charlie let out a sigh, though Theo didn't know if it was from frustration or relief. 'Is it serious?'

'Yeah it is.'

'How serious?'

'Life-changing kind of serious.'

Charlie smiled and sat down at his desk. 'I'm happy for you, genuinely. You deserve someone wonderful in your life.'

'But you'd prefer it if it wasn't someone from work.'

'I can hardly complain when I met and fell in love with Beth here. But we never kissed or hugged at work, we never even touched. I'm not sure how we should handle this. I presume you're trying to keep your relationship quiet for now.'

'Yeah, for obvious reasons. Roo also thinks that people will assume she got the job because we're together.'

'When did this start?'

'We got together the night before she started here. We

had no idea we were both working at Pet Protagonist until she showed up here on her first day.'

'That explains her reaction on seeing you when she walked into your office.'

'Yeah, it was a shock for us both. But after that she called it off, she didn't want people to judge me for sleeping with the new girl or judge her. But we got back together again last Tuesday night, after I told you that nothing was happening between us. When I was at your house, nothing *was* happening and I did wonder whether it would remain as a crazy, wonderful one-night stand. But I should have told you when we got back together and I'm sorry for that. It was just so new, and everything has changed so quickly. I just wanted to protect it and her.'

Charlie tapped his pen against his desk as he thought. 'How do you want to play this?'

'It *was* just a hug. And I absolutely know that isn't appropriate with other members of staff but it's not like you guys walked in on me shagging her on the meeting room table. And everyone knows we were friends before she came here. There is already gossip about the two of us because of that. I'm sure they will make of it what they want no matter what we say about it. So I don't think we need to address it. Not right now.'

'OK, it's your call. Is Aurora OK? She looked upset.'

'She'll be fine, thank you. She's been helping me with work at Little Paws and one of the animals she was helping yesterday has died today. I just wanted her to know before she saw a social media post about it.'

'Ah I'm sorry, I know how much these animals mean to

you. We lost our guinea pig last week. Just came down in the morning and she was dead in her cage. Beth was distraught and I'm not ashamed to say I shed a tear over her.'

Theo nodded. 'It is the hardest part about working with animals. Anyway, are we done here? I promise not to kiss or hug any more of our employees.'

Charlie smirked. 'Go on, get out of here.'

Theo got up and walked out. What he really wanted was to go back downstairs and see if Roo was OK, but he knew that would just make things worse. He could cope with Charlie challenging him about this, but he just hoped Roo wasn't going to get a load of grief for this too.

'So still denying you're doing the joggle-jingle with our CEO,' Brooke said.

'Can we not just call it sex?' Roo said, wearily. The new office couldn't come soon enough. This was never going to go away.

Any hope she had that Grace and Billie would be discreet and not tell anyone what they saw had been dashed as the whole office seemed to know about it not even an hour after Charlie had found them in the meeting room. The silly comments, looks and laughter had been almost non-stop since then. She was quite surprised that Brooke and Meryl had held off for this long.

'Are you having sex with Theo Lucas?' Meryl said.

'It was a hug. I'd had some bad news, I was upset, Theo gave me a hug. We're friends. That's what friends do.'

'Come on this is getting beyond a joke now,' Nate said. 'It could almost be classed as bullying.'

'I agree,' Ginny said, standing up. 'This has been really unpleasant to listen to over the last few days.'

'Then don't listen,' Meryl said.

'Hey, leave her alone,' Roo said.

'I just think, what does it matter if she's sleeping with Theo or not, that's their business not anyone else's,' Ginny said.

'I just don't like favouritism,' Meryl sniffed.

'What favouritism?' Roo said. 'I'm doing the job I was hired to do, and I'm being moved upstairs with a bunch of other people. How is that favouritism?'

'And if you're so interested in her sex life, let's talk about yours,' Nate said. 'Roo, did you know that Meryl was caught having sex with Daniel last year in the disabled toilet. Now that was hilarious gossip that was definitely worth talking about.'

Roo let out a laugh of shock and Meryl flushed bright red. 'That was a very long time ago.'

'You don't like it when the tables are turned do you? And Brooke is dating Stuart from accounts. Do I need to tell everyone what I caught you two doing down the back stairs near the fire escape last month because I haven't told a soul about that, but if you want to spread gossip about Roo, I think it's only fair.'

'No!' Brooke said, quickly. 'There's no need for that.'

'Then this needs to stop, both of you,' Nate said, firmly.

Brooke and Meryl looked suitably chastised. Roo nodded her thanks to Nate and Ginny for standing up for her. Although she knew it would only stop the gossip for a few days, she'd take the reprieve while she could.

Theo walked into Little Paws with all the donated scraps of meat from the local butcher. He knew the carnivorous animals would really appreciate it. Violet was there putting on her coat as she got ready to leave. She looked a bit happier today. Obviously, the news about the tree preservation order and the grant from the council had cheered her up; maybe it offered a chink of hope.

Violet gave him a hug. 'Good to see you. How are you doing?'

'I'm fine,' Theo said. 'How are you?'

'I'm good. I feel a bit more positive today. The total on Roo's fundraising page has reached £10,000 and with the council grant, we're definitely moving in the right direction. The tree preservation order has made me happy too. Adam will have to sell it for a lower price now.'

Theo didn't want to say that they weren't out the woods yet. There was lots that could still go wrong. But he would keep his worries to himself, it was nice to see her smiling again.

'It's good news,' Theo said.

'Right I'm off. I have poker tonight with the girls. Are you OK to lock up? There's no one else here and the front is already locked.'

'Sure, no problem.'

She waved goodbye and Theo picked up the bag of meat. All the animals would have been fed tonight but he could chop up the meat into small pieces ready for tomorrow. He grabbed a large knife and a chopping board and started chopping all the meat.

He heard someone knocking on the door at the front, or rather hammering. It must be urgent. He quickly went to answer it, wondering what injured animal was on the other side. He opened the door only to be met with Adam.

'What the hell is this?' Adam said, waving a piece of paper in the air.

'Hello Adam,' Theo said, calmly. He took the piece of paper from him, and his heart sank to see the tree preservation order. Of course, Adam was going to be mad over this and he hadn't really thought about that when it was going ahead. Theo stepped back to let him in and Adam barged past him. 'I appreciate you're upset over this, but—'

'Upset? You've just lost me £1.7 million. No one is going to buy the land now if they can't do anything with it.'

'Adam, no one is going to buy this land, anyway, you know that. You might get a farmer who would buy it for grazing land but not at that price. And the access for cattle isn't good. We spoke to Councillor Bishop, and she said the land at Little Paws would never get planning permission because it would be a logistical nightmare trying to develop it for building houses. It's too steep and there are rivers and small lakes and ponds. If you separate the land into three lots, as I said, the offer still stands for me to buy this land off you if you were to sell it at a fair price.'

But Adam was clearly too angry to listen as he paced back and forth across the floor.

'You've ruined everything. I know what you do here. Grandad told me.'

Theo shifted uneasily. 'What do you mean? We're just a wildlife hospital.'

'And I'm sure the council and the authorities would be very interested in the work you do with the squirrels.'

Theo's heart fell into his stomach.

'I heard the council have given you a grant to try and help save this place. They'd be taking that grant back and closing this place down if they knew what you did here, rescuing and rehabilitating squirrels, which is illegal. You'd get a massive fine too. Once you guys were gone I could bulldoze this place to the ground, apart from a few precious trees. That might make it much more attractive to potential developers.'

'Adam, please. We've built a successful charity here; we help thousands of animals every year. Don't destroy that for the sake of pettiness and revenge. We were just trying to protect what we've worked so hard to build.'

Adam shook his head. 'Get the council to withdraw the tree preservation order, or I'll tell them everything.'

With that he stormed out.

Theo swore under his breath. If the council found out about the squirrels, they would lose everything.

Roo opened the door to Orla's café and was pleased to see Fern there with her big dog Bones. Theo had gone to Little Paws to drop off scraps of raw meat from the butchers and she had gone home to get changed but she was going to go to his shortly for dinner. It was funny how easily and quickly they had fallen into spending every night together, how it just worked so well between them.

'Hey,' Fern said, giving her a big hug. 'Happy publication day. I've got my copy, *Captain Bones and the Search for the Lost Treasure* has a nice ring to it, eh Bones?'

Bones wagged his tail furiously, a big smile on his face.

'And I ordered one for my niece,' Orla said.

'Thank you both, that's very kind. The book has done really well, I'm sure Theo is very pleased.'

'And how are things with Theo?' Fern asked casually.

Roo didn't mind talking about it with Fern and Orla. Fern was his sister after all, she just wanted him to be happy.

'Well, I'm sure you already know we're together now.'

Fern grinned. 'Yes we know, Carrie has spies everywhere.'

Roo laughed. 'I am blissfully happy with him, but work is not easy. They already think I'm getting some kind of preferential treatment because I knew Theo before I started there. And of course, knowing Theo must mean I'm shagging his brains out. They've already decided we're having a relationship, even though there really isn't any proof. And the comments, looks and giggles are driving me mad. And then we made it ten times worse this morning when Theo was caught hugging me in the meeting room. He'd just told me Bluebell, a mole we'd rescued, had died and I was upset. It was just a hug but for everyone else it's the most exciting thing that's ever happened there. Me and Nate, the other lead designer, are getting our own office at the end of the week and it can't come soon enough.'

'That has to be exhausting,' Fern said.

'It really is. I love the job itself; I've had so much fun doing the illustrations for their new book, but this really has put a dampener on it.'

'Maybe you should just come clean about your relationship,' Orla said. 'Sure it will be a hot potato of gossip for the first few days but once everyone knows about it, the gossip will die down.'

'I don't know. That might help I suppose, but right now it feels like it will never go away. But it will have to come out at some point. I know Theo would love to take me to the ball on Friday and I want that too, but I don't know if it's too soon or we're just opening ourselves up for more gossip. Although at least by the end of the week I won't have to hear any of it.'

Just then the door opened and Roo turned around to see Theo walk in. He looked like he was carrying the weight of the world on his shoulders.

'Are you OK?' Roo said, giving him a hug. He held her tight, kissing the top of her head.

He took her hand and walked over to the counter.

'Adam is pissed off about the whole tree preservation

order,' Theo said. 'He just came to Little Paws, and I've never seen him so angry.'

'I did wonder how he would react to that,' Orla said.

'I should have seen this coming,' Theo said. 'I mean it makes sense for us, but it ruins all of his plans. Any hope of him negotiating with us has now gone.' He looked around to make sure no one was listening. Roo looked around too but the old couple in the corner were too busy chatting to pay them any attention. The rest of the café was empty. 'He knows about the SSS.'

'No!' Fern said.

'Oh crap,' Orla said.

'How does he know?' Roo said.

'Joseph told him. He obviously never realised Adam would use that knowledge against us. He is threatening to tell the council what we do if we don't remove the tree preservation order.'

'They'll close the place down,' Fern said.

'Can an order be removed?' Orla said.

Roo shook her head. 'From my limited knowledge of briefly working for a council department, they can be revoked but you have to have a really good reason. You can't just change your mind. And don't you think Councillor Bishop and her cohorts will want to know why? It will look really suspicious. I've even updated our fundraising page to say that we got this preservation order, how do I explain to all of our followers that we no longer want it?'

'I don't know what to do,' Theo said. 'This will ruin us. I haven't even told Violet and Lizzie yet; it will destroy them. If they close us down, then we'll lose our licence to rehabilitate wildlife; we wouldn't even be allowed to start over somewhere new.'

'What a mess,' Fern said. 'Surely we can reason with him. I know Adam, he's always seemed a nice man. I think he's just a bit stressed out because of lack of money and trying to repair his home before the baby comes.'

'He is a decent man. Well, at least, I've always thought so,' Theo said. 'I just hope he sees sense before he reacts and does something that can't be undone. His best course of action is to separate the land and focus on getting planning permission for the land across the river, as Councillor Bishop said. I did try to tell him that, but he was too angry to listen. If he decides to sell the land in three separate lots, he could come out of this financially a lot better off, and everyone wins. But he was so angry, I worry he's going to jump the gun and tell the council everything and then there's no going back. We're obviously not going to buy the land if the council shuts us down so he could lose out massively with that. I only hope Adam does the right thing.'

He sighed heavily and Roo's heart went out to him. 'I'm sure he'll calm down tonight and think about this logically.'

'I hope so.'

'Could you go and talk to him?' Fern said.

'Not tonight. He was furious. I could send him an email, reiterating what I said about getting planning permission for the other land, appealing to his better nature, explaining all the good work we do here. He might at least read that.'

'That's a good idea,' Orla said. 'Just don't mention squirrels in any written communication with him, because then he'd have proof – right now all he has is hearsay.'

'Good point,' Theo said.

They fell silent and Roo had no idea what she could say to make this better. It was bad enough when they were trying to raise funds to buy the place, but at least then they had hope. If Adam told the council what they had been doing, there was nothing left to do, nowhere to turn, not to mention the huge fine they could be landed with.

She squeezed his hand. 'Let's go home.'

He nodded and they said their goodbyes and walked out. They walked in silence over the hills towards his house. He opened the door and let her in. The smell of the casserole in the slow cooker immediately drifted over to them, making her stomach gurgle appreciatively.

'Shall I get dinner ready?' Roo asked, knowing there was some garlic bread in the fridge she could throw in the oven to go with the casserole.

'I think I'm going to have a shower, but please eat, you don't need to wait for me.'

She watched him go, unsure what to do. She wanted to take care of him, but she knew she couldn't take this worry away. This was the worst possible outcome since they'd found out Adam was selling.

She heard the shower run upstairs and she decided she'd go and join him.

She went upstairs, undressed in his bedroom, and then walked through into the bathroom. He was inside his large shower cubicle facing away from her, his hands against the wall, his head under the spray. She slipped into the cubicle and wrapped her arms around him, kissing his back.

He took her hand in his and held it against his heart and they stood like that for the longest time.

After a while, she let go of his hand and started massaging his shoulders, trying to ease some of the stress in his muscles. She ran her hands down his arms and all the way down his back, hoping it was helping in some small way.

She paused when he let out a groan of need.

'Christ, Roo, don't stop.'

She had been hoping to offer him some comfort but maybe she could do that in another way. She trailed her hands across his body, stroking and caressing rather than massaging now, then she replaced her hands with her tongue. She slid her tongue down the indent of his spine, and he turned around, cupped her face and kissed her hard.

'It's my turn now,' he said, his hands wandering all over her body as the water cascaded around them. She carried on stroking him, but it wasn't long before her body was humming with need as his hands explored everywhere.

'You are magnificent, Aurora Clarke, there is no darkness with you in my life, just sunshine and light.' He kissed her, pulling her close against him.

He suddenly pulled back, opened the cubicle door,

rooted around inside the bathroom cabinet for a second and then came back with a condom which he pressed into her hand.

He eased her back against a small shelf that ran the length of the shower and then he knelt down, kissing his way up her legs, his eyes on hers as he slowly inched closer to where she needed him. Finally, he kissed her right between her legs and she cried out, grabbing his hair, his shoulders, as he took her to the very edge of sanity with his mouth.

He took the condom from her hand while she was still trying to catch her breath. He dealt with it quickly and then urged her down on top of him. She straddled him and with his hands at her hips he moved inside her. She gasped, wrapping her arms around him for balance. He kissed her hard, kneeling up he took her with him. He leaned one hand against the wall the other arm around her bum, holding her close as he moved against her hard and fast. She wrapped her legs around him, taking him deeper and he made a strangled noise against her mouth. That feeling was building inside her, spreading out to every single part of her in blissful, glorious tingles and then she was falling, clinging on to him, shouting out his name and taking him with her.

He pulled back to look at her, his breath heavy against her lips. 'Thank you for helping to chase away the dark clouds.'

She stroked his face. 'It was my pleasure,' she smirked. 'Literally.'

CHAPTER SIXTEEN

The following night they drove to Lizzie's house so they could collect Barney, the juvenile squirrel, and release him in his home in Morgy Hill Woods. Lizzie was satisfied that he was now ready for release. Roo was quite excited about this part. She'd seen and helped many animals at Little Paws, but all of that rehabilitation was getting them ready to be released and she was yet to witness that wonderful moment.

'Are you sure you want to come tonight?' Theo asked. 'If we get found out I don't want you to get caught up in any fines, or worse, jail time, because of this.'

'I'm not missing this for the world. And I think, more than ever, we have to do this. If the council shut us down, we'll never be able to do this again. I don't even want to think about what will happen to the squirrels that are still rehabilitating under Lizzie's care, Tilly, Belle and the others. The council will have them put down, won't they?'

'It's highly likely they will. They can't legally release them so there is no other option. If it gets to that stage, we'll just have to do a mass release of the juveniles and adults and hope for the best for them. As for the babies... I don't know, maybe we can hide them somewhere until they are old enough for release, smuggle them out in a shoe box. The council would have the power to seize any squirrels they found on Lizzie's property. But I can imagine Lizzie chaining herself to the gates before she'd let them in, which may buy us a bit of time to get them out. But we're catastrophising here. Adam might know about the squirrels, but he might not know about Lizzie's involvement and it might not come to that if Adam sees sense.'

Roo sighed. There had been no word from Adam about whether he was still planning to go to the council about their illegal work with squirrels and there certainly hadn't been any word from the council. Roo felt sure they would hear the fallout straightaway if they knew. Maybe Adam was giving them a few days to rescind the tree preservation order or maybe he had calmed down enough to realise this was not the way forward for him.

Theo had sent him an email explaining clearly what Councillor Bishop had said about getting planning permission for the land over the river, and how desperate the council were for affordable homes for the locals, so they'd be more likely to approve it. He'd also laid out his offer to buy the land at Little Paws if it was priced as grazing or arable land. So far there had been no reply.

'Are you going to tell Lizzie and Violet about Adam's threat?' Roo asked.

He shook his head. 'Not yet. I don't think there's any point in upsetting them if this comes to nothing. Adam is a good man. I think Fern is right. He is stressed out right now because the farmhouse he's living in is in such a bad way. I was there the other day and there's damp and mould growing up the walls, the roof is in a terrible state, the windows are broken and draughty. That's no place to raise a baby. But I can't see that Adam will vindictively destroy a wildlife rescue charity because of this. Who would do that?'

'A man who is desperate and what you've just described sounds pretty bleak to me.'

Theo's mouth pulled into a thin line, and she knew that despite his bravado, he was still worried. But she understood his reasoning for not telling Lizzie or Violet. Adam's threat could be empty and purely given in a moment of anger. Poor Violet was already finding this whole thing really hard, the threat of Little Paws being forced to close would only add to her overloaded plate.

'What will you do about the tree preservation order?'

'I'm holding fire on that too. As you said, that will be harder to revoke than it was to apply it. And Councillor Bishop will want to know why. They threw us a lifeline with that preservation order as they couldn't give us the money to buy Adam out. I can't realistically go back to them and ask them to remove it without arousing suspicions. If Adam genuinely believes that removing the order and selling all the land as one big plot is his best course of action, he'll be chasing us up to make sure it's done. So, I'm taking a wait-and-see approach and hoping it doesn't come back to bite me.' He paused. 'Do you think that's the right thing to do?'

She smiled that he had asked her and put her hand on his thigh. 'We don't have a crystal ball – though that would have been handy over the years – so we can only make the best decisions based on the information we have. Your decision to not tell Violet and Lizzie and not have the order removed is based on the knowledge that Adam is a good man at heart and I think we must always hope for the good in people. We can't live our lives with doubt and mistrust, expecting to be let down. I did that with you. I'd been hurt in the past so I assumed I'd be hurt again and if I'd listened to that gut instinct to push you away, I would have missed out on being with one of the most incredible men I've ever met. So yes, always follow your heart, not your head.'

He smiled at that and squeezed her hand.

They pulled up to Lizzie's gate. Theo typed in the code on the keypad and the electric gates swept open, giving them access. They drove up to the farmhouse and got out.

There was no sign of Lizzie, so Theo knocked on the kitchen door and then let himself in.

'Lizzie!' he called.

'In here,' Lizzie called from the room that was now the nursery.

They walked in and Roo smiled to see Lizzie sitting in the rocking chair as she bottle fed one of the baby squirrels.

'Is that Tilly?' Roo asked softly.

'Yeah, she's doing really well. She really likes her food.'

Roo swallowed the lump in her throat as she thought about what would happen if there was no Lizzie, no SSS and no Little Paws anymore. Squirrels like Tilly would be put to sleep purely because some well-meaning member of the public had found her after she'd fallen out of her nest.

She watched as Lizzie fed Tilly the last of the milk and then popped the tiny squirrel back in the cage. They were doing something wonderful here, they had to fight to keep it.

'Do you guys have time for a cup of tea before you leave?' Lizzie said as she walked out.

Theo looked at Roo and she nodded.

'Yes of course,' Theo said.

'I've just put some tea in the pot so it should be ready now,' Lizzie said, pouring out three mugs as they sat down at the kitchen table.

'How's Violet doing?' Theo asked, taking a sip.

Lizzie sighed. 'She's better, putting on a brave face. I think that tree preservation order has given her hope and the fundraising total that goes up every day. But she doesn't want to talk about moving locations even though that might be the only option open to us. I've shown her some of the suggestions that Shay had for locations and she didn't even want to look at them. I think too many of her memories of Joseph are tied up with Little Paws and all the hard work and time she put into building it from scratch. She doesn't want to leave there, and I think if we have to go somewhere else we'll be doing it without Violet.'

'Violet is Little Paws, it won't be the same without her,' Theo said.

'I know, I said that to her too. But all of this has made her so sad. What are our chances here?' Lizzie asked. 'Now the tree preservation order has stopped the destruction of those trees, do you think Adam will agree to sell that land separately?'

'I don't know,' Theo said honestly, and Roo knew he didn't want to tell them about Adam's threat which could ruin any plans for negotiation.

Lizzie took a sip of her tea. 'Even if he did agree to sell it, we'd still need a few hundred-thousand pounds.'

Roo knew that Theo didn't want to tell anyone that he was considering buying the land at Little Paws because there was a good chance that Adam wouldn't want to sell it and he'd just be getting Lizzie and Violet's hopes up for nothing.

'Yes but—' Theo started.

'The crowd funding is going particularly well,' Roo interrupted. She didn't want Theo to put himself in a position where he promised to buy it and then couldn't. If Adam decided to charge more for the land than Theo could afford, she didn't want him to feel like he was letting them down. 'We've raised £20,000 so far and it's only been a few days since we set it up. I think we could easily reach a hundred thousand in a few weeks. Some of the smaller businesses have donated a couple of hundred here and there too and word is getting around.'

Lizzie's face lit up. 'Well that's something.'

'I think with the proceeds from the summer ball and a few of the other fundraising events it might be doable if Adam agrees to sell it at a decent price,' Roo said. 'Tell Violet not to give up hope just yet. We're going to do everything we can to save it.'

Lizzie smiled. 'Thank you, I'll tell her. That crowd-funding total is very promising. Well, I'm sure Barney is going nuts about being kept in his release box, if you excuse the pun. Let's go and get him. I'm sure he's itching to be out in the wild again. But let's hope his brush with captivity will teach him not to be so friendly with humans in the future.'

They followed her out of the kitchen and back outside.

'I've kept an eye on him over the last few days, the limp is gone, and he is eating and drinking just fine, playing happily with the two adults that I have in the outside enclosures so it's time for him to go back home. I'm hoping that he was near his drey when he was found and if you take him back to where he was found, he might be able to reunite with his family. I'm sure he has brothers and sisters in his litter that will be hanging around, even if his parents aren't. But he'll be fine by himself even if he can't find them. There are tons of squirrels up in the woods.'

'Do we know exactly where he was found?' Theo said.

'Luckily yes, we don't always get that, but the lady that brought him in was very precise. If you park your car in the main picnic area in Morgy Hill Woods and take the north path towards the little waterfall, there is another little picnic table along that path. There is a large oak tree right next to it and the woman said he came from there.'

'Great, that's really helpful.'

Lizzie opened a shed door and pulled out a picnic basket. There was squeaking noises coming from inside.

'I put some nuts in there which I thought might keep him quiet for a little while, but I bet he's snaffled them all already. Greedy little monkey.'

She handed the basket to Roo, and she could feel movement inside as Barney clearly wanted out.

'We'll take good care of him.'

'I'm sure you will,' Lizzie said. 'And take care of him,' she gestured to Theo. 'He needs a bit of TLC.'

'Again, I'm still here,' Theo said.

Roo giggled. 'I will.'

They waved goodbye and got back into Theo's car.

They drove off and the gates opened for them automatically as they approached.

'How long has she been doing the whole squirrel thing?'

'A while, even before it was illegal. She's been involved with wildlife rescue in one way or another her whole life. She makes me want to do more too but being a CEO takes a lot of my time.'

'Yeah, I can understand that. Do you think there will come a time when you move on from Pet Protagonist, find something you love?'

'That would involve selling the company and I couldn't do that. There are too many employees that rely on their jobs. If I sold Pet Protagonist I couldn't be assured that the person who bought it would keep the staff. Hell, they might even move locations, take the company to London or some other big city and the staff would have to leave anyway.'

'You could sell it to someone you know and trust.'

'You offering?'

She laughed. 'I've been given a very generous salary for my job as lead designer, but I imagine that would only cover one per cent of what the company is worth. But I do have -£386 in my savings, would that cover it?'

He laughed. 'Sadly not.'

'What about Charlie?'

'What about him?'

'You could sell it to him. You could trust him to keep the company exactly as it is. You've already said he practically runs the place and it's because of him that the company is such a success. Why not sell it to him?'

'You know, all the women I date, they all get really excited when they find out I'm a CEO of a successful company. You can practically see the pound signs in their eyes. I have never been with a woman who has encouraged me to sell off my success before.'

Roo blushed. It was none of her business what Theo did with his life. 'Sorry, I just want you to be happy. You have thirty or more years until you retire. That's a bloody long time to be stuck in a job you hate, especially when it takes up so much of your time.'

'And I appreciate that, more than you know,' he took her hand. 'But it's probably a bit more complicated than you think.'

'It doesn't need to be. You're the CEO. You can make it as simple as you like.'

He gave her hand a squeeze, but he didn't say anything after that, just kept his eyes on the road and she knew the subject was closed.

The night was drawing in and the sky was a pale, inky blue. It would be another hour or so before it was pitch dark, but the evening definitely had that twilight feel to it. A couple of bright stars appeared above them and the moon was shining brightly.

Theo turned off the main road onto a little side road that went straight to the heart of Morgy Hill Woods. In the day there would be cars parked all the way up the road on both sides as people enjoyed the walks around the woods. But as it was getting dark, Roo was surprised to see there were still a few cars parked up there.

'How come there are people still up here, it's a bit late for a walk through the woods?'

Theo smirked at her. 'What do you think they are doing up here?'

Roo laughed as the penny dropped. 'Really? People come up here to have sex?'

'Morgy Hill Woods are known for it. People do it in their cars or in the woods. It's quite the popular place. The locals call it Orgy Hill Woods.'

Roo laughed. 'Do they really have orgies up here?'

'I don't think so. More of a one-on-one thing, I think. When I've been up here at night to release the squirrels, I just see couples in their own cars, certainly no orgy action. But I've never brought a woman up here before. I have too much respect for the women I'm with to bring them somewhere seedy to have sex.'

'We used to hang out up here all the time as kids. I never realised it was that kind of place.'

'During the day it isn't. There are plenty of walkers and families that come up here but after dark it turns into something much more sordid.'

'Who knew that Apple Hill Bay was such a sex hot-spot? Don't the police come here to stop it if everyone knows about it?'

'I don't think they care. I'm sure they have better things to do than worry about a few people getting it on. We will have to be a bit careful, though. We don't want to release Barney if there is a couple nearby going at it like rabbits.'

Roo laughed. 'No, it might scar the poor animal for life.'

They parked up at the top near a big picnic area. There were lots of tables here but thankfully no cars, so they could get to release Barney in peace.

They got out and Theo picked up the picnic basket. 'This is the path to the waterfall, so we'll follow it until we come to another picnic table.'

He took her hand as they walked along and that made her smile.

'Can I just say one more thing about Pet Protagonist and then I promise I'll say no more.'

'You can say anything you want to me Roo. I don't ever want you to feel you can't talk to me. Even if I disagree with you or don't do what you want, doesn't mean you can't talk to me.'

She smiled at that. 'If you can't leave and you can't sell it, why not make your role more what you want? You're involved in so many of these meetings, early mornings, late nights, all through the day, but do you really need to be or are you just there because you're CEO and it's kind of expected? I bet Charlie is in most of those meetings anyway. And he thrives on that kind of thing. It doesn't need two of you to make decisions. You trust him to do a good job, so let him do it. And instead of CEO you could be CDO, Chief Design Officer, take on more of the creative side of things, especially with the new stories. You could design all of them and then pass it onto the rest of the team to iron out the creases. You're in charge up there, you could make the job whatever you want it to be.'

Theo was silent for a while and then shook his head. 'The company works seamlessly right now. In two years, it's gone from me creating a few books in my house to this hugely successful machine with over a hundred employees worldwide. And largely that's all down to Charlie and the people he has employed. I don't want to let him down when he's worked so hard to get us where we are. I feel like any change in the cogs of the machine, just to keep me happy, could have it tumbling down around us. And really, it's selfish to want something more than what I have. I should be happy, it's a massive success.'

She sighed. Perhaps it really was more complicated than she thought.

Up ahead of them she spotted a little picnic table

tucked into the trees on the side of the path. They had nearly missed it as the darkness was creeping in.

'Look, it's there,' Roo said and then looked around. 'And that's the oak tree Barney supposedly came from.'

'Right let's do it. Squirrels are most active in the morning and at dusk so his family may still be around.'

Theo placed the picnic basket on the table. Roo could hear Barney squeaking and moving around inside the basket. She wondered if he knew where he was.

They both looked around but there was no sound or sign of anyone else near them. They were obviously too busy getting over-friendly in their cars.

Theo carefully unhooked the lid on the picnic basket, opened one half and then they stepped back.

After a few moments, Barney poked his head out of the top and looked around. Within seconds he slid out the basket onto the table, moving so gracefully he was like liquid.

He started making little squeaking noises and Roo wondered if he was calling to his family. To her surprise, he hopped back in the basket, he was in there for a few seconds and came back out, his cheeks bulging with the remainder of the nuts that Lizzie had put in there for him.

He sat there for a few moments chewing on the nuts, seemingly not in any rush to grab his freedom. In between each nut, he'd make the same squeaking noise and then carried on eating. He was so laid back and it made Roo want to laugh. She'd thought he would run a mile as soon as the lid was lifted.

After a few minutes, another larger squirrel appeared

on the table and Roo let out a little gasp. It approached Barney, gave it a sniff, they squeaked at each other and then they both ran off, disappearing into the bushes.

Roo swallowed a big lump in her throat. 'We've just done something incredible.'

'Yeah, we have,' Theo said, putting his arm around her. 'And I know it's a big risk because of the legalities of it, but it's definitely worth it.'

'Do you think that was his mum?'

'Yeah, probably giving him a good clip around the ear for going missing and then a big hug as we speak.'

Roo laughed at the image and then she sighed. 'Barney is a fit, healthy, happy squirrel and so young. If we hadn't released him, the alternative of bumping him off just because a well-meaning member of the public incorrectly thought he was in trouble is just horrifying.'

'Wildlife rescue is a divisive subject. Many people hate foxes too. There are lots of people who own chickens and I imagine there isn't a chicken owner in the country that hasn't lost some or all of them to foxes at some point. Badgers supposedly spread diseases to cattle, and bats, mice and rats cause a lot of damage. Even butterflies are hated because the caterpillars feast on people's beautiful flowers and vegetables.'

'It just makes me so sad.'

He turned to look at her, cupping her face in his strong hands. 'Don't be sad. Be happy that you've saved a life tonight.'

She smiled. 'I am happy about that.'

He kissed her then pulled back slightly. 'Come on, let's go back to mine. I want to be with you tonight.'

'You can have me right here, as it's such a popular spot for sex,' Roo teased.

He kissed her again. 'For what I have planned I'd prefer a little privacy.'

He took her hand, picked up the picnic basket and they started walking back down the path.

'What do you have planned?' Roo said, loving the need he had for her.

'Well first—' Theo stopped talking as they rounded a corner. Another couple was walking up the path towards them and to Roo's dismay, she realised the woman was Danielle from Pet Protagonist. The man she recognised too as being one of the ones who worked in the printing room. They were giggling and kissing and hadn't seen Theo and Roo yet.

She quickly let go of Theo's hand. 'Should we hide?'

'I don't think there's time for that.'

He was right, a second later Danielle looked up and saw them. Her eyes widened and she looked embarrassed, probably about being caught in the act, or at least the prelude to it.

'Theo, Roo, what are you doing up here?'

The man snorted. 'What do you think they're doing up here. Same as us no doubt.'

'Actually Ryan, we were doing research,' Theo said, smoothly.

'Is that what they're calling it nowadays?' Ryan said.

'There is a waterfall scene in the new book, or at least there might be, we're playing with options. Aurora wanted to do a big, long waterfall but I wanted something that was more bouncing off the rocks on the way down, like Morgy Falls here. She's never seen it, so I was just showing her.'

'After dark,' Ryan said, snorting with laughter again.

Admittedly it wasn't a great excuse, but whatever they said, even if it was the truth about releasing squirrels, Ryan and Danielle wouldn't believe them. The reputation of Orgy Hill Woods proceeded them.

'It's a night scene,' Roo said. 'Theo wanted to show me how the moon bounces off the water as it tumbles over the rocks. I've got loads of photos for inspiration.'

'Photos eh?' Ryan guffawed and Roo decided she didn't like this man. 'You're into that kind of kinkiness, are you? Maybe we should take some photos of our own, eh baby?' He nudged Danielle but she looked really uncomfortable.

'I don't think so.'

It was quite obvious that Ryan was really drunk as he struggled to get his phone from his pocket. Finally he freed it.

'Ah come on, baby, we can take some great porno shots,' he said, and to Roo and Danielle's horror, he aimed the phone at Danielle's breasts.

'Stop it,' Danielle said, though that did nothing to deter Ryan from trying to get a shot.

Theo stepped forward and snatched the phone from Ryan's hand. He looked furious. 'You know Ryan, consent is an important thing in a relationship, but so is not being a complete dick.'

Ryan laughed. 'The big boss just called me a dick. Come on Danielle, let's go. I know just the spot to show you my d—'

'Danielle,' Theo interrupted. 'We're driving back into town now. We can give you a lift if you want.'

Danielle looked between Ryan and Theo and nodded. 'That would be great, thank you.'

'What?' Ryan looked completely shocked.

'I'm going home.'

Theo swiped Ryan's phone a few times. 'He didn't manage to get any photos.'

He handed back the phone then turned back to Danielle. 'Come on, we'll take you home.'

They started walking down the path towards the car, leaving Ryan looking stunned in the middle of the woods.

Roo squeezed Danielle's hand. 'Are you OK?'

'Yes, I just feel a bit foolish. I bumped into him in the pub tonight and after a few drinks he was all smooth and charming. When he suggested we come up here, it seemed like a good idea at the time.'

Theo opened the back door for Danielle and she got in. Then he opened the passenger door for Roo before climbing in the driver's seat.

'I'm sorry to interrupt your... evening,' Danielle said.

'There was no interruption,' Theo said. 'We really were working. And I would prefer to know you were safe so it's no problem to drive you home.'

They fell into silence.

Roo bit her lip, not sure what to say. They could hardly talk about the squirrels or what Theo had planned to do to her when they got to his house. And she hadn't been on too friendly terms with Danielle ever since Roo had sort of got promoted because she knew Theo, at least in Danielle's eyes. And now they had been seen by two colleagues at a well-known local sex hang-out, everyone at work would be sure to know that too. Could she ask Danielle not to say anything, or would that make it obvious there was something going on?

'Are you going to the ball, Danielle?' Roo asked, trying to fill the awkward silence.

'Yes, I'm going with a few friends. Are you going?'

Roo cleared her throat because she'd promised Theo a dance at the ball, even if it was a secret dance. But would it look odd that she was technically arriving alone? She couldn't exactly arrive with Theo.

'Umm yes, I'm looking forward to it.'

'Who are you going with?'

She cringed, knowing that question had been coming.

'You're going with Orla and Fern, aren't you?' Theo supplied, helpfully.

'Yes, there's a group of us going,' Roo said, relieved she'd got out of that.

There was silence again. Roo couldn't help wondering what Danielle made of finding her boss and her colleague in a local sex spot.

'Thank you for coming with me to see the waterfall,' Theo said, formally.

Roo smirked despite her worries. There was something quite sexy about Theo's professional formal persona. Or was it just that she found everything about this man sexy, even the way he looked after squirrels?

'I think we got some good photos to help with the design of *A Knight's Tail*,' Theo went on.

'Yes. I'm glad you suggested it. It's important to me to get it right,' Roo said.

They fell silent again as they drove into the town.

'Where do you live?' Theo asked Danielle.

'Lovegrove Lane.'

'Yes I know it.'

They drove for a few minutes before Theo pulled into her road.

'This is me,' Danielle said.

Theo stopped the car.

'Thank you for the lift,' Danielle said, getting out.

'Danielle, you're an attractive, brilliant and smart woman. You can do a hell of a lot better than Ryan Hancock,' Theo said.

Roo smiled.

Danielle nodded. 'You're right, I can. Thanks again.'

Theo nodded and she shut the door. Roo gave her a little wave. He waited until she was safely inside her house before he drove off.

'You are an incredible man, Theo Lucas.'

'Why?'

'Because you're a gentleman and a hero.'

She was definitely falling for this man, or had she already fallen?

'I think your rose-tinted glasses are firmly on when you're looking at me. But if you let me take you back to my place, I'll show you how I'm definitely not a gentleman at all.'

Her stomach clenched with need and desire. 'I'm looking forward to it.'

But she couldn't help worrying about what they would have to face the next day, or rather what she would have to face. Theo would be fine in his office, not exposed to any of it.

'Everyone will know about us being seen in Morgy Hill Woods,' Roo said. 'If Danielle doesn't say anything, then Ryan will. You just ruined his night of hot passion.'

'I know, I'm so sorry. I'm trying my best to present a professional front to everyone, but they've all made their own minds up about us and that hug in the meeting room wouldn't have helped. Now this will make everything a million times worse for you. We're a small company and the CEO dating an employee is a hot bit of gossip. I'm not sure what we can do.'

'It's not your fault. It just makes it really uncomfortable at work. I've tried keeping my head down, I've lied and that doesn't make me feel good and I have to work with these people every day. Thank goodness I'll be getting my own office soon, but I know it will be awkward as hell whenever I need to go back down to the main office to liaise with the design department.'

She rubbed a hand over her eyes. There really wasn't any coming back from this. No matter what happened now, she was always going to be the woman that slept with the boss and lied about it. No one would ever trust her again. And everyone would always think she was getting preferential treatment. And what would Nate make of it when the truth finally came out? She had to work with him every day.

'Are you thinking if we broke up then you wouldn't have to deal with this anymore?' Theo asked.

She looked at him in horror. 'That didn't even cross my mind. We're in this together, we will fight this together. It's frustrating and upsetting and I don't like it but I would sail the roughest seas to be with you. Breaking up with you is not an option. Worst-case scenario, we run away together to a little uninhabited island filled with hedgehogs, squirrels and foxes that we can feed and look after every day, and we can just forget the world.'

'That sounds pretty perfect to me.'

CHAPTER SEVENTEEN

Roo walked into work the next day almost cringing as she waited for the onslaught. Theo had left early again after kissing her thoroughly goodbye, which had made her float with joy before she remembered she had to face the Morgy Hill Woods gossip when she got to work. That had made her come back down to earth with a bump.

She walked over to Nate but she was aware of giggling and people watching her and whispering about her as she moved through the office. She tried to tell herself she was being paranoid and that they weren't whispering about her at all, but she could see they were all looking at her.

Nate excitedly patted the chair next to him. 'Oh honey, everyone is talking about you and Theo being caught at Morgy Hill Woods last night. Is it true?'

'We were there, but not in a romantic capacity. We were working.'

'That's not what everyone is saying,' Nate said, sympathetically.

'But it is the truth.'

Roo sighed. They'd all had their suspicions that something was going on between her and Theo, especially after the hug in the meeting room the other day and now it was confirmed, at least in their eyes, because they'd been having passionate sex in the aptly named Orgy Woods. But even that wasn't true.

'Taking photos of the waterfall in the moonlight sounds very romantic though,' Nate said.

'It wasn't romantic. Theo talked to me about the rocks and getting the texture right. And how he wanted the water to sparkle.'

'I'm sure he was the model of professionalism,' Nate said, not sounding like he believed her for one second. And truth be told she probably wouldn't believe her either. 'I'm going to get a coffee. Do you want one?'

'Tea please. Thanks,' Roo said.

Nate got up and ambled over to the machine.

Danielle got up and came over. 'I didn't say anything to anyone, thought you should know that. But no prizes for guessing who has been laughing and talking about it all morning.'

'I'd like to say thank you for your discretion but there wasn't anything to be discreet about.'

'I believe you. Theo was nothing but formal with you last night. There was no chemistry there at all.'

Roo studied her. 'Are you OK? Has Ryan been saying anything about you?'

'Yeah, that I'm a tease. But I can live with that. If I'd slept with him I'm sure he would be laughing and talking about that instead. At least I can keep my chin up. I still have my dignity.'

'Yes you do. You're well out of that.'

Danielle nodded. 'Thank you again for taking me home last night.'

'No problem at all.'

Danielle gave her a small smile and went back to her desk.

Roo logged into her laptop.

'So, you really were at Orgy Hill Woods last night?' Brooke asked.

Roo looked up and could see the look of distaste on Brooke's face. Meryl turned to listen too.

'We were there for work,' Roo insisted.

Meryl's nose wrinkled with disgust. 'I always thought Theo was a bit of a gentleman. I know he's slept with quite a few women, but he's always had a reputation for being respectful. Now it seems he's as sleazy as Ryan is.'

'I know, can you imagine going on a date with Theo and he takes you up there for sex. How disappointing,' Brooke said.

'We didn't have sex,' Roo said. 'We didn't even kiss up there. That was absolutely not part of our plan. It wasn't a date. We were discussing using a waterfall in one of the scenes of the new book and Theo said he imagined it like Morgy Hill Falls. I said I hadn't seen it and he offered to show it to me after work. It was not romantic. He didn't try anything when we were up there. We took photos of the waterfall and discussed work. That was it.'

Meryl and Brooke exchanged glances of disbelief. She didn't really care that they didn't believe her. In any other circumstances, she would think this was funny. But the fact that they thought that Theo was sleazy and creepy really upset her.

'Can you imagine if anyone from work asked to meet you at *Orgy* Falls after dark, I'd be running a hundred miles in the opposite direction,' Brooke said. 'But our boss? Eww.'

'Yes, I'd slap a sexual harassment complaint on him if that was me,' Meryl said.

'He was the perfect gentleman the whole time. He even insisted on taking Danielle home when she realised she'd made a mistake going there with Ryan.'

They clearly didn't believe her.

She tried to focus on her laptop, opening up the pages she'd been working on. She wasn't really sure what else she could say. But she could hear people talking about it and not even that quietly. None of it was nice.

She had to tell the truth about what they were doing. Well, sort of. She couldn't take back the lie about the falls featuring in the new book and she couldn't tell everyone what they were doing up there with the squirrels but she could tell them about the work they were doing for Little Paws.

She stood up, climbed on the desk and putting two fingers in her mouth she let out an ear-piercing whistle with predictable results. The room fell silent as everyone looked over.

'I'm sure you've all had a good laugh over the juicy gossip that Theo took me to Morgy Hill Woods last night. Well it ends here. While there were several cars with couples in them parked up there when we arrived, that was not the purpose of our visit. Many of you know of Theo's involvement with wildlife rescue. Last night he was up there to release some fox cubs. Foxes are a divisive subject for many, especially for people who own chickens and small furry animals such as rabbits or guinea pigs so it's not something he talks about to many people but that's the truth. Yesterday while working on *A Knight's Tail*, we talked about one of the scenes being set around a waterfall and Theo said that he imagined it being like Morgy Hill Falls. I said I'd never been. He said that as he was going last night anyway to release the fox cubs, I could come with him and we could look at the falls. We went to the wildlife hospital, picked up the fox cubs and took them to the woods to release them. We have to release them in the spot that they were found, he didn't just randomly choose Morgy Hill Woods. While we were there we went to the waterfall and took some photos of it to help with the design of *A Knight's Tail*. He did not kiss me and we absolutely did not have sex up there.'

There was silence in the room and she knew that half the people here wouldn't believe a word she said.

She looked round and saw Charlie and Theo standing in the doorway watching her and her heart sank. Charlie must be regretting the day he ever got in touch with her and offered her a job. She had done nothing but cause trouble since she'd got here. And what would Theo think about this outburst? He didn't look pleased at all. Neither of them did.

'Miss Clarke, can I have a word,' Theo said.

She sighed. Climbed down from the desk, grabbed her laptop and walked over to them.

Theo held the door open for her and she followed him upstairs in silence. He gestured for her to go in his office and she walked in and he closed the door behind him. Then he cupped her face in his hands and kissed her. 'You are the most spectacular, incredible woman I've ever met. I love you.'

Her heart leapt as he kissed her again.

She pulled back. 'You... You love me.'

He grinned. 'Completely and utterly.'

Then he kissed her again.

Just then, there was a knock on the door and they broke apart.

'Come in,' Theo said.

Charlie stepped inside and closed the door. 'Aurora, I'm so sorry you're going through this. I know you and Theo are together, but I haven't told anyone. I'm afraid the possibility that our CEO is dating the new girl is the most exciting thing that's happened round here since the managing director started dating the lead designer. I know what you're going through, I know how upsetting it is. Is there anything I can do to help?'

Roo shook her head. 'I just hate what they are saying about Theo and the frustrating thing is we weren't having sex in Morgy Hill Woods last night. We really were up there releasing wildlife.'

'I know, Theo told me what happened with the foxes and Danielle and Ryan seeing you. I can send a very stern email about gossiping in the office but it won't stop it. We can't stop people's opinions.'

'I know.'

Charlie sighed. 'We'll make sure your office next door is ready as soon as possible. At least that will stop you hearing some of the comments. And maybe it will die down a bit once you're up here.'

In reality, she knew this would never go away. Although she had an idea to make it stop once and for all but she didn't relish the thought. There had to be something else she could do.

'Thanks Charlie.'

He nodded. 'I'll let you get on with your work.'

He walked out, leaving the door open.

Theo went to close it after him, but she shook her head. She was determined that if anyone walked past, they would see nothing but professionalism in here.

Roo walked towards Pet Protagonist later that night. She hadn't told Theo she loved him and she knew she should have said it back because she did, she loved him with everything she had. She'd just felt scared about putting her feelings out there, as if by telling him she loved him would somehow jinx it and it would come to a crashing end.

This was too important to her to lose. But she had to trust in him, and them.

Regardless of her outburst earlier that day, the gossip about her and Theo had continued and it had made her die inside listening to people talk about Theo like he was some creepy sleazeball for taking her to Morgy Hill Woods. She had kept her head down and hadn't engaged with it hoping it would die down, but it was all everyone could talk about. Theo was such a good, kind, decent man, he didn't deserve that kind of disrespect. She knew she had to do something to stop it and when she'd got back to her little beach hut, she had reached a decision that made her heart break.

She opened the door to the office and could see the printing room was in complete darkness. She walked upstairs to the main office. She knew Theo was staying late because he had a video call with someone in California and as they were eight hours behind, he had to stay late to talk to them. She was surprised to see that there wasn't anyone in the main office either. Most people worked nine to five but there were those that preferred to get in late on some days and work late to make up for it, but there was no one there tonight. She went up to the top floor and could see all the offices and meeting rooms up there were in darkness too, but the lights were on in Theo's office and the door was open.

She popped her head round the door and could see he was busy typing away on the computer. She knocked softly on the door and he looked up a smile spreading across his face as soon as he saw her.

'Hey, I was just finishing this email and then I was going to come and see you. You didn't have to come back here to meet me.'

She swallowed. 'I'm here in a professional capacity.'

He frowned and she handed him the letter.

He looked at it in confusion and then opened it. He looked at her in horror. 'You're leaving?'

She nodded even though she felt sick inside. She loved this job, she didn't want to leave.

'Why are you leaving? Is the job not challenging enough for you? We can make it more challenging, we can give you more responsibilities. Whatever you need, we can adapt the job for you.'

She shook her head. 'I love this job. I've been so happy this past week or so, I love doing what I'm doing.'

His face cleared. 'It's the gossip about us. You don't want to put up with that anymore. You tell me who it is and I swear I'll sack every single one of them.'

'It's everyone Theo, everyone is talking about us.'

'I know it must be hard to deal with that all day but it will die down soon. And when you have your own office you won't have to hear it.'

'You don't understand.'

'No I don't.'

'They're talking about you. They're saying you're creepy and disgusting because you took me to Morgy Hill Woods to have sex. You are the most incredible, kind, generous man I have ever met and I can't bear for them to have that opinion of you when you are so decent and wonderful. They're only talking about this because we both work here. If I wasn't here, there wouldn't be anything to gossip about.'

'I don't care what they think about me, I don't care what anyone thinks or says about me, the only person's opinion I care about is you. Why do you care what they say?'

'Because I love you.'

He stared at her in shock. She hadn't meant to blurt it out like that but now it was out there and she couldn't take it back.

She cleared her throat. 'I'm so in love with you it's like my heart has swollen in my chest to accommodate my feelings for you. I have never felt the way I feel right now for anyone before. And it kills me to hear people saying horrible things about you when they're simply not true. Before I came here, people respected you, the women all thought you were a gentleman, which you are and I've ruined all of that for you. I need to protect you and this is the only way I can see to stop it.'

A smile spread across his face and he stood up. 'Firstly, if they genuinely believe I'm that kind of person then they will think that if you leave or stay and I honestly don't care what they think.' He moved over to the door, closed it then locked it and she frowned. 'Secondly,' he took her face in his hands. 'I love you so much it consumes me and there is nothing that we can't face when we're together.'

He kissed her and the way he did she knew instantly why he'd locked the door, despite the whole building being empty.

He gathered her in his arms, holding her tight against

him. He trailed his mouth across her cheek to her neck, whispering that he loved her as his mouth passed by her ear and it made her feel weak.

'Is this crazy that we feel this way, so quickly?' Roo said, as he slid her dress strap over her shoulder, his mouth following it down her arm.

'Sometimes we need a little crazy in our lives.'

She knew he was right, she'd take this kind of crazy in her life any day.

He slid her other strap down and her dress slithered to the floor. She wrapped her arms round his neck, pressing herself up against him as she kissed him hard but she was surprised when he slid one hand inside her bra running his fingers across her breast. She gasped against his mouth.

She quickly struggled to get his shirt off and giggled against his lips when one of the buttons pinged off in her haste.

'I'm taking that out of your pay.'

She laughed as she pushed the shirt off his shoulders and it joined her dress on the floor.

He lifted her and she wrapped her legs around him as he carried her to his desk. He sat her on the edge, kissing her as he removed her bra and knickers.

He moved back, undoing his trousers. 'Say it again.'

She smiled. 'I love you.'

'Christ, no one, outside of Carrie, Shay and Fern has ever said that to me in my life. I never realised how much I needed to hear it, or how much I wanted to hear it from you more than anyone.'

'I'll tell you every day, a thousand times and I will mean it every time. I will shout it from the rooftops if that's what you want but right now I need something from you.'

She ached for him, felt her need for him bubbling beneath the surface.

He grinned and suddenly swept all the paperwork from the desk onto the floor. She really hoped none of that was important.

'Lie back.'

She lay down on the hard surface and cried out when he suddenly kissed her right between her legs. It was such a wonderful, delicious shock she arched off the desk. He moved his mouth lower capturing that exact spot where she needed him, driving her wild and within seconds she was falling apart, shaking and screaming out his name and telling him she loved him over and over again.

As she tried to steady her breathing as she came down from her high, she leaned up on her elbows to watch him strip completely naked. He slid her back across the desk and then climbed up on top of her, pinning her to the desk with his glorious weight as he kissed her.

He pulled back slightly and reached into his drawer to grab a condom. 'I love this desk,' Theo said, dealing with the condom. 'If I ever leave, I'm taking this desk with me and installing it in my house so we can do this every damn day.'

'You might have to build an extension on your tiny cottage to fit this massive desk in your house.'

'It would totally be worth it.' He gathered her legs around his hips and the next thing he was inside her.

She stroked his face as he stared down at her in wonder. 'I love you.'

He smiled. 'I love you too.'

He kissed her, slowly moving against her, adoring her body with every touch and she almost laughed that she had been so worried about saying those words because she knew with him, she had finally found her forever.

Theo was sat in his office chair with Roo sat on his lap, a blanket he'd grabbed off the back of the sofa wrapped around her and he couldn't stop kissing her.

Finally he pulled away slightly, stroking her face. 'I'm so happy right now, I can't even tell you.'

She smiled up at him and then frowned. 'But what about what everyone is saying about you?'

He shrugged. 'I honestly don't care. And you leaving isn't going to change what they think of me. You won't have to hear it anymore, but they'll still think it and say it.' He leaned forward and picked up her letter of notice that was miraculously still on his desk after almost everything else had ended up on the floor. He ripped it in half.

'You can't do that, it's a legal document.'

He ripped it in half again. 'I'm not accepting it. It won't solve anything so why leave a job you love?'

'But the gossip is more exciting because the CEO is sleeping with one of his employees. If I wasn't here, it would just be CEO has a girlfriend and no one would really care about that. Let me do this for you.'

'Absolutely not. Besides, it would still be creepy, sleazy CEO has a girlfriend, if that's what they choose to believe about last night. I suspect most people don't think that, it's just a juicy piece of gossip. But I've worked with most of these people for over a year. If they genuinely believe that's the kind of man I am, it says a lot more about them than me.'

'But how can you not care?'

'I grew up being told I was worthless and hundreds of other insults my birth mum threw at me. And that's not true. I am worth something to the right people. Those are the only opinions I care about. Look, I think we tell them we're together. The summer ball is Friday night and if we go together there will be no doubt in anyone's mind that we are dating. To have that confirmed will be the biggest gossip, more so than a possible dalliance in Morgy Hill Woods. Next week you'll be in your own office with Nate and they will be all gossiped out by the end of the week. Once we are open about it, there will be no more suspicions, or excitement. It will just die down and go away.'

Roo sighed and he kissed the frown above her eyes.

'It will be OK, I promise. Come to the ball with me. Let's show them how much we're in love and how happy we are together. There can be no hate for us after that.'

She had tried denying their relationship, she had tried skirting around it, she had tried keeping her head down and not engaging and she had tried standing on the desk to make a big announcement and nothing had made any difference. Maybe it really was time to tell the truth.

'I'll come to the ball with you.'

He smiled and kissed her.

Her stomach rumbled and he laughed. 'Let's go home and I'll cook us something to eat. Then I'm going to make love to you in my bed and I'll make sure all of your worries are the furthest thing from your mind.'

She laughed. 'I like the sound of that.'

CHAPTER EIGHTEEN

The following night Roo and Theo were working at Little Paws. It was something of a relief to be able to work together without people staring and giggling at them every time Theo came over to her to discuss work. The comments about Theo and Morgy Hill Woods had continued. Roo hadn't bothered addressing any of them, she'd just kept her head down and focused on work.

Theo went to put three little hoglets back in their cage just as someone rang the bell out in reception. She went outside to see a man carrying a box.

'Hello, how can I help you?' Roo said.

'Hi, I've been doing some landscaping work in my garden and I disturbed a nest or burrow or whatever you want to call it. Anyway, I found these baby rabbits. I just took the top layer of soil off and there they were. It didn't even look like a proper hole, they were just under the surface. I covered them back up and kept an eye on them all day but there has been no sign of Mum and I wonder if I scared her off. I didn't know what to do so I brought them here.'

'You did the right thing keeping an eye on them for a while and then bringing them in.' Roo peered in the box he'd put down on the reception desk and saw four tiny little rabbits, cowering in the corner. Their eyes were all open which was a good indication of their age. They'd had very similar sized rabbits brought in a few days before and Theo had told her then that they were old enough to be left alone. They'd been released the day after they'd been brought in. She put the lid back on. She certainly wasn't an expert though so she'd let someone else make that decision.

'Let me just take a few details off you, including your address. If they are fit, healthy and independent enough to be left alone, we like to release them in the place they were found if that's OK with you.'

'Yes of course.'

Roo moved to the laptop. 'Could I also ask if you would mind giving a small donation. At the moment we are trying to raise funds to buy this place off our landlord who wants to sell the property. If we can't save it, there will be no place left to bring baby rabbits to, or any other sick or injured animal.'

He looked at her with wide eyes. 'I guess his name is mud round here.'

'He's not the most popular that's for sure. It takes a special kind of heartless person to want to close down a wildlife hospital.'

Just then Theo walked into the reception. 'Adam, hey, what are you doing here?'

Roo's heart leapt. 'You're Adam? As in—'

'The cruel and heartless landlord you were just telling me about, yes that's me.'

Theo's eyes widened as he looked at her.

'I'm so sorry, I didn't realise.'

'It's OK,' Adam said, looking like it definitely wasn't OK. 'I knew the decision to sell wasn't going to be a popular one but it is just business at the end of the day and I have to do what's best for me and my family.'

'And you're clearly not heartless,' Roo said. 'If you care enough to bring in these baby rabbits.'

'I'm sure there's a heart buried in there somewhere,' Adam said, dryly.

Theo moved to the box to look at the rabbits. 'Ah these are only a few weeks old, you were right to bring them in.'

Roo frowned slightly. That was almost the exact opposite of what Theo had told her a few days before and those had been smaller than the ones Adam had brought in. Although Theo probably didn't want to make Adam feel bad for bringing in the rabbits when he should have left them alone.

'Let's just make sure we've got all the details of where exactly you found them,' Theo said.

Theo took a few moments to take Adam's description of where he found them and then Adam turned to go.

'While you're here, do you want to have a look around?' Theo said.

'What?'

'You've not been here before, have you? If nothing else it might give you an idea of the kind of land you are selling. It might help you make decisions about any offers that come in.'

Adam rubbed his hand across his jaw. 'Sure, OK.'

Theo stepped back to let him in to the examination room. 'Come this way.'

Adam walked through, Theo followed him and Roo was left cursing her stupid big mouth.

'This is the examination room,' Theo said. 'We'll assess, treat and feed all the animals in here until they are ready to be weaned onto solids. Once they are on solids we try to keep as hands off as possible which will help with their rehabilitation into the wild. I'll take you down to the cages now where the baby animals are kept before they are moved outside to the enclosures that are more in keeping with their natural environment. With us here in the cages we have four sets of baby hedgehogs or hoglets, three baby foxes, two baby barn owls, a slow worm, a shrew, a vole, an adder and a pole cat.'

'I've lived here all my life and I've never seen some of those animals before, especially in the wild. I don't even know what a shrew looks like.'

'I'll show you,' Theo said.

Ordinarily, he would never take the animals out of the cages just to show people, but he thought Adam might actually start to feel some kind of empathy for the animals if he could see them. He wanted Adam to see the importance of this place and seeing rare animals like shrews and voles might help with that. Theo had no idea where Adam stood with telling the council about their illegal squirrel dealings. Adam certainly seemed calmer today but there had been no word from him since his outburst on Monday night, three days before.

He put a glove on to minimise the contact with the shrew and carefully lifted it out the cage. 'This is a common shrew, but despite the name it is quite rare to see them. They are a protected species.'

'Oh look at its nose. That's amazing. I've never seen anything like it.'

'They are complete characters.' Theo carefully put it back and it disappeared back under the leaves in a huff at being disturbed.

'That's our vole,' Theo pointed at another cage where the vole was sitting quite happily chewing on a bit of fruit. 'They're a protected species too and on the endangered list. So it's important that we're able to rehabilitate them and release them back into the wild.'

Adam peered through the cage and smiled. It was clear he had an affection for animals too, the fact he brought the baby rabbits in today gave Theo some hope.

'Did you say you have an adder too?' Adam asked.

'A baby one. It appears to have been attacked by a bird of prey.' Theo pointed to the small snake curled up inside a log. 'But the wound isn't too bad and it's possible the snake might have bitten the bird to get away.'

Adam bent down to have a look.

'And all of these will be returned to the wild?'

'That's our intention with every animal that comes through that door. Sometimes the injuries are too severe, we had a mole die the other day after being attacked by a cat. Sometimes they aren't fit for release in the wild and they go to specialists who will look after them for the rest of their life. But the majority of the animals we look after are returned to the wild. Shall I take you down to the outside enclosures?'

Adam cleared his throat. 'Yes, it would be good to see the quality of the land.'

'Follow me.'

Theo took him outside. 'Out here we'll have some of the babies when they are big enough and independent enough to be outside. We bring them here so they can adapt to their natural environment before they are released. Right now it's a little early in the season to have too many babies out here but the enclosures will soon fill up as the babies get bigger. Right now most of our guests out here are adults with injuries. We have an otter, an adult fox, a hare, two badgers, three hedgehogs, various birds, two rats, and a few bats.'

'That's quite the mix.'

'Good people like you bring them in and we look after them, no matter what they are. Some are hit by cars, some attacked by other wildlife, some just get sick or get injured falling out of trees or flying into fences or windows. So we do what we can.'

Adam was quiet for a moment. 'I'm not sure I'm a good person.'

'You are. Anyone who cares enough to rescue baby animals is good in my book. I'm sorry for what Roo said. I think the possibility we might lose this place has hit us all hard. Especially Violet.'

Adam made a noise of disapproval. 'I never liked her.'

'What? Violet is lovely. What is there to not like about Violet?'

'I don't know. She and my grandad got together not even a year after my nan had died. It just felt so disrespectful. Nan and Grandad were together for fifty years and then in walks Violet. And the worst of it was that Violet was Nan's friend. It felt like such a big betrayal.'

'I don't think a relationship was on either of their radars. Joseph spent a lot of time here helping to build the enclosures and then helping out once it was up and running because he was so lonely at home without your nan. He just wanted a project to keep himself busy. I don't think either of them planned to fall in love. But they did and whatever you might think about Violet, she made your grandad very happy in the last few years of his life.'

Adam sighed. 'He did love it here, I know that. I saw the photo album you deliberately left at my house and he looked so happy caring for the animals. And with her.'

'I started working here to honour his memory as I knew how important it was to him,' Theo said. 'I never expected to love it so much. The work we do here is so important and I want to be a part of it.'

Adam didn't say anything for a while so Theo kept pointing out various animals. But finally he spoke.

'I'm sorry for the way I acted on Monday. That was unnecessary and over the top.'

'Mate, you've been under a lot of stress with the house and now a baby on the way. It wasn't our intention to make life harder for you, we were just trying to protect Little Paws.'

'I know. I did speak to my estate agent about splitting the land into two or three lots but he seemed to think I'd get more money leaving it as it is, one big sale. But I spoke to another estate agent, and he said it would be far easier to sell the land over the river separately to the rest of it. I know it's early days, but I've only had one person interested in the property so far and he said he wasn't going to put an offer in, so I think your part of the land is putting people off or the old farmhouse is. I don't know what to do for the best.'

Theo chewed his lip as he thought. 'I still think the land over the river is your cash cow and I'm not just saying that because a separate sale would benefit me. It's flat, got good road access, great views. It's perfect for development.'

'I've been turned down twice for planning permission. Paid a small fortune for architects to draw up some plans.'

'Did the plans include development on this land?'

'Yes, on both sides.'

'That's what your problem is. Building houses on such a steep bit of land could cause all sorts of issues. Adapt the plans to just show development on the other side of the river and see if they go for that, Councillor Bishop said you most likely would get planning permission if you just did that side. If you can get planning permission for that part of the land you'd probably be able to sell that for the same price you're selling the whole thing.'

'Do you think so?'

'Yes definitely. And the offer still stands for me to buy this land off you. That would be a very quick sale if you wanted to go ahead with that. At least that would give you some immediate money to help with the renovations of the farmhouse and to pay the architect to update the plans for over the river.'

'I'm thinking about it.'

Theo nodded. 'We're looking at other options too.'

'What does that mean?'

'We're looking for a new location to move Little Paws to. My brother is researching different places. He's found somewhere about fifteen miles from here so it's not ideal and it's smaller but it would be cheaper than if I was to buy this place off you. We're going to look at it tomorrow. But I'm sure you'd still get offers for this place once we'd left. I'm sure someone would find a use for it. Some farmer might pay for grazing land.'

Theo saw worry cross Adam's face at the very real possibility that no one else would touch this land with a barge pole, especially now with the tree preservation order in place, although he wasn't going to bring that up again.

'So you're basically saying don't think about it too long,' Adam said.

'I'm not rushing you. Like you said, you have to do what's best for you and your family. And we have to do what's best for Little Paws. We only have five months until we have to be out of here. If we agree a deal tomorrow on this other land, and the sale goes through very quickly, say six or eight weeks, then we'd have three months to build the new enclosures and get the animals transferred over there before we have to leave here. We have to move quickly. And I totally appreciate you might want to wait to see if you can get planning permission on the other land first before you decide whether to split the sale into different lots, but that could take many months and sadly we don't have that luxury of waiting. It took nine months to get this place up and running so we can't afford to wait around hoping for a good outcome.'

Adam was silent and Theo hoped he had given him something to think about, not just about selling the land to him separately, but about how important Little Paws was. But they did need a decision fairly quickly so they knew where they stood: could they stay or would they have to go all in on finding somewhere else? It was true that Shay had found a place fifteen miles away but it wasn't suitable for their needs and far smaller but land for sale without any kind of planning permission was a lot harder to find so they might not have any choice.

'I'll talk to Marilyn and have a decision for you by tonight,' Adam said.

'I'd really appreciate that. At least then we know one way or another. I'll speak to Violet about holding out on offering on this other place until we hear from you.'

They'd arrived back at the front of the building.

Adam nodded. 'Thank you for showing me around.' He

turned to go but then turned back. 'And umm... would you keep me posted about the baby rabbits.'

'Of course. And... what about the squirrels?'

'What squirrels? I don't know anything about any squirrels.'

'Thank you.'

Adam gave him a small smile and left.

Theo let out a heavy breath. He only hoped what he'd said had been enough.

Theo was pacing around his house waiting for the phone call from Adam. It was approaching nine o'clock and there still hadn't been any word. Roo was curled up on his sofa, reading a book or at least attempting to, but he knew she was having trouble concentrating on it, she had gone back and read the same page two or three times.

It had been such a relief to hear Adam didn't intend to pursue contacting the council over their illegal squirrel handling. They just needed him to agree to sell the land separately now.

The phone suddenly rang, and he looked at the screen and saw that it was Adam.

He sat down next to Roo, answered it, and put it on loudspeaker so Roo could hear. She took his hand.

'Hi Adam.'

'Hi, I've had a chat with Marilyn and we're happy to go ahead with selling the land at Little Paws separately.'

He glanced at Roo and knew her huge smile was mirrored on his face too.

'Adam, this is wonderful news, you don't know what it means.'

'Yeah, I do. I could see how much it meant to you today. It's something you were so passionate about. You're an advocate for those animals and we need people like you in the world to fight for them, even those that you're not supposed to fight for. Which is why I have a condition of sale.'

Theo frowned.

'I will sell the land, but I will only sell it to you. The deeds will be in your name not Violet's.'

Theo thought about it for a minute. Little Paws was Violet's, she had started it all, she had got it where it was today. Could he really take it away from her?

'I know you think this is mean and petty because I don't like the woman, and maybe, if I'm honest, that's probably part of it, but in truth, she's what eighty-two, eighty-three? She might not be here in ten or fifteen years and I want the legacy of Little Paws to continue long after she's gone. I don't want there to be any complications after she's gone where someone else could take that land. I know you will look after it and the animals in your care for many, many years.'

Theo chewed his lip. He did make a fair point. As much as he didn't want to think about Violet's death, she wouldn't be around forever.

'OK. I can accept those terms. What price will you be selling the land for?'

'I spoke to my estate agent as soon as I left you. I asked him what he thought your land is worth as grazing or arable land. He thinks around one eighty-five to one ninety. Is that doable?'

'Yes.'

'He's going to come first thing tomorrow morning and have a proper look at the place, I presume that won't be a problem?'

'Not at all.'

'I've instructed him to take down the listing for the whole land and once he has a price he'll create a listing for the land at Little Paws which will probably be live by lunch. I'll contact you when it is and you can make a formal offer through them.'

'OK, thank you, really. This is fantastic news and I really do think financially this will be the best thing for you too.'

'I do too. I'm going to use some of the money to pay the architect to tweak the plans to just show development over the river. We want to take the time to get it right so we get the planning permission and sell it at a decent price but the rest will be used to do the farmhouse up.'

'I think that's a great idea.'

'OK, well, I'll be in touch tomorrow.'

'Thanks again Adam.'

They said their goodbyes and hung up.

Roo squealed with excitement and hugged him. 'I'm so happy for you.'

He held her tight. 'I'm happy too. I'm happy for Violet

and Lizzie and all the staff. Little Paws means so much to so many people.'

'It's a bit weird about the Violet clause though isn't it?'

'He doesn't like her because he feels she muscled in on Joseph too soon after his nan's death, so I think this is part of that. But I guess he has a point that Violet won't be around forever, as much as we'd like her to be. Selling it to me will ensure its legacy for many years to come.'

'I don't like the idea of planning for Violet's death but it does make sense. Do you think Violet will be OK with that?'

'I think she will be delighted that we can save Little Paws and we don't have to move. And she will understand that keeping it in my name helps to protect it. But let's give her a call and tell her the good news.'

He quickly called Violet and after a few rings she answered.

'Theo, is everything OK?'

'Yes, I didn't wake you, did I?'

'Oh no, I was just reading a few more chapters of the latest book from my favourite crime author.'

'Well, I have good news. Adam has agreed to sell the land at Little Paws separately to the land over the river. He is going to try again to get planning permission for the land over the river and if it's a success he'll put the land up for sale for a price that reflects that but it's completely separate to any deal he makes for the Little Paws land.'

'Oh that is good news. How much does he want for it?'

'Violet, I'm going to buy it. He's told me a price that I'm happy with and I'm going to buy it.'

Violet's voice caught in her throat. 'Oh Theo, no I can't let you do that, you work hard for your money and—'

'Little Paws is important to me, the work we do, the work I do there, it's something I'm really passionate about and I want to secure its legacy for many years to come.'

Violet was silent for a moment and when she spoke her voice wobbled. 'Theo, thank you, so much, I don't know what to say.'

'Adam did have a condition of sale though, he wants to make sure there can be no claims on the land in years to come, when you're no longer with us, he wants to ensure Little Paws can still continue. So the deeds will be under my name. The rescue centre will be mine.'

Violet was silent for a moment.

'It's still yours Violet, you're still in charge, this is just a formality.'

'It makes perfect sense,' Violet said. 'And we need some young blood in the place, help turn it around, make it better. You've got a good head on your shoulders. I for one will be excited to see what you do with the place.'

He was silent for a moment as he digested her words. He was going to be responsible for Little Paws, going forward and that was something he was going to take very seriously. He cleared his throat.

'Well, I don't want to celebrate just yet until he's formally accepted my offer but it looks really good. I thought we'd announce it at the ball tomorrow night, tell all the staff and volunteers the good news.'

'Great idea. Thank you, Theo, you've lifted such a huge weight from my shoulders.'

'It's my pleasure. The estate agent will need full access tomorrow morning, nine o'clock.'

'I will be there to welcome him myself.'

Theo grinned at that. 'Thanks Violet.'

He said goodbye and hung up.

'I'm so excited for you,' Roo said, giving him another hug. 'Little Paws makes you happy and you need to fill your life with the things that make you happy.'

He held her tight and smiled. She was so right.

CHAPTER NINETEEN

'I love this office,' Nate said, standing at the window of their new office, staring out at the sea. 'Look at that view.'

Theo and Charlie had spent the morning getting desks out of the downstairs storeroom and moving them upstairs to the room next to Theo's, making a huge desk area in the middle of the room so they could spread out all their illustrations. Theo had fitted two desktop computers and phones in there and they'd just been told to get their stuff and move in.

And while Roo could appreciate the stunning sea view and she loved that she would no longer have to hear the gossip anymore, or what they thought about her getting her own office, she kept on looking through the open interconnecting door into Theo's office. She hadn't had a chance to talk to Theo that day to get a progress report. She knew Theo was waiting for the listing for the land at Little Paws to appear so he could make a formal offer. She couldn't wait to hear that everything was confirmed. She felt really nervous waiting, wondering if Adam would change his mind, or if the price would be more than Adam had originally said. He knew how desperate Theo and the staff at Little Paws were to get the land; if he was an arse, he could try and charge a lot more knowing Theo would probably pay it.

'Of course the view in there isn't bad either,' Nate said.

She looked up and saw that Nate had spotted her watching Theo, although not for the reasons he thought.

'Sorry, we're waiting for an important call.'

Nate sat down. 'We?'

She bit her lip. Nate had been really supportive and had stuck up for her against Meryl, Brooke and the others that had gossiped or commented about her. She had successfully managed to avoid directly lying to everyone about her relationship with Theo, apart from Nate and she felt bad about that. As they were outing themselves that night at the ball, she might as well come clean with Nate now.

But the way he was smiling at her, she felt like she didn't need to tell him, he already knew.

'You know, don't you.'

'Of course I do. I'm an expert in these things.'

'How did you know?'

'Well, I had my suspicions, the same as everyone else, but when I said that lie about him being with a redheaded woman, you didn't seem shocked or sad or angry, you were just grateful for the cover. You knew it was a lie. And the only way you would know it was a lie was if you were with him.'

She smiled. 'Oh, that's crafty. Nate, I'm sorry I lied about it. That morning when I was late and said I was at the dentist and you asked me if I'd just had sex with the CEO, I said no and that we weren't seeing each other. I feel bad about that. But I didn't feel like I could tell the truth.'

'Oh honey, of course you lied, I don't blame you for that. You could hardly come out and tell everyone you were sleeping with the boss on your first week in the job. Want to know how I met my husband?'

'Go on.'

'He was the CEO in a company I worked for.'

'Oh my god.'

'I've been in your shoes. The worst thing was no one even knew he was gay, something he was keen to keep quiet so we had to be so careful. The sneaking around thing was deliciously exciting to start with, but then it got really frustrating. So I get it, I really do.'

'Well thank you for being so understanding.'

Nate waved it away like it was nothing. 'But now we're being honest about this, you have to tell me everything.'

Roo laughed. 'You won't be getting that from me.'

'Or me,' Theo said, and she looked up to see him standing in the doorway. 'Although I will tell you I'm in love with this wonderful woman.'

Nate squealed with excitement and Roo smiled.

'Roo, can I borrow you for a second?' Theo said.

'Do I need to put my headphones in, so I don't hear you two at it like rabbits?' Nate said.

'No need, we're always strictly professional at work,' Theo said, and Roo had to suppress a smile at that.

She followed Theo into his office and he closed the door.

'Little Paws is now mine.'

'Oh Theo, that's wonderful.'

'The estate agent was there at nine this morning and the listing appeared half an hour ago. I put an offer in and I've just heard back from the estate agents that Adam has accepted my offer. So that's it, I own a wildlife rescue centre. Well, I will do in a few weeks. There's no mortgage, no surveys or anything like that to be done so it should go through relatively quickly.'

'You've done something incredible. I'm really happy for you.'

Theo nodded. 'Now I need to go and tell Charlie.'

Roo frowned in confusion, but then Little Paws was their charity partner, so he probably should be told.

'I have some things we need to talk about, but we can do that tonight at the ball. I'm still holding out for our dance on the lake.'

She smiled. 'I'm looking forward to it.'

He gave her a kiss on the cheek and walked out and she was left wondering what he wanted to talk to her about.

Theo walked into Charlie's office. Charlie was on the phone and he flashed him a smile as he talked to whoever it was on the other end. Theo shut the door and after a few moments, Charlie finished the call.

'Hey, you alright?' Charlie asked.

'You got a few minutes?'

'Of course.'

Theo sat down and played with the cuff of his shirt for a moment as he thought about what to say.

'I wonder if you would consider buying me out.'

Charlie's eyebrows shot up. 'What?'

'Not all of it. Say ten per cent, then you would have the majority share of the company.'

'But you're the CEO, this is your company.'

'Not if you bought me out. It would be yours and rightly so. You have done everything for this company, you've got it where it is now, it's successful because of you. I'm just the bloke who came up with the idea and designed the software. Everything else has been you.'

'We're a team.'

'That's kind of you to say but you've basically carried me the last two years. The company is yours.'

Charlie stared at him in shock. 'Are you leaving?'

'Yes. I've just bought Little Paws and I intend to make that as successful as I possibly can, using some of the business skills I've acquired from you over the last few years. That place is important to me, it's something I'm really passionate about. I feel I can really make a difference there. Pet Protagonist was a hobby, a bit of fun.'

'And now it's not.'

'Being a CEO of a big international company was never on my to-do list. That's a Charlie thing and you do that so well.'

Charlie let out a heavy breath. 'I had no idea you weren't happy. I've been so focused on the business I didn't stop to check.'

'I'm insanely proud of what our business has achieved in such a short amount of time, and I am happy with what you've done, more than happy. It just isn't for me anymore. And look at it this way. As CEO you can bring Beth on as MD. She was always wasted as a lead designer when she has business qualifications coming out of her ears.'

Charlie gave a small smile. 'She would love that. But is there anything I can say to change your mind?'

'No, I'm sorry. The last few weeks I've realised I need to do the things that make me truly happy. And I want to do the right thing for you. You've earned this. I do have some conditions though.'

'What are your terms?'

'I'm obviously still going to get a share of the monthly profits.'

'Of course, it was your idea, your computer program and you'll still have shares in the company.'

'If you wish to keep me on the payroll as technical support I'm always happy to tweak and adjust the computer program to your needs or make any repairs if there's a glitch. But most importantly, I want a guarantee from you that every single member of staff keeps their jobs and that includes Roo.'

'I have no complaints about her work. I've seen the designs she's done for *A Knight's Tail* and I'm very impressed. And with you gone, at least all the gossip surrounding her will die down.'

'That's what I'm hoping for too.'

'You're not leaving for her, are you?'

'No, I'm leaving for me, but I'm hoping that it will help her at the same time.'

Charlie nodded. 'I have no intention of getting rid of any of the staff. As you are aware, we are taking more on.'

'I'd also really like it if you stayed here in Apple Hill Bay. People rely on their jobs and if you move, people might not be able to work here anymore.'

'There's no fear of that, I grew up here and never want to leave. I want Hope to grow up playing on the beach every day like I did. It's possible we may need to extend at a later stage, but I'm thinking of moving the printing press to a place across town so we can reclaim the bottom floor for more staff. Or we move to bigger premises, but it will be in Apple Hill Bay no matter what we do.'

'OK good.'

'How much do you want for your ten per cent?'

'Whatever you think it's worth. I have no worries you'll try to fiddle me. Are you OK with this?'

'Your terms?'

'Me leaving. I don't want to cause any problems for you or let you down, but I figure you'll just carry on being your brilliant self without me.'

'I'll be sad to see you go, of course, but we've known

each other for too long for it to affect our friendship. Plus you're Hope's godfather so it's not like this is goodbye.'

'Definitely not. I'll be round every week for our weekly chess game. One day I might beat you without Beth's help.'

He grinned. 'I look forward to it. And you're not letting me down, not at all. I want you to be happy. I'll manage without you.'

'Get yourself a brilliant MD, if not Beth, someone you can trust completely. That's what I did and it makes everything run really smoothly.'

Charlie grinned. 'Thanks mate. When are you thinking of leaving?'

'I don't want to leave you in the lurch. And it will be a while before Little Paws actually becomes mine. Shall we say six weeks?'

'Sounds good. I'll get all the paperwork sorted.'

Theo nodded. 'Thank you for making this so easy. I've known for a while I wanted to move on, but I didn't know how to tell you and was worried I'd be letting you down.'

'I hope you'll be very happy and if you ever want a job as lead designer, I'd take you back in a heartbeat; all the fun with no responsibility.'

Theo smiled at that. 'That thought did occur to me and it's something I might do in the future, but I need a bit of a break for a while and to concentrate on Little Paws too.'

'I understand. Are you still coming to the ball tonight?'

'Oh yes. I've decided to go out with a bang – me and Roo are going together.'

Charlie laughed. 'Good for you. Personally, I found it so much easier once everyone knew about me and Beth.'

'Hopefully that will help Roo too. Right, I better get on with some work.' Theo stood up and Charlie stood up too. To his surprise, Charlie came round and hugged him.

'It won't be the same without you.'

'I'm sure everything will run like clockwork as always. The company is in very safe hands and there is no one else I would trust with it.'

Charlie pulled back. 'Thank you.'

Theo clapped him on the back and walked out, feeling so much lighter already.

CHAPTER TWENTY

Roo was waiting nervously in her beach hut for Theo to pick her up. The thought of walking into the ball at the hotel hand-in-hand with Theo was making her stomach churn. She didn't want to hide their relationship, she was proud to be his girlfriend, but she didn't want to be the subject of everyone's gossip either, especially as she had been denying it for the past few weeks. And once they came clean, everyone would believe that they really did go to Morgy Hill Woods for sex. But she supposed the sooner everyone knew, the sooner they could get all the gossip out of the way and move on. It would be old news in a week.

There was a knock on the door and she rushed to answer it. Theo was standing there looking absolutely gorgeous in a tux. His eyes widened when he saw her, his gaze travelling down her dress.

'You look incredible, Roo,' Theo said, softly.

'You're looking pretty damn sexy yourself.' She stepped forward and kissed him. He wrapped his arms around her and kissed her hard.

She pulled back slightly to look at him. 'Let's just stay here and make love all night instead.'

He smirked. 'Now that is an unbelievably tempting offer but I'm looking forward to sweeping around the dance floor with you in my arms.'

'In front of everyone?'

'Yes. You make me so damned happy and I want everyone to see how happy you make me, how completely in love I am with you. But I'll make you a deal. We go for a bit, have a couple of dances, I'll do my big speech about Little Paws and then we'll sneak out and I'll take you somewhere beautiful.'

She smiled. 'OK.'

She grabbed her bag and walked out, locking the hut behind her.

The night was warm and the sea was flat calm, under a flamingo sky. They walked along the path that was lit with little lamps until they got to the car park. But instead of walking towards his battered old Land Rover, he guided her towards a long silver Rolls Royce.

'Is this for us?'

'Yes, I hired it for the evening, I thought we should arrive in style. I was going to hire a driver too, but I intend to make love to you in the back of that later and I didn't think the driver would want to witness me ravaging you.'

She laughed. 'Very considerate of you.'

'I'm thoughtful like that.'

He opened the door for her and she slid inside the plush leather interior. He got inside the driver's side and drove off.

It wasn't long before they reached Merryport Castle, a splendid, beautiful location to hold the ball. Theo parked the car and got out hurrying round to her side to open the door for her. She got out and admired the lights in the trees and the red carpet leading up to the entrance of the fairytale castle. Music was drifting out from the ballroom as couples arrived in all their splendour.

Theo took her hand as they approached the entrance and she took a deep breath. There was no going back after this.

They handed their tickets in and Roo could already feel a few people staring over at them and they hadn't even gone into the ballroom yet. Theo didn't let her hand go as he led her straight onto the dancefloor. There were only a few couples dancing, everyone else was mingling round the bar or the buffet table. He gathered her in his arms and started moving around the room. She glanced around to see people's reactions and as she thought, almost every single person in the room was staring at them.

Theo captured her chin and turned her face towards his so he could kiss her. She smiled against his lips as she kissed him back and everyone else in the room was forgotten.

He pulled back slightly. 'I love you so damn much, Aurora Clarke, nothing else matters.'

She smiled and kissed him again, not caring what anyone thought.

Eventually they pulled back and carried on dancing around the room, his eyes on hers the whole time.

Other couples joined them and they danced through song after song after song.

As one song finished, Theo gave her a kiss on the cheek.

'I'd better go and give my speech.'

'Good luck.'

Roo looked around as Theo made his way to the stage. The room was filled now with the Pet Protagonist staff, the Little Paws staff and volunteers and everyone's dates and friends. She spotted Carrie dancing with Antonio, Fletcher and Fern dancing together and then she saw Orla dancing with Shay and looking ridiculously happy.

'Hello.'

Roo turned around to see a very pretty blonde-haired woman in a gorgeous green dress.

'I'm Beth, Charlie's wife.'

'Oh hello,' Roo said, giving her a hug.

'Lovely to meet you. I've heard so much about you and how you've completely turned this one's life around,' Beth gestured to Theo.

'He's done the same for me too. I'm completely head-over-heels in love with him.'

Beth grinned. 'I bet it's been so hard the last few weeks, sneaking around.'

'The gossip about us and him has not been kind. But

I'm in my own office now and I'm loving the peace and quiet.'

'Yeah, sometimes it's better to just let them get on with it and if you're not there to hear it, even better. I also wanted to say thank you for your help with the whole Sally debacle. I know that wasn't easy to basically grass on someone on only your second day, but I do appreciate your honesty. The things she was saying about me and Charlie were horrible and just not true. With her gone, I feel like I can come back to work for Pet Protagonist now. I'll be in for a few days a week starting from next week and then full time in six weeks. You're looking at the new managing director and I'm so excited.'

'Oh congratulations,' Roo said, then frowned. 'But what about Charlie, what is he doing?'

Beth's face fell. 'Sorry, I thought you knew, forget I said anything. Charlie asked me to be discreet about it and I blab it to the first person I speak to. Hazards of being a stay-at-home mum for a year, you forget how to have adult conversations. Oh look, there's Violet, I must go and say hello. Lovely chatting to you. You and Theo will have to come for dinner one night.'

With that Beth hurried off leaving Roo more confused than ever.

Theo switched on the microphone and tapped it a few times to get everyone's attention. Everyone fell silent, looking up at him expectantly.

'Thank you all for coming,' Theo said. 'This week saw the release of our latest book, *Captain Pet's Name and the Search for the Lost Treasure* and already we've reached five thousand sales. Every single member of our team works so hard in writing, designing, producing, printing and marketing the books and I want to thank you all for helping the company go from strength to strength.'

There was a small round of applause.

'And I want to thank all the staff and volunteers from Little Paws that have come here tonight. As you are all aware, Little Paws was facing closure as Adam Larch, our landlord was selling the land. I'm pleased to tell you that Adam has agreed to sell the land at Little Paws separately to the rest of his land and this morning I put an offer in for the land which was accepted. So Little Paws gets to stay and buying the land means it will be protected for many more years to come.'

There were gasps and cheers around the room and everyone erupted into a big round of applause.

'Thank you, and to celebrate, all the drinks at the bar for the next half-hour are free.'

There was another cheer at that before everyone rushed off to the bar. Theo handed the microphone back and hopped down from the stage.

Roo watched as his family and several other people came over to congratulate him, Carrie giving him a big hug. Lizzie came over to hug him and to say thank you too. She and Violet would never know how close they had come to losing everything, and it was better that way.

Finally, Theo was free and he walked straight to her.

'I believe you owe me a dance on the lake?' Theo said.

She smiled. 'Of course.'

He took her hand and they walked out the open patio

doors. The night was warm, the stars and the moon were shining brightly above them. Little lanterns lit the way into the gardens and along the path towards the lake, which reflected the stars and the moon like a mirror.

They reached the shores of the lake and Theo led her across a small wooden jetty to a wooden bandstand in the middle of the lake that was strewn with tiny fairy lights.

He took her in his arms and started dancing with her. She could hear the faint sound of the music drifting out through the open doors.

'You look so beautiful tonight,' Theo said. 'I can't believe how much my world has changed in the last few weeks since you came into my life. I love you so much.'

'I love you too. You make me so happy.'

'Well, I have some news about that, about being happy. And this was all you. After our chat the other day about you wanting me to be happy and how you knew Pet Protagonist wasn't giving me that, I had a long think about what would make me truly happy and I came up with two things. Firstly, I want to work with wildlife. I want to do that every day, not just a few hours here and there. So after Adam accepted my offer to buy Little Paws I went to see Charlie and I asked him to buy me out. He's going to buy ten per cent of my shares so he will be the majority shareholder and the new CEO. In six weeks, I'll be going to work for Little Paws full time.'

'Oh Theo, that's fantastic news. I'm so happy for you.'

'I'm excited. I also feel like I can do so much more for Little Paws to help them raise money and awareness. Merchandising is something we can look at, a monthly lottery and as you suggested, getting businesses to sponsor enclosures. Maybe we can do a newsletter letting people know more about the animals we're rescuing and what we're doing? I'm looking forward to putting my mark on the place.'

'This is wonderful,' Roo said.

'I'll still get a profit of the shares of Pet Protagonist and I'll stay on the payroll as technical support. I built the program at Pet Protagonist so if there are any problems or adjustments need doing I can do that but I can easily do that from home. And I trust Charlie to keep everything as it is; he won't be making redundancies, or moving to London any time soon. So your job will be completely safe.'

'Well that's good. Although I wasn't too worried. I really love my job but I've always been able to find work and because of my skills and experience I can do a lot of jobs at home. When I eventually find a home.'

'And that brings me to the second thing that would make me truly happy. I want to spend the rest of my life with you. You make me so completely and utterly happy. I want to come home to you every night and wake up with you every morning.'

She stared at him in surprise and she realised he was shaking.

'Don't panic, I'm not asking you to marry me, although I will, one day. But your time at The Little Beach Hut Hotel is coming to a close and with the school summer holidays fast approaching the likeliness of you being able to extend it is not very good. So I thought maybe you might want to move in with me, at least until you get your own place. Or forever, whichever you prefer. The house has always been ours anyway, it kind of makes sense to make it more permanent. But I know it's very early days with us and you might not want to move that quick. But I do have two bedrooms at my house so you can have your own space and I can spend some nights with you in your room and you can spend some nights with me in my room and—'

She put a finger over his lips. 'You buy a wildlife rescue and sell off the majority shares in your multi-million-pound company without batting an eye, but ask me to move in with you and you're a bag of nerves.'

He smiled and let out a heavy breath. 'Because I want that more than anything.'

'I love you, so much, nothing would make me happier than to live with you at Little Haven, marry you one day, and to spend the rest of my life with you. Yes. Of course the answer is yes.'

He grinned and kissed her and she knew right here in his arms, she had found forever.

EPILOGUE

Roo sat on the balcony in Little Haven watching the sun start its descent from the sky, leaving wispy clouds of tangerine and damson in its wake. On the cliff side, only a few metres from the back of the house, four fox cubs were playing together, under the watchful eye of their mum and dad. Dolphins were leaping through the waves at the end of the headland and she felt like she could sit there forever watching them and never get bored.

It had been a year since she had officially moved into Little Haven and she loved it here so much. It was peaceful, tranquil and she got to wake up in Theo's arms every single day. She couldn't be happier.

She loved her job at Pet Protagonist, Nate was brilliant fun to work with and she loved being involved with the illustrations from the very start. She'd become good friends with Beth, who was an excellent MD, and Roo and

Theo would have dinner with her and Charlie at least once a week. The gossip about her and Theo had died down quite quickly after they had outed themselves at the summer ball the year before and was quickly replaced with more gossip and speculation about the real reason why Theo was leaving. One of the wild guesses she'd heard was because Charlie had caught them having sex and had fired Theo, which had made them both laugh.

Theo had started as CEO of Little Paws instead and it was a job he absolutely thrived in. He loved working with the animals and came home smiling every single day. He had made the charity so much more profitable with merchandising, a lottery and corporate sponsorship, it was easy to see he was made for that role. She helped out on weekends too and she loved working side by side with him.

He had still stayed on in a technical capacity with Pet Protagonist, helping with the computer program whenever it was needed. He'd even done some illustrations for some of the new books, but that was freelance work so it was flexible and he worked from home. But at least he was still allowed to do some of the fun stuff, which is why he'd created the company in the first place.

She heard the door open and Theo let himself in. She ran to greet him, she had some exciting news.

He caught her in his arms and she wrapped her hands around his neck and kissed him.

'Hello, my love,' Theo said. 'How was your day at work?'

'Good, really good. How was yours?'

'We released a badger up at Morgy Hill Woods – release days are always emotional, in a good way. But I wanted to show you something.'

'Sure.'

He took her hand and led her to the sofa and then fished around in his bag, pulling out a book.

'So Charlie and I had a chat about a new range of books to celebrate a pet owner's life events; birthdays, anniversaries, graduations, weddings, new babies, et cetera, with the pets helping out on these important days and getting into mischief along the way.'

'I love that idea,' Roo said.

'So this is one I've been working on as a prototype, see what you think.'

Theo handed her the book, titled *Clarke's Parents get Engaged*, featuring a cute English Setter puppy on the front, holding a diamond ring.

'Clarke is a great name for a dog,' Roo grinned. 'Dad would have loved this.'

She opened the book and started reading. It was all about a puppy called Clarke that was trying to get the engagement ring to his human dad in time for the big proposal but mishaps and chaos ensued delaying the pup and at one point even losing the ring. Finally the pup managed to get back to his house with the ring just in time for the big proposal.

'I love this,' Roo said, turning the penultimate page to see a cottage exactly like Little Haven, nestled into the cliff side above a beautiful beach and Clarke the puppy running up the garden path with the ring in his mouth.

'Hey, that's our house,' Roo said.

'I may have used it as inspiration.'

She turned the last page to see a couple that looked very similar to her and Theo, with the man on one knee and Clarke looking happily on in the foreground and just the words. 'Will you marry me?'

'Theo, this is perfect, what a great idea. But why haven't I heard about this?'

'It was just an idea we had, it's still in the very early stages yet. What do you think of the illustrations?'

'Well, I love that you used Little Haven for inspiration. And the couple look a bit like us so I like that too.'

'I only used us and our home as a loose inspiration, it's not us obviously, as we don't have a puppy called Clarke.'

Suddenly there was a yapping outside the door.

Roo looked at Theo in confusion. Was it one of the fox cubs?

'We'd better go and see what that is,' Theo said.

Roo went to the door and opened it and outside on the step was an English Setter puppy wagging his tail furiously, big smile on his freckly face as he climbed out the box trying to get to her.

'Oh my god, Theo.' Roo bent down to scoop up the tiny puppy and carried him back into the house. 'He's beautiful.'

She knelt down on the floor and released the puppy and he climbed all over her, licking her face excitedly.

'His name is Clarke,' Theo said, kneeling down in front of her.

Tears filled her eyes. 'You bought me a puppy.'

'Yeah, I felt like he needed a loving home.'

'Well, he'll certainly get that with you, you're the most kind and generous person I know,' Roo said, kissing him.

She stroked Clarke's ears as he chewed on her dress. 'He's so gorgeous.'

Suddenly she remembered the book, the puppy helping his human dad to propose in a house that looked like Little Haven.

'Oh my god,' Roo said, her hands going to her mouth.

Theo smiled and undid a ribbon attached to Clarke's collar, slowly pulling off a diamond ring.

'Theo,' Roo choked out as he reached for her hand.

'Aurora Clarke, I love you so much, you have made me so damned happy every single day and I want to make you that happy for the rest of my life. Will you marry me?'

She leaned forward and kissed him hard, nodding and crying as she did.

'Yes, yes, a million times yes.'

He grinned and kissed her back.

He pulled back and slid the ring onto her finger, a beautiful oval diamond surrounded by tiny opal beads so it glistened in the setting sun spilling in through the patio doors.

He went to kiss her again but she stopped him.

'Wait, I have news of my own.'

He smiled. 'More exciting than this?'

'Maybe.' She smiled and took his hands, resting them on her belly. 'We're going to be parents.'

He gasped. His eyes widening in shock. They'd talked about having children of course, though it had always been something they'd said they'd wanted to do in the future, after getting married. But sometimes fate took things into their own hands.

A smile crept onto his lips and when he spoke his voice was rough. 'I'm going to be a dad?'

She nodded.

He leaned forward and kissed her hard, stroking her belly gently.

Clarke wandered off to find something far more exciting to play with as Theo rolled her carefully back onto the soft rug on the floor.

'You've just made me the happiest man alive, saying yes, giving me this gift. I love you so much,' Theo said.

'Do you think we're crazy, getting married, raising a puppy and having a baby all at the same time?'

'Sometimes we need a little crazy.'

If you enjoyed *The Cottage on Strawberry Sands*, you'll love my next gorgeously romantic story in the Apple Hill Bay series, *Christmas Wishes at Cranberry Cove*. You'll get to know more about Theo's brother, Shay and his friend, Orla. It's out in October

.   .   .

And you might enjoy *Meet Me at Midnight*, an enchanting witchy romance that sparkles with magic and love. It's still the small town romance you've come to expect from me, but with a magical twist. It follows on from *The Midnight Village* but can be read as a standalone as it follows a different couple. It's out this summer

ALSO BY HOLLY MARTIN

Midnight Village Series

The Midnight Village

Meet Me at Midnight

Apple Hill Bay Series

Sunshine and Secrets at Blackberry Beach

The Cottage on Strawberry Sands

Christmas Wishes at Cranberry Cove

Wishing Wood Series

The Blossom Tree Cottage

The Wisteria Tree Cottage

The Christmas Tree Cottage

Jewel Island Series

Sunrise over Sapphire Bay

Autumn Skies over Ruby Falls

Ice Creams at Emerald Cove

Sunlight over Crystal Sands

Mistletoe at Moonstone Lake

The Happiness Series

The Little Village of Happiness

The Gift of Happiness

The Summer of Chasing Dreams

Sandcastle Bay Series

The Holiday Cottage by the Sea

The Cottage on Sunshine Beach

Coming Home to Maple Cottage

Hope Island Series

Spring at Blueberry Bay

Summer at Buttercup Beach

Christmas at Mistletoe Cove

Juniper Island Series

Christmas Under a Cranberry Sky

A Town Called Christmas

White Cliff Bay Series

Christmas at Lilac Cottage

Snowflakes on Silver Cove

Summer at Rose Island

Standalone Stories

The Secrets of Clover Castle (Previously published as Fairytale Beginnings)

The Guestbook at Willow Cottage

One Hundred Proposals

One Hundred Christmas Proposals

Tied Up With Love

A Home on Bramble Hill (Previously published as Beneath the Moon and Stars

For Young Adults

The Sentinel Series

The Sentinel (Book 1 of the Sentinel Series)

The Prophecies (Book 2 of the Sentinel Series)

The Revenge (Book 3 of the Sentinel Series)

The Reckoning (Book 4 of the Sentinel Series)

A LETTER FROM HOLLY

Thank you so much for reading *The Cottage on Strawberry Sands,* I had so much fun creating this story. I hope you enjoyed reading it as much as I enjoyed writing it.

One of the best parts of writing comes from seeing the reaction from readers. Did it make you smile or laugh, did it make you cry, hopefully happy tears? Did you fall in love with Theo and Roo as much as I did? Did you like the seaside town of Apple Hill Bay. I would absolutely love it if you could leave a short review on Amazon. Getting feedback from readers is amazing and it also helps to persuade other readers to pick up one of my books for the first time.

If you enjoyed this story, my next book, out in the summer is called *Meet Me at Midnight.* It's still the small town romance you would expect from me but this one has a slightly magical twist.

And if you want to read Shay and Orla's story, you'll find that in *Christmas Wishes at Cranberry Cove*, which will be out this autumn.

Thank you for reading.

Love Holly x

ACKNOWLEDGEMENTS

To my parents, my mom, my biggest fan, who reads every word I've written a hundred times over and loves it every single time, and for my dad, for your support, love, encouragement for my stories and for cooking celebratory steak every publication day

For my twinnie, the gorgeous Aven Ellis for just being my wonderful friend, for your endless support, for cheering me on, for reading my stories and telling me what works and what doesn't and for keeping me entertained with wonderful stories. I love you dearly.

To my lovely friends Julie, Natalie, Jac, Verity and Jodie, thanks for all the support.

To the Devon contingent, Paw and Order, Belinda, Lisa, Phil, Bodie, Kodi and Skipper. Thanks for keeping me entertained and always being there.

To everyone at Bookcamp, you gorgeous, fabulous

bunch, thank you for your wonderful support on this venture.

Thanks to my fabulous editors, Celine Kelly, Kerry Barrett and Johnny Sharp.

To my lovely agent and the team at Lorella Belli, thanks for all your hard work taking my books to different countries.

To all the wonderful bloggers for your tweets, retweets, facebook posts, tireless promotions, support, encouragement and endless enthusiasm. You guys are amazing and I couldn't do this journey without you.

To anyone who has read my book and taken the time to tell me you've enjoyed it or wrote a review, thank you so much.

Thank you, I love you all.

Published by Holly Martin in 2024
Copyright © Holly Martin, 2024

978-1-913616-52-6 Paperback
978-1-913616-53-3 Large Print paperback
978-1-913616-54-0 Hardback
978-1-913616-55-7 audiobook

Cover design by Emma Rogers